Michelle Meets Her Match

Charlotte S. Snead

Jan-Carol
Publishing, Inc

"every story needs a book"

Michelle Meets Her Match
Hope House Girls Series
Book 5
Charlotte S. Snead

Published December 2020
Little Creek Books
Imprint of Jan-Carol Publishing, Inc.
All rights reserved
Front Cover Photograph: © Pololia / Adobe Stock
Copyright © 2020 Charlotte S. Snead

ISBN: 978-1-950895-66-3
Library of Congress Control Number: 2020949702

You may contact the publisher:
Jan-Carol Publishing, Inc.
PO Box 701
Johnson City, TN 37605
publisher@jancarolpublishing.com
jancarolpublishing.com

Michelle Meets Her Match

Chapter One

ARRIVING AT JOHNS HOPKINS

Michelle pulled up a chair in the cafeteria, noticing two beautiful white girls across from her. She was used to their type and was not intimidated as she once was; after all, she was a doctor, trained at Cleveland Clinic, and her best friend was a white Christian music star who had won Dove awards and was up for a country music award this year. Smiling to herself, Michelle thought she would strike up a conversation. She was new here and needed to make friends, but she had someone more important to talk to first.

She bowed her head and crossed herself. "Father, once again I am humbled by Your favor," she mouthed silently. "Thank You for this opportunity to study at Johns Hopkins. Give me favor with my superiors. Help me to work diligently, to absorb all You have for me here, and to become the best pediatrician I can be. Let me give life to the living and eternal life to the dying in the name of the Father, the Son, and the Holy Spirit."

Looking up, she saw that the women had fallen into a respectful silence and were smiling at her with genuine warmth.

"I hope I didn't disturb you," Michelle apologized. "This is my first day, and I don't want to start off on the wrong foot. My name is Michelle Logan."

"Hi, Michelle. I'm Sandy Collins, and this is Pat Owens. She's a newbie, and I'm showing her around. I'll add you to the tour if you like. Where are you from?"

"I completed my pediatric residency at Cleveland Clinic and worked there for several years. I'm here for a fellowship in pediatric critical care."

"Welcome to Baltimore. Johns Hopkins has an amazing critical pediatric reputation. I'm sure you have heard of Dr. Ben Carson, right?"

"*Gifted Hands?* Sure! Who hasn't?"

Michelle had demonstrated the proper awe, so Sandy responded with warmth. "He's retired now, but sometimes he likes to make rounds with the residents. Maybe you'll meet him today."

"I'd be so honored!"

Sandy leaned forward. "You don't sound like you're from Ohio. Where are you from?"

"I grew up in Boston and lived there all of my life, until I made a huge mistake and took a wrong turn and a short detour. I've lived in Ohio since I was fourteen."

"Oh, an intrigue. Do tell us, or am I being too invasive?" Pat wanted to know.

"I used to be tongue-tied and shy, but I got over that. Since God turned my life around, I have too much gratitude to hold back sharing what He has done in my life."

"I thought you were a Christian," Sandy said. "I am, too. I'd take you to my church, but you're a Catholic, right?"

"Yes, but I have no qualms about going to other churches. My best friend in the world is Missy O'Malley. Have you heard of her?"

"She's my favorite Christian singer! Where did you meet her?" Sandy squirmed excitedly in her chair, leaning forward.

"Let me tell you about Hope House, a maternity home in Columbus, Ohio. Tragic circumstances brought Missy there. It's all in her book. She was raped by three vicious boys and became pregnant. She was a life-long Christian, she was very pro-life, and she didn't once think about abortion.

When she came to Hope House, she'd never left West Virginia in her life. She called herself a 'mountain maid.'"

"Did you know she's performed with her birth daughter? I saw them at a church in Arlington, Virginia, last summer. They shared their story, and everyone in the auditorium was bawling!" Pat dabbed her eyes.

"I've met Tiffany. Isn't she beautiful? She has her uncle's red hair, just like the O'Malley side of the family. Have you seen the family in concert?"

"No, but I have some of their DVDs. You really know Missy O'Malley? What's she like?"

"We were young when we met at Hope House. My father was angry with me for getting pregnant and sent me off as soon as he found out. He wanted me to have an abortion, but we were Catholic, and I was horrified. I'd read Pope John Paul's *The Gospel of Life*, and I couldn't believe he would consider it for a moment! When I refused, someone told him he could ship me out of state to a maternity home, and that's how I got to Hope House. I was there a couple of months before Missy. She had a loving family. Her mother's a saint, and it broke Missy's heart to leave, but she wanted to protect the family from scandal, and she was also afraid of those boys. But she stayed home until she began to show. They were poor, and she wanted to work. She was already showing when she came. She was the first real friend in my life, and she prayed with me when Christ became apparent to me."

"Please tell us more. This is fascinating. I want to know all about it."

Pat nodded at Sandy's words, adding her own urging. "We're all here a day early, right? Do you have time? No meetings or appointments?"

"Missy says I should write a book about my life, but it's pretty dull. Have you read hers?"

"I bought it at the retreat! Oh, you must be...? She gave you another name. What was it?"

"Hannah. She referred to me as Hannah in her book. Samuel's mother took her son to the tabernacle and gave him to God, if you remember. Missy gave us all different names to protect our privacy. She says ours is our own story to tell, but she wants to do a series and call it *The Hope House Girls*."

"Do you know what ever happened to the girl who ran away?"

"No one has heard from her, but we pray for her every time the Hope House girls have a reunion."

Sandy stood. "If we're all okay with it, let's move over to the sitting area. I'm going to get some more coffee."

A large, very black man, too big to be unobtrusive, moved nearby, putting a stack of books on the table and opening one of them. The women paid him no mind and settled in to listen.

Chapter Two

BEGIN AT THE BEGINNING

"'Kay, let's begin at the beginning," Sandy urged. "So, your dad sent you away, and Missy's didn't?"

"Missy's father abandoned the family. He was an alcoholic. She didn't know where he was at that time. You'll have to get her book from Pat to learn her story. It's called *Recovered and Free*. I was an embarrassment to my family from the time I was conceived. Mother was forty-four when I was born and was high up in the governor's cabinet. She was secretary of health and human services for the state. Abortion wasn't legal in our state then. She could've gone to New York but decided she'd be an example, and they could get a maternity leave bill out of her experience. I was born, but her career didn't miss a beat. They hired nannies. My father was—still is—a high-powered attorney. Harvard Law.

"Our home was a mansion, but my childhood was lonely. My brother and sister were away at private schools when I was a child. HJ—that's Herman Junior—was in prep school and followed my father to Harvard, and my sister was at another exclusive academy, shooting for Vassar, and she went there. I was the disappointment—a big, ugly child who was awkward and wore thick glasses. When I was ten, I went with my parents to a fundraiser for Senator

Kennedy. Ted, you know? Father was chatting with him and asked him about private schools in Washington. The senator wanted my father to move to Washington and work on his staff; token black, you know. Father didn't want to be on his staff, but he accepted a position at a firm in Washington that defended many of the senators. Anyway, that night I overheard him say, 'I'm going to have to educate her well because...look at her. She's going to be huge. She's only ten! And dark. And not the smartest.'

"Senator Kennedy said, 'But, Herman, you are tall and dark. She takes after you.'

Father told him, 'Look at her mother. She's fair, and so is her sister.' In the black culture—not so much now, but when I was ten—my father thought it was fine for a man to be dark, but not the women. 'If I don't get her well placed, she'll have to live on a trust,' he told the senator. Those words completed my miserable self-image. Already lonely and shy, I knew I was an accident, and now Father was saying I wasn't pretty or smart and that I wouldn't amount to squat."

Pat handed Sandy a tissue and mouthed a derogatory name for the man who made their new friend feel like pond scum. "Did he defend Senator Kennedy after Chappaquiddick?"

"Oh, no. Father was a straight arrow. Much as he loved and respected Dr. King, he was grieved over his...extra-curricular activities. Lovely family, the Kings. Such a tragedy. Alveda, his niece, is the CEO, or whatever you call it, at Priests for Life now."

"I've heard her on TV," Sandy said. "She's a good spokesperson, and so intelligent! But you must be, too, and I can't believe your father said that about you."

Michelle's hearty laugh rang out like a glorious carillon. "Don't fret, ladies. Missy demonstrated the love of Christ and brought me into God's family. I'm the Bride of Christ, the fair one, accepted by the beloved. One night at Hope House, she and another girl short-sheeted my bed. Our house-mother was upset because I was shy, sort of a misfit, and she feared they made me feel rejected. Missy and Cathy were standing outside my room, laughing hysterically. They burst into the room, and Missy loved on me. She hugged me so tight I thought I'd cry. Mrs. G. fussed at them and said, 'Games are over, children. Make up that bed right this minute.' She started to pull me into her room to comfort me, but I wasn't crying because I felt rejected. I was crying because, for the first time in my life, I had friends who played with me.

"Five of us went through an intense time at Hope House. Because my father made me feel I wasn't smart, I didn't do as well as I could have in school, especially in math. Missy tutored us all and convinced me I was smart. 'Who told you that you aren't smart, girl? It took me weeks to get this concept, and I explained it to you once...' Michelle then snapped her fingers and said, 'And you got it. Just like that!' Because of her, I was able to skip high school and take the GED test. I started community college in the fall. Missy found the best in everyone and encouraged us to reach for it. That's the heart of her ministry. Her songs do that. Did you know she didn't want to be a singer? She considers herself a wife and mother, and she's an interior decorator."

"I can't believe that! She's such a natural on stage," Pat said. "But let's get back to your story. What happened at Hope House? I know Missy placed her baby. What did you do?"

"That would be such a tough decision," Sandy added, "but I saw Tiffany with her birth mother and her mother on stage, and it was a good choice for all of them."

"Laura—she's named Betty in the book—was the first to place. One day at Hope House, we were in Missy's room, and Laura, Missy, and I climbed our Mount Moriah. Remember in Abraham's trial, when he offered Isaac to God? We did that. We placed our babies on the altar. When Laura's baby was born, Missy told her she was like Jochebed, the mother of Moses, who placed her baby in a basket and put him in the river, where the pharaoh's daughter would find him. When Missy had Tiffany, she told me, 'It was the best thing I ever did, and the hardest.' And it was. Missy was with all the girls when they had their babies, but she had left before my daughter was born. Laura stayed in Columbus, though, and she came over to be with me."

"If you don't mind my asking, how did you get pregnant? I mean, you said you were shy and awkward. Were you raped, too?" Sandy rested her hand on Michelle's arm when she asked.

"No. This guy—he was kind of a nerd, too—took advantage of me. He told me he loved me, and I fell for it. Both of us were young and inexperienced, so I got pregnant, and he dropped me like a hot potato. He never loved me. He only wanted to have sex and be one of the guys. I had to tell my parents. I don't think he ever told anyone. Maybe he did. He transferred to another school, and his forwarding address was never given."

"What a jerk!" Pat leaned back and crossed her arms.

Michelle touched her new friend's hand, feeling her sympathy and appreciating it. "He lost, big time. He never knew he had a daughter. I got to hold my daughter and caress her tiny face. Her parents are lovely. They were mature, ready to be parents, and they gave her the love she needed."

Sandy sniffed into her crumpled tissue and foraged around in her briefcase to find another for Pat. "After you surrendered your baby, did you go back to Boston?"

"My folks lived in Washington by then, but I'd found love and a relationship with God at Hope House. Laura, Candy, and Cathy stayed in Columbus. Cathy went off to Wheaton after we attended two years at community college together. I lived with a lovely family in my church and got an associate degree before transferring to the university. Then I went to medical school at Ohio State. After she married, Cathy moved back to Columbus, and she and her husband opened a counseling practice. Missy still lives in West Virginia. Laura told me Missy sang to her when she was in labor, and she felt the presence of God when she sang. All the girls said that. Cathy and Candy kept their babies, but that's their story to tell. All of us supported each other's choices. Each of us did what she had to do."

"You're strong, to do that and to tell us about it with calm acceptance, even joy." Sandy agreed with Pat, and both women hugged her.

"I was young. The adoptive parents are wonderful folks and wanted a baby. God works for the good of those who love Him and are the called according to His purpose. Even my father's attitude shaped me. He made me work hard. I was determined he wouldn't have to fork over a dime, and I refused his offers. He did send Hope House a lot of money. Sometimes, through college and medical school, Mother would send me a check, and I could get a new outfit or buy books. Today, in many ways, blacks have an advantage, and I was female, too. I'm grateful for every equal opportunity I got. I made the most of it, believe you me. I made excellent grades and did nothing but study and work with at-risk youths in Cleveland. You want to see our troupe?" Michelle opened her laptop.

The tall man who lingered nearby asked politely if he could watch, so they scooted their chairs.

Michelle pointed to each teenager, told his or her name, then said something about their backgrounds. Some of them had been referred by the courts, and one of the girls had a baby she juggled on her hip. "What we do is enact their stories. Johnnie was on probation for knifing his mom's boyfriend. Dixon had robbed some convenience stores because his mom was an addict and his kid brother and sister had no food." She continued with their stories, explaining that they went to schools and churches with the programs, to warn their peers and urge them to make better choices, and they also raised money for the shelter that enabled them to stay in school. "That took a lot of time, so between school and Kids with Hope, I've had no other life. Maybe with this fellowship, hard as it is, I'll not be so torn."

"I don't know how you feel about this kind of thing, Michelle, but I have a word from God for you." Sandy leaned forward and began to speak. "God wants you to know He loves you with an everlasting love, and He is pleased. Now He wants you to rest, to cease striving, and to abide in His love. 'Come away with me, my love, my fair one,' He says, 'and let me hold you a while.' Be comforted, revel in His love, and draw strength for the journey ahead." Sandy shrugged. "Make of it what you will, but I felt God wanted to tell you that."

Weeping, Michelle gasped out, "Thank you. That's comforting." She looked up at the stranger. "You got caught up in a chick event. Sorry."

Looking into her brown eyes—his were almost black—the man said, "I am not sorry." He spoke in a deep voice that suited his size. He had a kind of British accent, and the smile creasing his ebony face seemed as wide as the sea; Michelle could easily drown in it.

"God brought me here," he said. "We were appointed to be here. But I will tell you more of that another time." He reached out to take her hand. "I am Marcus Mansour. I, too, will be in the pediatric department. I am an oncologist and a pediatric surgeon. I have a fellowship in pediatric oncology. I am sure we will see a great deal of one another, and that thought pleasures me."

The girls exchanged knowing glances and moved away. "If you want to tour the campus with us, we'll be in the girls' room. But, uh, if you don't want to, we'll catch you tomorrow at orientation." Pat stood, and Sandy joined her, but Michelle and Marcus stood staring at one another, hardly noticing them slip away.

"Where are you from, Marcus?"

"I am from South Africa. I have been here three days, and I have been looking for you. Now I have found you."

He beamed, and Michelle turned to putty. She sank in a chair. "What do you mean? You don't even know me. You've never met me."

"I, too, am a believer in Christ. God showed you to me in a dream. He said I would meet you here and that you would be my wife."

"Hold on, Mr.—Dr.—Mansour."

"I know this sounds strange, but in Africa we are more used to the ways of God's Spirit. I should not have told you so soon, but I am excited. I am not a stalker. I promise you this. I am a simple Christian, like you. Let us get to know one another and see how this goes. Would you do that?"

"Can you hold off on that marriage thing? It sounds weird, you know. It isn't every day a strange man comes up and says he dreamed I would be his wife. I didn't have a dream. Sorry."

Marcus chuckled, a deep bass sound that came from his chest. "Yes, Dr. Logan. It surprises even me. I saw you in Johannesburg when I was applying to come here. I was waiting for my papers—the travel visa and the student visa—and I was quite discouraged. I had a dream, and God told me I would come here and meet my wife. And she was you. But first I will court you. Will you allow that?"

"We could date, sure, but first let's hang around the hospital, okay?" Michelle thought she would follow him to the ends of the earth if only to see him smile again, but reason had to prevail, didn't it?

Chapter Three

MICHELLE

Michelle never dated much. She thought she had found the right guy several years ago; she even took him to a Hope House reunion. He met the girls at the reunion but soon faded away. She assumed the emotions of that weekend—the depth of the testimonies and the lives of Christian service her friends and their spouses had—drove him off. He transferred to another residency. He had said he was a Christian and made nice with Laura's husband, the pastor, but the distance became too insurmountable to overcome.

Thankfully, her mother had re-entered her life, traveling to her college graduation. She'd been accepted to the medical school and got a significant grant. Her mother gave her a cell phone so they could keep in touch. And they did, all throughout Michelle's time in medical school, her time at the pediatric residency, and the years she worked at Cleveland Clinic. Her mother fretted about her loneliness; she wanted Michelle to try again, as she wasn't getting any younger. But Michelle, despite her confession to Pat, still felt herself large and awkward. She had been taller than her boyfriend, and maybe that was part of why they broke up. She wore flat shoes, but still, she was five feet and ten inches tall, and she had no way of getting around it.

She pulled out the new phone her mother had given her when she had met her at the Baltimore airport, planning to restore her family, ecstatic they would be close. Michelle had her doubts. It was the latest smart phone, and the technology would help her immensely; she used it to find her way to the nearby hotel. She was grateful for her mother's gift because her savings would be depleted during this fellowship year. Losing money would be worth it, though, as she yearned to know more about helping her little patients who were critically ill.

She had chosen a nearby hotel because she could walk to the hospital. On the walk back to it, she thought about the disturbing man she had met. He was beautiful. Much taller than she, and that was a nice change. Unheard of, really. But his claim to have seen her in a dream in South Africa was the strangest come-on she'd ever heard. Did he really think God told him to marry a woman in a dream? Ridiculous. He'd seemed so sincere, though, and she felt something—a zing, maybe—when he smiled. He had such a wonderful smile; it took over his face. His eyes glowed, and laugh lines framed them. She had to admit that she liked that smile, and she smiled just from thinking about it. She walked around a tree and watched the red and orange leaves fall. She looked up, lifting her hand to catch them as the wind pulled them off and they floated in the air.

The doorman opened the door for her. She had to do something about cutting expenses, and the thought caused her to start praying about where she'd live. She couldn't afford this hotel, for sure. She dialed the number Pat had entered in her phone earlier, and they arranged to meet the next morning. Sandy had volunteered to give her the tour, but her preoccupation with the tall, dark, and handsome, though oddball, stranger had separated them. Seeing the girls waiting for her at the door the next morning lightened her spirits. She missed her friends in Ohio, the troupe she had worked with for three years, and her Hope House friends, who were more than family to her. She didn't expect to see her mother's hopes for a restored family come to pass, and her father had made no attempt to see or talk to her in fourteen years, so she needed some people in her life.

When she got to work, Sandy linked her arm with hers and urged her to the cafeteria, where the food was more than decent, and cheap. Michelle explained her need to get out of the expensive hotel, and the girls exchanged a glance. The night before, they had felt led to invite her to room with them. Cutting the rent for their apartment three ways would do them a favor, as well.

Michelle bowed her head in the middle of the noisy cafeteria, but this morning two new friends linked hands with her. She already had much to appreciate, and she wanted to thank God. Lifting her head, she looked around and saw confusion and anxiety among newcomers. They were just as lost as she was in the vast complex that made up Johns Hopkins.

After the general session, Sandy led them to pediatrics, where she and Pat were in training, and then took Michelle up to oncology, figuring she'd spend a lot of time there, as well. Michelle glimpsed Marcus. He towered above everyone, but he didn't bend like overly tall people often did, as she once did, until her mother made her stand straight. Her mother was tall but beautiful, light-skinned, and willowy. Mrs. G, the Hope House house-mother, used to say God made her and that He makes everyone perfect. Sometimes she thought He'd made a mistake with her.

Chapter Four

MARCUS MANSOUR

Marcus saw, or felt, Michelle Logan when she came into oncology. He thought she looked at him. He hoped she did. An awareness of her presence brightened the day. He wondered where she was staying. He had found a dump of a boarding house, but it was near the hospital. After medical school and two residencies in surgery and oncology, he didn't want to ask his father for any more help, though he loved his papa deeply and missed him immensely. His longing for his parents and his home had been twisting like a knife until he had spotted her yesterday. When he had talked to her, why had he blurted it out that way? She probably thought he was crazy. But he'd been so excited, so sure. God was faithful. He didn't need a woman in his imagination; he needed a woman, as his papa always teased. Oh, he wanted a woman. He was ready for a family. He had spent many long years celibate, and he hoped it would end! She was here, and he prayed the rest of his dream would come to pass. Soon.

He jolted when he realized the department head had spoken to him twice. With a smile, the older doctor asked him if he had jet lag. Marcus didn't tell him he'd been here three days, and he certainly didn't tell him he was looking for his dream woman. He wanted his Christianity to be apparent in the way he lived and the excellent care he gave. He didn't want it to be distorted with some mystic stuff he hardly believed himself. But it was her—her face, her voice, and even her Amazon goddess stature. He forced himself to pay attention, which was easier when she and her two friends moved away.

He'd never experienced a tingling awareness such as the one that had come over him, and he longed to see her again. He forced himself to listen to instructions, learn the log-in codes, check out the protocols, and meet the staff. He even heard himself respond to a challenging question accurately, earning a compliment. The department head, Elliot Campbell—not of the Campbell's orthopedic fame, he assured them; Campbell's Orthopedics being the classic textbook of orthopedic surgery—pulled him aside. He'd been looking at his curriculum vitae and recognized that Marcus was well trained in South Africa. He suggested that Marcus should assume greater responsibility, even perhaps earn more of a salary, and he agreed to try without pay for a time, to see if he could fulfill his mentor's expectations.

Although he was encouraged, flattered even, he wanted to find her. Why hadn't he entered her number in his phone? He had seen the girls do that. Oh. Right. He was trying to convince her he wasn't a stalker after his stupid presentation of himself as some fanatic. The lunch crowd thinned out before he entered the cafeteria, but still his eyes swept the large area. And landed on her. By herself. How terrific was that? He made his way to her, balancing his tray in his hand, and she glanced up. His heart stopped. Would she send him away? He hesitated. She smiled, which didn't help his heart return to normal. She waved him over to the chair beside her.

She had seen him in the oncology department, and they spoke about Dr. Campbell and the staff, the rooms, and the technology. He thought he was coming off much more professionally this time. She told him her new friends had invited her to room with them and asked his opinion. She wanted to know if she was taking a chance. After all, she hardly knew them. So he told her that his living situation wasn't too pleasant, and sharing expenses was a good idea. But he also advised her to keep her pocketbook in sight until she make sure. She laughed, and he liked the sound. It was rich. Melodious. Perfect. Like everything about her. Funny, he was usually a cautious man, always careful about his friendships. But God had never led him astray, and he was convinced that God was moving.

* * *

Michelle moved from her hotel that weekend. On Saturday, they lugged her books and suitcases up the two flights to the apartment. Since Sandy and Pat were planning to share a room, they moved the second bed into one bedroom, and that night Michelle slept on the couch. She attended Sandy's church, and in the afternoon, they bought a bed and desk for the second bedroom.

Michelle's father sent a significant check and told her he would have his used Audi delivered to her that week. In the curt note, he said he was proud of her accomplishments. He hadn't attended her graduation from college or medical school, so she was surprised. She guessed he had gotten her address from her mother, who insisted on paying her cell phone bills so they could stay in touch.

Work began on Monday morning. Sandy and Pat were nurses. Sandy was on peds, and Pat worked on an oncology rotation, so Michelle worked with Pat. They had gone to high school and nursing school together, though Pat was a year behind. Michelle carefully ironed her scrubs even though the girls had told her they were drip dry and that no one ironed them.

Marcus had attended a different orientation, but they spoke in the cafeteria. In the days following, she lunched with him when she could, and they ran into each other on the oncology floor. The staff grew used to seeing them together. They didn't have much free time, but they saw each other when they could. Her roommates programmed his phone number in their phones because, if they couldn't find Michelle, she was usually with him, or he knew where she would be.

Because Marcus was on the pediatric oncology wing, Michelle bumped into him constantly. He was brilliant and hard-working, and she came to admire him. She scrubbed with him on several cases, as a pediatrician had to be present in these risky procedures. Right away, she figured out he wasn't a nutcase, and his tenderness with his little patients grabbed her heart.

Three weeks later, they finally had the same night off, and by this time she was comfortable being alone with this unusual man. She had her father's old Audi at this point, so she picked him up at his boarding house in a marginal neighborhood. She leaned over and pushed open the car door. "This is kind of a sketchy neighborhood, Marcus. Are you sure about living here?"

"Sketchy?"

"That's colloquial for not so nice, maybe even scary."

His booming laugh filled the car. "Look at me! I am a large man, correct? No one bothers Marcus Mansour. But in this fancy car, maybe I should be careful, huh?"

"It's old. My father gave it to me. He sent me a check for the move and gave me his old car. It's the first thing he's given me since I got pregnant. You heard that, right? Weren't you eavesdropping on my story?"

She thought Marcus reached out a hand to touch her cheek, but he dropped it to his lap, then said, "I was shameless. I listened to every word. I wanted to learn every detail about my...about you. I am moved by your faith and your courage. Truly, God has His hand on you."

"I couldn't have made it without Him." Michelle flipped on the turn signal and moved over a lane. "I thought we'd go to the harbor. Lots of nice seafood restaurants there. You aren't allergic, are you?"

"No. I live by the coast, and we eat lots of fish. One of the interns took me during the first days I was here. I would like that, but isn't it 'sketchy,' as you say?"

"Sometimes, but it is early, and I am with a large man. I should be safe and secure," she teased.

"I will keep you safe. I hope to keep you safe the rest of my life."

Michelle pulled into the parking area. "I thought we weren't talking about that for a while."

"Is that 'sketchy,' too?"

"No, only places are sketchy, not conversations between friends."

"I like that we are friends. It is a beginning."

They got out of the car and walked to the payment box. "My mother heard I had a date, and she was thrilled. She bought me a credit card and said it was her treat." Michelle looked up—far up—which was unusual for her height. She didn't usually look up at people, even men. She was afraid he might be insulted about her paying for their dinner, but considering where he lived, she didn't know what kind of money he had.

He was quite comfortable, saying with a smile, "Then we should eat well, correct? And tell your mother 'thank you.'"

"I will." She thought he made a move to take her hand, but he stopped himself and offered her his arm instead. "I thought we'd go there." She pointed up to a restaurant overlooking the harbor. "It has a lovely view. Mother suggested it."

"I will have the loveliest view, looking at you across the table."

"Marcus, are you flirting with me?"

"I'm trying. Is that all right with you?"

"It was a lovely thing to say."

"Good. And I am glad you saw your mother. Did you get along well?"

"Mother has reached out to me. She came to my medical school graduation without my father, and she gave me a phone when I graduated from college, to keep in touch. She still pays for upgrades and the monthly bills."

"This is good. I'm glad for you. And your father gave you the car, so reconciliation is coming." Marcus reached for the door and held it.

"If you have any visions or dreams about that, let me know. I haven't seen my father in fourteen years."

Marcus let go of the door and turned her to face him, cupping her elbows with his hands. "Fourteen years! I could not go for fourteen days without talking to my papa, nor could I go fourteen months without his embrace."

She shrugged. "It is what it is." She could tell he wanted to hold her, to comfort her, but her eyes were blurry, and she motioned to the door. "Shall we?"

Marcus pulled it open and signaled for a table for two with his fingers. Michelle gave the maître de the reservation. He waved with an elegant gesture, and they followed his directions to their table overlooking the harbor. "Welcome to Philippe's," he said. "Your server is Bonnie. She will be here directly."

Marcus picked up their conversation. "I'm in such pain for you about your father."

"Once again, remember my story. I didn't mind not having him around. My father was not proud of me. He thought I was ugly. Too big and too black."

"That is enough!" Marcus stood beside her chair and pulled her up, turning her around and standing back to look at her. "You are magnificent. Exquisite. This is the first time I have seen you in a dress. I am overcome."

Michelle was afraid he might kiss her right there. She looked around, and people were watching them. "Marcus, you're embarrassing me. Sit."

Holding her chair, he pushed it forward as she sat. "I was going to tell you how nice you look tonight."

"Thank you." She looked at the table, then out the window. "It is a lovely view."

"And I repeat, I have the loveliest view of all, looking across the table at you."

"Would you stop?" He looked wounded. She covered his hand, and his smile appeared again. She gave a little sigh and hoped his dream would come true. He looked more than nice himself. He had on a dark blue sport coat over a blue shirt and a blue and red striped tie. "Tell me about your papa."

The waitress intervened, opening huge leather menus and placing them in front of them. "I'll take your drink orders and let you look over the selections." She went on to tell them the specials for the night, then left. Soon another server arrived with Michelle's Earl Grey and Marcus's coffee.

They went ahead and ordered before picking up the conversation. "Papa is a large man like me, but fortunately I have my mother's hands."

She turned the hand she still had covered. His fingers were long and tapered, almost delicate, and she remembered the scalpel in his hand as he made fine incisions, and almost wept. "God gave you these hands. Fine and strong. Perfect for a pediatric surgeon."

"I use His gift as He wills it. But back to Papa. He is an international diamond merchant and travels all over the world. He will be in Canada next month, and he will come to see me. You'll meet him. He is eager to meet you, the woman of my dream."

"You didn't tell him, did you?"

"Papa knows all of my dreams, but he did think this one was a bit far-fetched."

"He's not the only one!"

"It was you. I saw you in my dreams, and God said, 'She will be your wife,' as clearly as I am talking to you."

"You know how crazy that sounds, don't you?"

"I do. I am not a mystic, but this is true, and I believed it when I woke. My father, not so much. He laughed and said I needed a woman, so I made one up. He worried because I didn't date much, but you understand what residency is like."

"For Christians, anyway. Some of the residents in my program slept with anything that walked in the door."

"But not for you and not for me."

"You heard the part about my having a baby, didn't you?"

"But that was in secondary school, when you were very young. I was sad for you. You felt unloved by your father, and you became prey for a boy who used you. But I am glad he, the one who left you with child, abandoned you, because you are here with me tonight and—"

She held up her hand to cut him off. "We're getting to know each other, remember? More about your family," she encouraged.

"My mother is a teacher, devoted to her students. She teaches in an excellent private school in Cape Town, but on Saturdays she goes out to the poorest of the poor, in a section outside the city called Cape Flats, and teaches all day to all grades. She gives their teachers lessons for the week, teaching them to teach. Papa adores her, says she is like a Mother Teresa. Mama scoffs at him, but it is true. She works hard. Her students in town become doctors and lawyers, capitalists and government ministers, and her students in the county become teachers and merchants, and some rise into the professions."

"She sounds like a wonderful woman, your mother. How many brothers and sisters?"

"My brother is three years younger. One night my mother answered a student's call for help. Papa was out of town, so she went alone because she thought one of her students needed her. Instead, she was knifed in the belly. She lost her baby, her womb, and part of her intestine. We thought she would die. She was still in a coma when Papa flew home to be by her side. He fasted until he was emaciated. I prayed, 'Please, Father, don't let me lose them both,' and God heard my cry."

"How old were you?"

"Eight. She lost so much blood, you see, and her injuries were severe, life-threatening. She was in the hospital two months. Papa is tender with her, but she is healthy now. Nevertheless, he didn't travel for two years. When the doctors discharged her, can you guess the first place she wanted to go?"

"To her poor students in the country."

"Yes! And Papa was angry. 'I never want you to teach there again. You cannot. Please, Alicia.'

"But she took his hand and said, 'Harry, they did not cut out my heart, but you will.' Of course, he let her go, and he took her himself. We all went that day. I remember the people running beside the car in the crowded, dusty street, laughing and crying. My brother was five then, and he couldn't figure out why there was a parade.

"'It's for your mother, Dennis. She is the saint of the slums. Look at all who adore her,' Papa told us. Dennis plastered his nose to the window, and I wanted to, as well. But of course, I was too old."

"She's been back there ever since, hasn't she?" Michelle asked.

"She has, and now many of the staff at the private school go with her."

"And what does your brother do?"

"He's a priest. The funny thing—God's cosmic joke, right?—is that I am built like Papa, and my brother is built like Mama. Slender. Tall. Lighter skinned. But he has Papa's hands. He laughs about God exchanging our hands. He says he needs big hands to present infants to the congregation after baptism and to lift the chalice high before God and the people when we feast at the Lord's table. Right now, he and his wife and two sons are in England, where he is getting an advanced degree at Westcott in Cambridge."

"Obviously, he's not a Roman priest."

"No, we are in the Anglican Communion, which is called Charismatic Episcopal in this country."

"Oh, I've heard of them, but I've never been to a service."

"You would be comfortable. We are very 'high church,' as they say. I found a wonderful church last Sunday. Where did you go?"

"I've gone to church with Sandy, but maybe I could visit the one you attended." Once again, his lethal smile melted her toes.

"I'd like that very much. How about desert?" Pressing her hand on her stomach, Michelle shook her head. "Come on," he urged. "I'll split the Mocha Bombay with you."

"Oh man, I read about that! You're on."

He did look forward to the last course, but mostly Marcus wanted the evening never to end. He ordered the desert and two spoons. Before she reached for one, he held a taste to her lips. "You first. Tell me how it is."

"Mmm, this must be served at the wedding feast of the Lamb. Have I died and gone to heaven?"

Chuckling, he took a bite from the same spoon and agreed. After they scraped the plate, he ordered another cup of coffee, and she ordered another cup of tea after excusing herself to use the restroom. When she returned, Marcus reached for his billfold, but Michelle reminded him it was her mother's treat. After they settled the bill, he took her hand and suggested they take a walk. "You said it was sketchy, but it is still light out, and it seems to be well patrolled."

"I don't know if you read about the racial tensions in Baltimore. It's not the same as it used to be, but I'm with a large man, right?"

"I will keep you safe." They walked to the railing and looked out over the harbor. The sun still hovered over the water. "It is a long way from my home in South Africa."

"Are you homesick?"

Marcus didn't want to appear weak, but he was honest. "Yes. I love my country, and I love my family."

"You are blessed."

He took her hand and pointed with his other. "Is that a tourist boat? Perhaps we could come if we ever have an afternoon off. What time do you have to be in tomorrow?"

"Seven."

"I took seven, as well, so I could go to church Sunday. I would love to escort you. I will get a taxi."

"I know where you live now. Tell me what time, and I can swing by." Michelle noticed him feeling in his pocket.

His phone must have been on vibrate, and when he glanced down, he said, "Excuse me. It's Papa." The look on his face as he greeted his father sank another of cupid's arrows in her already-riddled heart. "Papa, how are you? Where are you? Kenya? At De Beers mines? And where is Mama? School will start for her soon. No, I'm not at the hospital. At this moment, I am walking along the harbor in Baltimore with the world's most beautiful woman." He laughed. "Mama for you perhaps, but Michelle for me. Every bit. Yeah, sure."

He handed her his phone, and she cradled it with both hands. "Mr. Mansour, nice to talk to you. We aren't that far yet. We only met less than four weeks ago." She laughed. "Yes, he did, but—Yes, I'd say so. He is most attractive. He says he looks like his father." His father laughed and called him a rogue. Michelle handed Marcus back his phone.

"Okay, Papa, thanks. I'll call you later. Maybe tomorrow, then. I love you." He put the phone back in his pocket. "You have charmed Papa. What did you say?"

"He asked if I should be calling him 'Papa.' And then he asked if you had told me about your dream and agreed it was...what did he say? Rather mystical. Almost unbelievable. But he wanted to know how I felt about you."

"I'm happy you find me attractive."

"Get over yourself. Every female in the hospital is swooning over you."

Putting his phone back in his pocket, Marcus took her hand, turning with slow steps toward the parking lot. "We'd better go back. Seven comes early in the morning. Although I don't want this evening to end." He paused and peered at her face. "Are you among those women you say are 'swooning' over me?" The edges of his mouth twitched.

Michelle cut her eyes at him. "Could be."

"I hope so, because I am rejoicing in the one whom God has chosen." Michelle fell silent. "May I kiss you?" Without words, she gave her permission, and he leaned a bit to taste her lips. Putting his head on her forehead, he whispered, "That was nice." He leaned toward her, putting his hands on either side of her cheeks, and she raised her face to receive another kiss, this one somewhat deeper and a whole lot longer. He blew out a long breath when he let her go.

"You should know that that kiss was nice for me, too, but I didn't have a dream, nor did I hear God say I should be your wife, or anyone's wife. I tried that once. I went with a guy in my program at Cleveland Clinic. I thought we were headed for marriage, but my past turned out to be too intense for him. Laura, a pastor's wife, was sure he would be the one when he went to a Hope House reunion with me, but after that night we drifted apart. He learned about my father, and since he was a couple of inches shorter, maybe he agreed that I was too big and too black. Maybe he was too Christian to marry a woman who'd had a baby." She saw his dark eyes shooting fire, but she also saw an intense sadness in them.

"He was no Christian. He has no understanding of God's grace and His redemptive power."

"I did sin, but I confessed my sin, and my advocate took it up with the Father. I feel forgiven."

He didn't say a word, but he kissed her again—a soft, gentle kiss—and took her hand, pulling her close to his side.

Without a word, they walked back to the car. When they got there, she offered to let him drive, but he said she knew the route better. She popped on the GPS, which was programed to his address. "In America, we sing a

Christmas song. It goes, 'Over the river and through the woods, to grand-mother's house we go. The horse knows the way to carry the sleigh..." She giggled, breaking the solemnity. "The GPS knows the way." She patted the dash. "Good horsey."

Chapter Five

PAPA MANSOUR

When Marcus and Michelle bumped into one another as they were leaving after their afternoon shift Sunday evening, she offered him a ride home. They chatted about the church service that morning, Michelle admitting she liked it. They agreed to go out for coffee, but Marcus had blood on his scrubs, so he convinced her to wait in the lobby while he ran upstairs to change. His phone rang, and once again she watched the joy in his expression as he saw it was his father.

"I completed my shift, and Michelle brought me to my place, but we are going for a cup of coffee. I'll let you talk to her while I go upstairs and change." He handed her the phone.

"How are you, Mr. Mansour?"

"How are you and my son doing, daughter?"

"We had a lovely time Friday night, but you should know that the place where he lives is not in a nice neighborhood. It probably isn't safe. He laughs at me, tells me he is big and bad and not afraid, but Baltimore has become lawless, and boys run in gangs." Looking across the cracked linoleum floor in the lobby of the old building, she saw paint peeling off the walls. "Plus, it's dirty and run down."

"When I come, we will see about that. I'm coming to Canada soon, and I'll see my son then. Will you save time for me to meet you? I will let Marcus know when I'll arrive."

Michelle assured him she'd make every effort to meet him. Seeing Marcus coming down the stairs, she began her goodbye, but he interrupted.

"Before I let you go, tell me, when he told you about his dream, you said it was...what did you call it?"

"Weird."

"Yes, it was unusual, but I will tell you that my son hears God. He has from an early age. When he was two, he sat up from his sleep and told us his aunt was dead. Two hours later, we received the call from my father confirming it was so. And he is a faithful man, my son. A good man. He will be a good husband. A good father."

"I see it every day, sir, when we work together."

"You see it already?"

"We work together a lot, and I see him with his little patients. His tenderness and care. You should be proud. He is an excellent doctor. And he treats the staff with kindness. Everyone loves him."

Marcus took the phone. "Papa, you ask too much."

"Have you kissed her?"

"I'm hanging up now." Marcus looked over the phone at Michelle.

"Aha! This is important in a marriage, son. The kissing must have fire."

"Goodnight, Papa. I love you, even if you are too much in my business."

Michelle heard the booming laugh. Did his father call him a rogue? "You didn't talk to him very long. Why did you hang up?"

"Did he ask you too much?"

She chuckled. "He asked how we were getting along, and then he gave me a glowing report of all your good qualities." Marcus lowered his head and shook it. "But I told him I already knew what a good man you are and that he should be proud of his son, the good doctor that you are." Marcus lifted his head and gazed into her eyes, and she knew he wanted to kiss her.

"Come. Let's get the coffee, and let me tell you what a good doctor you are. How you calm the fears of the little ones. How you diagnose their bodies and pour the love of God into their souls."

Rising from the plastic couch, she took his hand. "Lead the way."

They drove out of that neighborhood, went to a Tim Horton's, and talked about his father's visit. When his father came, the department head was going to give Marcus two days since his family lived so far away, and Marcus was going to let her know so she could arrange some time to meet him. As they walked out of the coffee house, she shivered.

"Cold?"

"No, I—" She pointed. "It's a shooting star. Did you see it?"

He put his arm around her. "Maybe it will be a sign for you. A sign of God's blessing."

"I don't wish on stars."

"Neither do I, but I believe in signs and wonders. A star led the wise men to Bethlehem."

She didn't answer, but when she dropped him off, she put her hand on the side of his face. She blinked back tears and gave him a quick and gentle kiss.

* * *

When Mr. Mansour arrived, he came in a day before his son's scheduled time off. He met Michelle briefly when he drove the rental car to the hospital. She would be off the second afternoon of his stay, she told him. To his son, he pronounced her lovely, teasing him about the beautiful babies she would give him. When he visited his son's the room at the boarding house, he agreed with Michelle, calling it a "rat trap" and promising to find him a better place before he left. When Marcus protested, insisting he should live on his salary and that rents near the hospital were high, Mr. Mansour argued that Marcus had earned a marvelous opportunity to train at the best hospital in the world. A decent place to live? This, a father could do.

"Thanks, Papa."

His father put his arm across his shoulder and pulled him close. The two big men were never uncomfortable showing their affection. His father wanted him to stay at the hotel with him, but Marcus said his room was close to the hospital and that he had to check in the next day. His father spent the morning searching for a good property for his son. He put a deposit down, but he waited for his son's approval before signing a lease. These man-children of his had their pride, which was a good thing.

Marcus was overcome when he saw it that afternoon, but his father reminded him that he would soon be married and that he must get a decent place for the two of them. "From your lips to God's ears, Papa. We can pick her up for a brief visit, but she's been working since seven. She will be off the day after tomorrow, and we can have the whole day together."

When he called her, she suggested that she could meet them at his father's hotel for supper when she got off.

"Tell me about this woman. Does she resemble your dream, or did you see her features in the dream?"

"She is the exact woman in my dream. Her face, her voice, her laugh. The moment I saw her, I recognized her." He told his father about the day they met and how they were now working together. "She's amazing. She has a gift for calming the children. When I cannot get through their hysteria, I call her. She picks them up through all the wires and tubes, holds them in her arms, rocks them, sways side to side, and even sings. One day I stood at the door and watched. I couldn't take my eyes off her. I felt God's presence. Michelle held the little girl, and when the phlebotomist came in for the second time to draw blood, we had no more trouble. She walked out the door and whispered, 'Where did the little hellcat in this room go?' This is who Michelle is.

"The only time we have disagreed was over a patient I scheduled for surgery. She blocked the surgery, saying he was coming down with something, but I thought it was necessary immediately. I thought his problems were entirely due to his need for surgery. She insisted on another blood test and stood her ground. She was right. If I had operated before we treated his infection, he could have died. She's an excellent diagnostician. Sometimes she gets in trouble for slowing surgeries down, but she is careful."

Glancing at his watch, his father asked if they needed to go somewhere to pick her up. Marcus told him she was driving over but that perhaps they should walk downstairs to meet her. When they got to the front door, she was turning in.

She gave the valet a tip when she got out of the car. Seeing them, she smiled. She stretched out her hand to Mr. Mansour, but he pulled her into his arms as if he'd known her all her life. She cried—like a child, she cried—so Mr. Mansour held her, rubbing small circles on her back.

Harry Mansour felt that his heart was strangely connected to this precious daughter, and he was as convinced as his son that she was God's chosen for him and for his family.

Michelle stepped back, embarrassed, explaining she'd worked a double shift and had been on her feet since 7:00 a.m. She sniffed, and Harry pulled his handkerchief out of his pocket, wiping her eyes and nose with a father's touch, and then Marcus put his arm around her shoulder and walked her to the dining room.

From what his son had told him, and from what he had seen within their brief introduction, Harry thought that she was unusually quiet this evening, though she was gracious and conversant.

Marcus seated her, pushing her chair in and touching her shoulder, and she turned to his father. "Mr. Mansour—"

"Please, it's Harry, or better yet, call me 'Papa.'"

She started crying again. Marcus squatted beside her and pulled her head to his shoulder. He dabbed her eyes with his own handkerchief.

Harry placed a hand on her arm. "You had a hard day?" He didn't know what to do with the weeping woman before him.

She was surrounded by love—masculine love—from a father and a son. "You really don't mind if I call you 'Papa'?"

"This son and I hope it will soon be so."

"You see, my father... I never called him 'Dad' or 'Daddy.' If I called him anything, it was 'Father.' And he never held me like that. Never. That was a new experience for me." She lifted her eyes, and tears still stood on her lashes.

How cruel. A man who did not show love to his daughter. "You will call me 'Papa.' It is settled." He looked at his son. "Now, my son, you make it so." *God help me, I will show this daughter the love of the Father. Please, Sir, help me to do this.* Harry watched as Marcus kissed her forehead before taking his seat, and Harry tried to ease her discomfort by telling her about his son's new apartment. After they selected their dinners, he said, "You were right, daughter. That place where he was living..." He shuddered. "That place is not habitable."

"I have inhabited that place for over two months."

"It didn't even have a bathroom! What were you thinking? We will pay off your lease."

"It leases from month to month."

"Month to month? That should have been a clue, for heaven's sake," Michelle said.

Harry laughed. "Indeed, a giveaway. Who lives there? Drug dealers moving to their next hideout?"

"All right, you can help me move tomorrow."

"Where did you bathe?" Michelle asked.

"I have a sink in my room, and a toilet and bathing facilities are shared down the hall."

"That is just gross! I've seen some skanky people in that building."

"Another idiom, but it needs no interpretation." He shook his head. "I run in the mornings, and I bathe in the hospital showers."

"Thank God! I don't want you to carry something into the hospital, or give it to me."

Michelle did brighten up when she got some food in her system, and she told Harry about her training at Cleveland Clinic. She started working for the hospital after finishing. He wanted to ask about her family, but given what she had shared already, he thought he'd wait for another time.

Because of her long day, she left after dinner. They fretted about her driving alone and made her promise to text when she got to the apartment, but she assured them she had an underground parking garage. The two men went to the room on the sixth floor, and Harry asked Marcus about her family.

Marcus filled his father in on what he knew of her past and present, omitting the story of her baby. That was hers to tell. He told him that her father and brother were Harvard-trained attorneys; that her father worked in a high-powered firm in D. C.; that her brother was in DOJ, America's office of national justice; that ger mother had a job in Health, Education, and Welfare, another government agency; and that her sister-in-law taught at Georgetown. They were Catholics, he told his father, but nominal, and she liked the church he had found in Baltimore. "She is deeply devoted to God. I see her pray over her patients, sometimes with them, and we pray together."

"This is good, to share your faith. God chose well." And he told his son about his overwhelming sense that she belonged to him and to this family.

"She is the other half of me."

"As it should be."

"I feel the strangest connection. Even before I see her, I know when she is in the oncology unit. I have an awareness of her presence, and it's comforting. And when she is with me in the operating room, everything goes better. One day she was late, and surgery had started. I was having a particularly difficult time tying off a bleeder. She moved the scrub nurse aside to stand beside me, which she doesn't usually do, but maybe she sensed my desperation. I was sweating. She told the nurse to clean the field, and she wiped my forehead. I felt like God touched me. Stronger. Surer. And I saw what I had to do. Immediately, I tied it off."

"She is a helpmate suited for you."

"I thought it would be hard to have her in surgery because she's beautiful and I love her. But when we work together, we are both focused on the patient."

"How long after you walk out of the room, huh? Not long. And then you want to hold her in your arms and caress her. When will you marry?"

"She finds it hard to believe my dream."

"You must admit, it is unusual, but you have always heard the voice of God. Even knowing that, I didn't believe until it came to pass. She has many hurts, and to trust a man will be difficult. Did her father truly say those things to her? I prayed to God that I could show her the Father's love."

"You did, Papa. You don't know how much healing you poured into a rejected child."

"She is a strong woman, then, to have overcome such a loveless childhood. God has given you this precious, wounded child to love. You must love her well."

"She hasn't seen him in over a decade."

Harry's jaw dropped. "Her own father? My heart is broken." He wiped tears. "Dear Jesus," he whispered.

"Her mother came to her medical school graduation. She gave her a cell phone so they could remain in touch, and they see each other often. They live in D.C. I'm meeting her for lunch when she comes over one day next week."

"Good. Win the mother, and you will win the father."

"I thought Grandfather respected your skills in the diamond industry."

"It was a long time coming, son. A long, hard battle." He shook his head as if to clear the memories. "Let's go to bed. You have to go in tomorrow?"

"Only for a little bit. We can settle things in the apartment, and the next day Michelle will be with us all day."

* * *

Marcus and his father had moved him out of the boarding house and into the new apartment when Michelle joined them the next afternoon. They drove over to his hotel, and once again she felt a father's arms around her, a kiss on her cheek. She reached up and, with a feather-light touch, caressed the side of the older man's face. He took her hand and asked her to help him find gifts to take home, tucking her hand in his arm as they went down the line of shops.

The following day, on her day off, they drove to Washington, wandering the National Gallery of Art and the main Smithsonian, then had lunch in the Air and Space museum. Marcus's papa loved these buildings. He pointed up to the old planes hanging above them, and he wanted to see the simulated deck of a warship. He could almost hear the waves, feel the spray, and smell the salt air, he told her.

Michelle initiated the hug when they parted, and she glowed as she reveled in his praise. She was beautiful, she was kind, she was a good doctor, and she was the perfect wife for his son, he told her. God had chosen. Choking back tears, she said, "I love you, Papa," and he drew her into his arms and held her. She clung to him for a long time.

When she stepped back, he said, "You set up this wedding, and Mama and I will be here."

Chapter Six

MARCUS MEETS LOUISE LOGAN

Marcus hoped he could be half the man his father was. His papa was good at loving. Michelle didn't argue about the wedding, but she didn't bring it up when they were alone, and he wasn't sure where to go in the relationship. He knew, even without his divine revelation, this woman was the one for him, but he was determined to continue the courtship. Every time his father called and she was near, they talked, and when he asked if they had set the date, she would laugh and say, "Not yet."

If not now, when, Lord? How long must I wait? Give me patience, Marcus thought.

He went to a nearby café with Michelle so they could meet her mother for lunch. Michelle waved, and the older woman stood and hugged her daughter.

"Mother, this is Marcus Mansour, the doctor from South Africa I've told you about."

"The oncologist. I've heard a lot about you. Michelle has the highest respect for your work."

Marcus felt his heart sink. *She respects my work. Not a word about us.* Marcus took Mrs. Logan's hand. "I respect hers. She is an excellent diagnostician. The best. She keeps me on my toes."

"I'm glad you're here and that I finally get to meet you. You're all she talks about, a regular paragon."

Some better. I guess no daughter would confide she lusts after a guy. I hope she feels a touch of lust. I'm no paragon of virtue when I think about her daughter, that's for sure! he thought, but he said aloud, "Excuse me. What did you say?"

Michelle asked him if he knew what he wanted to eat, and Mrs. Logan urged him to sit, inviting him to call her "Louise," and launched into questions about his family in an interview style.

Finally, Michelle rescued him. "Mother, you're giving him the third degree. Let him eat!"

"I'm sorry, but I know you must get back to work, and your father wants to know the answers to all of these questions."

Marcus reached for Michelle's hand under the table as he saw the bitterness tighten her mouth.

"Since when does my father care about me or my relationships?"

Thank God, we do have a relationship! He swiveled his head to look at Louise, realizing she looked hurt.

"Please, dear. You know your father cares."

"He cares about his precious reputation, not so much his big, ugly daughter."

"Where do you get that?"

"Oh, Mother, we both know you and Andrea are beautiful, and Father is proud of you, but I am the black sheep, if you'll pardon the expression."

Louise was indeed a beautiful woman. She was tall. Not as tall as Michelle, but close to 5'9", Marcus guessed, and she had hazel eyes and a sleek, willowy body. Louise straightened her hair, but he preferred Michelle's close cut, which shaped her curls to her skull, defining her long, regal neck. Once again, he turned his head. This was beginning to feel like a tennis match as the women lobbed one comment after another at each other.

Louise covered her daughter's hand. "Can we put all this unpleasantness behind us? You've never even met your nephews, and I do want our family to come back together."

"Mother, I have to protect myself from toxic relationships. Neither Father nor HJ has attempted to reach out to me, and I've been here since July."

I need Papa here to help me bolster her ego after this conversation.

The women studiously avoided further conflict, talking about banal topics: a concert her mother attended, funny things Michelle's roommates did, the new puppy the boys wanted, and Beatrice's objections. All non-controversial. Nothing to draw them closer or further apart. When they rose to go, Louise offered them a ride, but Marcus declined, saying they'd enjoy the walk.

"It looks like rain. You'd better get along, then."

"We'll finish our coffee and head out. Thank you for lunch, Louise."

"We must do it again sometime." Michelle's mother kissed her on the cheek and waved her fingers.

Marcus wondered what he could say. "Lovely woman."

"She is. I look like my father."

Missed it. Guess I heaped it on higher. I wish she could believe her beauty. She is such a goddess!

"Ready to go?" She pushed her chair back and started for the door.

He pushed it open, and the wind snatched it from his hands. Leaves were swirling in eddies above their heads, and huge splatters fell on their upturned faces. Marcus noted some abandoned umbrellas by the door and asked the manager if they could borrow one.

"Take one. They've been hanging around for months. I think the striped one is a double size."

"Thanks." Marcus tried to shelter Michelle with his body, but the wind flapped their pant legs and attempted to rip off their jackets. They jogged toward the hospital. Despite the umbrella, they were soaked in the slanting rain. Grabbing her hand, he tried to run against the storm. A giant burst of air turned the umbrella inside out, and pellets of hail stung their arms. Marcus lifted his head into the downpour and hollered, "God, are you angry with me?"

An angry surge of thunder rolled. And the wind ceased. And the sun came out.

Michelle stood, dripping, staring at him. "Who are you, Marcus Mansour?"

He shook his head, his own eyes as wide as hers. "I'm an ordinary guy, a humble Christian who loved you before we met. Maybe God wants to prove Himself to you."

He offered her his hand, and each step they took squished. He opened the door into the basement at the back of the hospital and noticed her shirt was glued to her, revealing all of her delightful curves. He sucked in his breath as his body responded to her. To keep from looking at her, he pulled her fiercely to his chest and held her tight against him, lowering his lips to hers in a deep and hungry kiss. Wrong move. Now she could feel the firm length of him. He stepped back. "I'm sorry. I shouldn't have... I didn't mean for that to happen."

"I was as much into it as you were." She broke away and led them up the stairs, still squishing water with every step. She giggled.

The beeper on his waist went off, and he stood by a window on the first floor to punch the number on his cell phone. "Yes, sir, we got caught in the rain. Yes, she is." Michelle's phone cut off in the middle of a ring. "They're looking for both of us. Fifth floor."

On this fateful day, they met Cassie Stewart. Dr. Campbell told them he wanted them both on this seemingly hopeless case, so they walked in together. The patient had been referred by a hospital in the eastern pan-handle of West Virginia, and they had sent her in a last-ditch effort to treat brain cancer. Bald, yet still beautiful, with soft creamy skin, she took them in with solemn, huge blue eyes, all but trembling in fear.

Michelle twirled in front of the ten-year-old child. "Look at me! We got caught in the rain." She shook her head and sent flying drips. Cassie smiled. Michelle took her hand. "Glad to meet you, Cassie Stewart. Dr. Mansour and I are your doctors here. I'm Dr. Logan. He looks big, but don't be afraid; he's really a teddy bear."

Cassie's eyes darted over to him, and Marcus grinned. "You're not sup-posed to tell, Dr. Logan. How will I frighten the others?" He lifted the child's hand and pinched her skin gently, then looked up to see if Michelle saw her dehydration, and they exchanged a nod. Marcus grabbed two towels out of the bathroom and tossed one to her. They dried off as best as they could. "Did they tell you that you wouldn't stay in this room? Dr. Logan and I hang out on the eighth floor most of the time, but we're waiting for a bed. If we like you, we'll take you upstairs with us." Curving his hand under her chin her chin and then touch her nose lightly, he asked, "What do you say, Dr. Logan? Shall we keep her?"

"Oh, she's definitely a keeper. What do you say, Cassie? Shall we keep you?"

"Where's Mama?"

"Did you come in an ambulance?"

The girl whispered, "Yes."

"Did they turn the sirens on for you?"

"Sometimes."

"She'll be here in a little bit. In traffic, you got ahead of her. How about I wait with you while Dr. Mansour finds you a room upstairs?"

"I'd like that."

"I'd like you to drink for me, as much as you can." Michelle poured water in a glass and bent a straw to her dry lips. "Do you like Ginger Ale?" Her head moved from side to side with effort. "A little more, sweetie?"

"They told me she'd be on the eighth floor," a healthy, larger version of Cassie said as she stepped into the room, "but Dr. Mansour told me where you were. Hi, baby, how was the trip?"

Cassie held out her thin arms, and her mother lifted her. "I'm so tired, Mama."

"I know." She looked over to Michelle. "Dr. Logan?"

"Michelle Logan, Mrs. Stewart."

"Suzanne Stewart. Dr. Mansour says I'll like you."

"You'll have to forgive him. He's a bit prejudiced, but you won't find a better doctor."

"He said the same thing about you. You guys work together a lot?"

"All the time. I'll watch him carefully, Cassie, so the old teddy bear won't hurt you."

"I like him. He's funny."

"Who is funny?" said the man in question, pushing through the door. "Teddy bears aren't funny; they're cuddly. Will you cuddle with me, Cassie? I'm going to carry you to your room."

Michelle opened her mouth, but he interrupted her. "Rules are made to be broken, Dr. Logan, and this little girl breaks all my rules. Put your arms around my neck, pumpkin."

An aide came up to them with a gurney, but Marcus shook his head. "I've got her."

Michelle pushed the elevator button, and Marcus swept in, the wisp of a child swallowed in his arms. The entire space of the elevator was filled with his presence, his gentleness. "Cassie says she's tired, Dr. Mansour. I thought she could nap a little?"

He pressed his lips on the child's forehead. "Does that sound good to you, precious?"

When they got out of the elevator, he proceeded down the hall, but Michelle showed Suzanne Stewart to the hygiene station. She was familiar with the protocol and scrubbed up to her elbows, then applied the antibiotic lotion. They got to the room and found Marcus holding the girl in his lap.

He looked up. "We needed a bit of a cuddle, but she's ready to stretch out now." He gently placed her under the covers. "Dr. Logan is going to give you a little cup to drink so you can nap. Sweet dreams."

Suzanne sat beside her daughter until her chest rose and fell. "I've met an angel. A huge, black angel. Two of them."

"Marcus might qualify, but I sure don't, except for the huge, black part." Seeing the child's mother was at the breaking point, Michelle took her to the consultation room, where Marcus was inputting on the computer.

Suzanne sat in a chair Michelle offered, and Marcus rolled his beside her and took her hand. "I need to ask your expectations. Is Cassie's father part of the picture?"

"Yes. We're in constant touch, but we have three other children. Between us, we trade off, but since she's gotten...so bad, he has a hard time." Her lips trembled. "I do, too." She took a bedraggled tissue out of her purse. Michelle handed her a fresh box and a trash can for her shredded one. "We don't have any expectations, really. We've been told Cassie is beyond hope. We figured the hospital sent her here to die."

Marcus blew out his breath. "We can provide comfort care to mitigate her pain, but we can consider some options. It may not be successful, but we're willing to try."

"I can't stand to see her suffer anymore. I feel selfish. We've put her through hell—surgery, chemo, radiation. What would you do if she were your child?"

"You've had her in treatment for four years?" Marcus looked at the screen in front of him. "Since she was six?"

"They said it was very aggressive. We had hope after the surgery, but..." She looked at him, tears swimming in her eyes

"I don't think internal radiation would hurt to try, and it's not painful. Why don't you and your husband pray about that?"

"We've never been... We don't exactly go to church."

"God will meet you where you are." Marcus stood and touched her shoulder. "Ask Dr. Logan or me any questions you want, and we'll give you the best answers we can."

Michelle stood, and Suzanne realized the consultation was over. The ball was in her court, and she looked wary of making these decisions.

"Are you going home, Mrs. Stewart?" Michelle walked with her toward Cassie's room.

"I can't leave her. I have a three-year-old, a seven-year-old, and a twelve-year-old at home. I miss them. Their sister has been sick for most of their lives, and all of Julie's."

"Julie's the baby?"

Suzanne nodded. "When we got pregnant, Norman suggested an abortion. Neither one of us were fans of abortion, but we were consumed with

Cassie's care. Norm adores Julie, maybe because we almost didn't have her." Suzanne rubbed her nose on her sleeve, and Michelle held up the tissue box. Grabbing a handful, the mother turned her eyes, which were Cassie-blue, on the doctor, asking, "Do you pray, too?"

Michelle followed her into the room. "I do. Would you like me to pray with you now?"

With the mother's permission, Michelle prayed, placing Cassie in the Father's care, asking God to guide their decisions, to relieve Cassie's suffering, and to bless and strengthen this family and grant them peace.

"Thank you. And no, I won't be going home. I can't leave her here alone in a strange city, a strange hospital."

"I'll arrange for a sleeping chair and some linens, then, and we'll see you tomorrow."

Michelle went to look for Marcus and found him coming out of another patient's room. He told her that Mr. Hawkins was going home tomorrow, and they rejoiced. His prognosis looked better.

"Ready to go?" he asked. "If you give me a ride, I'll provide your dinner. I have some roast chicken in the refrigerator, and we can toss up a salad."

"It's a deal." Michelle matched him stride for stride, and they headed for the stairs. Eight flights, nine to the basement. Their daily exercise.

"She's a heart thief." Marcus broke the silence.

"A what?"

"Papa would meet a particularly precocious child, or a special-needs one, and say, 'This one's a heart thief. She'll steal your heart.' Cassie's one of those."

"Yeah."

"You know we can't do much."

"You think she's hopeless."

"For man. Who knows what God will do?" He stopped and turned her to face him. "Guard your heart, Chelle." And he touched the one lone tear trickling down her cheek.

They rode to his apartment in silence. He put the chicken in the microwave to warm, and they stood side by side to wash and cut the veggies. The simple meal was sufficient. After they ate, they went to the pleasant living room. She sat on the black leather sofa, and he was in the matching chair. He nodded to the big screen TV on the wall and said he never had time to watch it. They discussed the few options available, Marcus holding out for implanting radiation near the vestiges of the tumor, the resistant, stubborn spots.

Later, holding her hand, he walked her to the door, and this time it was only three flights down to her car.

He kissed her briefly. "You know I love you."

"I love you, too," she replied before cranking her car and pulling off.

* * *

Suzanne and her husband agreed to one more course of treatments, and Cassie seemed more comfortable afterward. Norm, her father, made it in over the weekend, leaving her brothers and baby sister with relatives. Marcus liked the guy, and he could read the misery and pain in his face. Her father held Cassie in his lap, stringing the IVs off to the side. She dozed, and he leaned his head back on the chair. Suzanne went home for the day. Marcus wondered how long it had been since they had shared the comfort of lying in bed together, holding each other, and making love. His gut twisted.

"My insurance agreed to try this." Norm looked up at him. Cassie was asleep on his lap, her thin fingers tangled in the front of his shirt.

"We're out of options here," Marcus replied.

"I know, doc. I didn't figure... But Suzanne wanted to give it a try. One last shot, you know." Marcus sat beside him. "Cassie sang me some songs today. She seems happier, more peaceful."

"Michelle spends a lot of time with her. She likes to sing to kids."

"Dr. Logan? She is the sweetest woman, so gentle and kind. Suzanne loves her."

When Cassie stirred in her father's lap, he asked her if she wanted to eat, but she wasn't hungry. She took some juice and lay back on his chest, whispering, "I love you, Daddy."

Kissing her softly on the forehead, he told her he loved her, too, and Marcus thought his heart would break. "Nothing to do, then," the father said.

"We'll keep her comfortable."

Seeing Suzanne coming in, Norm rested the shell of his little girl on the sheet and tucked the covers over her, leaned to kiss her forehead.

"I'm glad you had a safe trip. Are the kids okay?" Marcus asked.

"They never want me to leave. Maybe it won't be much longer." She broke down, and Norm took her in his arms while Marcus slipped out.

When he came back, the couple was gone. Michelle stood alone, her head leaning on the window, and stared into the dark. He moved beside her, and she said, "I knew you were here. How did I know that?" She turned to face him.

They tried to be circumspect in the hospital. Although everyone knew they were a couple, they remained professional. Standing several feet away, he could feel the heat of her. If he touched her, they would burn up. Maybe they would turn into a crisp, and he wouldn't have to watch this child die.

"I know when you walk on the floor, even if I'm in a room," Marcus replied. "I feel your presence, and it calms me. I feel strong and powerful. Although sometimes I want to grab you and kiss you silly." He got a chuckle out of her, which was what he intended, but he knew she had to face the reality before them. "She's getting weaker. She told her Daddy goodbye, and I think she knows. He said she sang him some songs."

"She likes 'Fairest Lord Jesus' and 'Jesus Loves the Little Children.' She likes to hear stories about Jesus, and Suzanne listens as intently as she does."

* * *

45

Over the days and weeks that had passed, Marcus's conviction had grown firmer. Michelle seemed to have feelings for him, and he wrestled with what he should do next. One night he was walking home in the dark, trying to walk off his need for her, and the wind picked up. He wrapped his coat around him and brooded. His love burned inside of him. This tall, magnificent woman was his Valkyrie, his magnificent black goddess. She held his life in her hands, and he hoped she would choose life for him, and soon.

Louise called him later that night. After asking where Michelle was and learning she wouldn't be off until 11:00 p.m., she asked how things were going between them, and he told her his fanciful notion.

"Valkyrie. Isn't that Norse mythology?"

"She holds my life in her hands."

"I wondered. Herman wants to know your intentions."

Marcus bit off a retort. As if the man had any right to know. "I will marry her as soon as she allows it, Mrs. Logan, but she seems to have a visceral mistrust of masculine affection."

Louise hesitated. "She has every right to be bitter, you know."

"I know."

"Did she tell you...?"

"About the baby? Yes, she did. And about being sent away to school when she was what? Ten? Twelve?"

"Can we make it up to her?" He remained silent. "Will you help us?"

Marcus rubbed his hand over his eyes. *Father, what do I say?* "I will always stand with Michelle. If there are 'sides' to this, I'm on her side."

"Good. She needs someone to be on her side."

"But I will pray. God is a Redeemer, the author of reconciliation. He has reconciled us with Himself. She is a woman of faith—strong faith—and given a chance, I trust her to do the right thing."

"That's all I can ask. Is she all right? She hasn't talked to me in a while."

"We're losing a tough battle. A little cancer patient. Ten years old. She's taking it pretty hard."

"I didn't know," she replied in a small voice.

"Now you do." Marcus hung up. He felt petty, but the ones who should have been on her side all her life had not been there for her, and he was angry.

Pulling his coat back on, turning his collar up, and jamming a hat on his shaved head, he went outside. He walked, not counting the blocks, but he found himself near his old neighborhood, where he saw a bunch of thugs beating an old man. Enraged by injustice in general, cold fury swept over him. He pulled them off, tossing first one and then another to the side. Cursing, they threatened them.

"I've walked the streets of Soweto, boys, and I've seen the worst and learned the worst, and if you want to taste a piece of me, come on." The look in the giant man's eyes pushed them back, and they fled.

Marcus picked up the dirty, smelly old man and tried to think of the nearest shelter. He reached for his cell and punched 911. An ambulance was dispatched, and he surrendered the man to the EMTs, explaining the situation and guessing he was homeless. Police arrived as the ambulance pulled off. Marcus gave them his contact information, and they said they'd get ahold of him to identify the attackers, asking if the victim had been robbed.

"He didn't have anything to rob. It was senseless violence."

When Marcus didn't hear from Michelle later, he figured she was tired, because they usually talked when one or the other got off late. He missed the sound of her voice, but when he went in the next morning, he learned that Cassie had died a few minutes before he had arrived, and Michelle had been with Suzanne all night. He knew she must've been exhausted. She went to the doctor's lounge to lie down, and he peeked in, finding her asleep.

Later, he learned she went down to pediatrics and worked the 7:00–3:00 shift. His pager beeped, and he dialed oncology.

"Dr. Mansour, Dr. Logan has been sitting in Cassie's room in the dark for over an hour."

"Didn't she get off at three?"

"She arrived shortly after three, and she's been here ever since. I hate to tell her, but the body's been taken, and we need to turn the room around."

He strode to the stairs and went up to the floor two steps at a time. He nudged the door and saw her in the dark, frozen, curled into a ball in the only chair. "Michelle?"

Her large, empty eyes sought his face, and his heart broke. He dropped to his knees beside her and pulled her into his arms. "We lost this one, baby. We can't win them all. She fought the good fight, and because of you, we'll see her again."

"I want Papa to hold me." Her voice was as broken as her heart.

"I'll do the best I can." He pulled her up, wrapping his arms around her until the dam burst. He didn't try to shush her. She needed this, and he knew it. He felt like weeping himself.

"Take me home with you. Aren't you about ready to leave? I thought you left. You signed the death certificate."

"I had some other patients to see, but I'm finished now."

"Take me home."

Marcus wasn't ready for this. He wanted to hold her, to love her, entirely inappropriately, but he couldn't tell her no. He picked up her purse and took her hand. This time they took the elevator to the garage, and he drove her car to his apartment. The silence was soft, poignant. They didn't need words. They both loved Cassie and had hoped against hope that the treatment would be the breakthrough. He led her into the apartment. She walked into his arms again, and he held her. What else could he do?

"Sweetie, I don't think this is such a good idea."

"What?"

"For me to bring you here. Maybe in a while we'll take you home."

She clutched him. "Don't leave me. I need you. Why can't I stay?"

"I love you. And when a man loves this much, he wants. I want you. It's driving me crazy. I'm trying to wait, but God knows it's hard. I've waited all my life for you." His lips sought hers, and she responded with passion. He stepped back. "Do you know what I mean?" Tears slipped down her cheeks, and he kissed them and then groaned.

"Why haven't you asked me to marry you?"

Taking her by the hand, he led her to the couch, where they sat facing one another. "Whenever I mentioned making you my wife, you stopped me. You said we needed to get to know one another. I didn't want to push you away. I was waiting for you to say something."

"We've known each other five months. We've been together in crisis situations. I know you as well as I've known any man. I thought when I called your father 'Papa,' that was a clue."

Marcus leaned his head back. *Six weeks ago! She's been ready that long? We could have been married by now.* "Sweetheart, I'm a man. We are clueless. You must spell it out to me. Will you marry me?"

"Yes! Yes. I love you. You're the one I will love for the rest of my life. I've waited all my life for you, too."

"How soon? Yesterday would have been good. Last week would've been even better."

Michelle giggled. At least she wasn't crying anymore. "We'll have to ask Father Manny about that."

"I'll call him right now." And he did, explaining they wanted to move quickly. He put the phone on speaker, and they responded together. Yes, soon, she agreed. Yes, they had remained celibate. It meant a great deal to them. At the end of the conversation, they determined they could be married by Christmas if they did six weeks of counseling in three. Marcus disconnected, their first appointment scheduled. "Can we do this? I don't want you short-changed. I want you to have a wedding. Every bride deserves a wedding."

"I don't want a big wedding. We need to check with your folks to see when they can come."

"And yours."

"Mom will come. She likes you."

"I like her, too. You don't think your father will come?"

"I doubt it. It will be short notice, and he's too busy."

"You will ask?"

She blew her breath out, struggling for composure. "I'll ask."

Marcus emailed his father, and the phone rang. He was up late because he was traveling. They worked out a time to skype with his mother, and they sent out save the date announcements that afternoon.

Marcus and Michelle ordered Chinese delivery and talked about their plans for a small wedding while they ate. The meal was interrupted by a call on Michelle's cell from Cassie's mother.

"Michelle, I'm sorry. I was so upset while packing up Cassie's things that I forgot to tell you. Before you got there, Cassie looked up into heaven. Her last words were, 'Mama, I see Jesus coming for me. Don't be sad.' She never regained consciousness. You should know that, and I want to go to church with you this Sunday because I want to be with her one day. Would you see if your pastor would do her services?"

"I'm with Dr. Mansour now. We'll ask, but I feel confident he will. He has prayed with us for Cassie. I'm sorry we—"

"You did all you could. I know that, and Cassie loved you both. You know that. God brought you into our lives to prepare our child for her heavenly home. She doesn't hurt anymore. I'm glad for that. I wanted you to know."

"Thank you, Suzanne. She changed my life, and I'll remember her always. Keep in touch, unless it's too painful. We understand. I love you, too. Goodnight."

Michelle described the conversation to Marcus, and they rejoiced. The testimony brought on another bout of tears, however, and Michelle fell asleep on his shoulder. He eased her down on the couch and covered her with a blanket. Then he sent a quick text to her roommates and wrote a long email to his brother.

He heard her moving at about a quarter to 5:00 a.m., but she'd fallen asleep around 7:00 p.m. last night. He'd turned in himself at about 9:00 p.m., but sleep was hard to come by with her in his living room. He shoved himself out of bed and saw her coming out of the bathroom. "Hi, want coffee?"

"That'd be good. My clothes are pretty wrinkled since I slept in them."

"I texted Pat and Sandy." She rubbed her eyes and stretched. He looked away. "Uh, I could get you a robe if you want to throw your clothes in the washer."

"Not a bad idea."

He got the robe but decided she should put her own things in the washer. He didn't feel comfortable handling her undergarments. She wandered into the kitchen, wrapped in his robe, which dragged behind her, and he tried not to imagine what was underneath, or not. He swallowed, handing her a cup of coffee with cream.

"Thanks, you know the way I like it."

Okay, not going there. "I have something for you. Papa sent it last week." Marcus went into the bedroom and returned with a small box. "It may need to be sized, but it's a ring. I hope you like it. Please tell me if you'd rather pick something yourself."

Taking the box in both hands, she flipped it open and gasped. "I can't! It's too much."

"He's a diamond merchant. What can I say? You should see Mama's."

"It's beautiful!" She slipped it on. "It fits perfectly."

"Papa has a pretty good eye. I noticed him holding your hand and turning it over."

"You know I can't wear this at the hospital." She held out her hand and rotated it. The facets sparkled, dancing across the room. "If we're sealing this with a ring, can I have a kiss?"

"Probably not. At least until you get dressed." He averted his eyes.

Looking down, she saw the neckline of his robe gaping open. She drew it together and clutched it while he turned his face away.

"Twenty-three days, God help me." Marcus rubbed his head. He kept it shaved, as it made it easier to keep a sterile field. Michelle wore her hair cropped close to her head so she didn't have to fight the curls. He thought she looked elegant, almost regal, with her long, slender neck. He got another cup of coffee and drank it too quickly, swallowing it in a gulp.

Awareness dawned on Michelle's face. She dropped her head. "I should've gone home."

"Probably. Let me get you a shirt to wear under that at least." Going into his bedroom, he brought out a T-shirt, and she went into the bathroom. He heard the shower and sat down at the table, putting his head on his crossed arms, his imagination running wild, thinking of her naked body and the water running over it. When the shower cut off, he thought about her toweling herself dry, and then she came out. Without looking at her, he told her he kept new toothbrushes in the second drawer. She thanked him, left, and came back. The robe was tightly tied when she crossed the kitchen to put her clothes in the dryer.

Twenty-three days, Marcus reminded himself. He put bacon in a pan and scrambled some eggs, telling her to sit still and not move. She giggled. He wondered if she knew what she was doing to him. "I have to be in by six-thirty."

"I can be ready by then. All I need is the clothes to be done."

"All I need is the clothes to be *on.*"

"Only for twenty-three days."

He groaned. "You're killing me."

She smiled. "Be good."

"I'm trying. Get dressed, and I'll get the car and meet you out front."

Chapter Seven

NOT A SMALL WEDDING

Because Father Manny was flexible with his schedule, they completed a long appointment that week, and he gave them some books to read. By the end of the week, over a hundred people indicated they wanted to attend. They were surprised, as it was short notice and a busy season. Michelle was thrilled that Cathy was flying in and that Missy planned to drive. Marcus's brother couldn't come because he was standing for examinations. Marcus was holding his breath about her father, but when he stopped by her apartment that evening, she was angrier than he'd ever seen her.

Marcus stepped back. "Whoa, what's wrong?"

"My father! He's planning to walk me down the aisle as if the last fourteen years didn't happen. He just assumed. He gave me away years ago. The nerve of him! I have a good mind to tell him to go jump off a cliff. I hope he breaks his neck."

Although Marcus understood, he choked back a laugh. To hide his twitching lips, he drew her into an embrace and kissed the side of her face. Collecting himself, he suggested they pray. They certainly didn't want him to break his neck until he confessed to the Savior, did they?

His arms stilled her rage. She knotted her fingers in his lab coat. "Pray for them who despitefully use you. Daddy dearest wants to add another hundred people to the guest list. All his Washington cronies. But he said he'd pay for the reception. How he can pull it off in such a short time is beyond me. And he still hasn't talked to me. All of this was by email!"

Marcus shook his head. "We can't fit that many people in our little church. We'll talk to Father Manny. We're late already."

As they drove to the church, Michelle frantically texted and asked the priest's advice on the numbers and her estranged father wanting to be a big hero.

Father Manny was chuckling as he swung the doors open and ushered them in. Marcus winked at him.

"If I weren't so needy, I'd delay this wedding," Marcus teased. "And if I didn't want it to be a sacred occasion, I'd elope."

Michelle glared at him.

"I'm teasing, sweetheart. We'll figure this all out."

"Yeah, in less than three weeks?"

"I've already contacted a friend who is a priest in Washington," Father Manny informed them. "He has a large building. When the Episcopal Diocese put it up for sale, a wealthy parishioner bought it and donated it to the congregation. We can take your scheduled day off, Michelle, and have our one-on-one as we drive over to look. It's beautiful, and it will work out fine. Our first order of business appears to be your father and the pain he has caused you. You said you haven't seen him in four-teen years?" The wound was lanced, and the bitterness poured out. As a minister, the good father had heard such tales of rejection, and his heart reached out to Michelle. "Marcus is right. We need to pray."

Michelle looked up. "We learned to choose forgiveness at Hope House. I learned I must choose. It's not how we feel, but obedience and feelings will follow the choice."

"You had some good counsellors."

"Excellent, Father, and deeply spiritual." She bowed her head. "Dear God, again I choose to forgive my father. He is lost, and he needs You. May my forgiveness touch his heart. Help me, Holy Spirit! Let this be a beginning of restoration."

Marcus saw her struggle and put his hand on her shoulder. He missed his own father, who would know what to say.

Michelle bitterly noted that it wasn't about love, but showing off his daughter, the doctor.

"It's a start," Father Manny said. "But we need to get back to completing this workbook. Did you do the next chapters?"

The couple handed over their papers, and they went over the answers.

* * *

On Michelle's day off, Father Manny picked her up. Because he knew the way, he did the driving to Dr. Mondalah's church. "He, too, is African," he explained, "but he's from Rwanda. Otiano was from the Tutsi tribe. Do you remember the civil war in Rwanda?"

"Isn't that where the Hutus and the Tutsis butchered each other in the 90s?"

"Yes. Otiano was at seminary when the bloodshed began. By the time he made his way home, his mother and father, all of his siblings, and his entire village were ransacked. Everyone he loved was murdered."

"And he's still a priest? Makes my petty forgiveness issues look insignificant."

Father Manny stretched out his hand and covered hers without taking his eyes off the highway. "Yours were pretty significant for a little girl, but you are triumphing over them by the grace of God. Marcus is wise and gracious to encourage you to include your father and ask him to attend."

"I emailed him last night and accepted his offer to pay for the reception. My small wedding is out the window. He's arranging the venue and catering."

"And to escort you down the aisle?"

"He didn't ask me my permission. He assumed. But I thanked him. If he doesn't refer to me as his big, black, ugly daughter, I won't hit him."

Father Manny didn't try to bite back his laughter. He let it loose, and it was contagious. She joined him. "Michelle, you really need to get over the poor self-image he planted in you. You truly are a beautiful woman. Marcus is right. You should go to Africa. You would be surrounded by beautiful black women, though none lovelier than you."

"My father is from Mississippi. In our history, the racially mixed women who were well-kept mistresses of wealthy white planters were fair-skinned."

"You have a rich color, and Otiano, Marcus, his family, and I will surround you with blackness."

"My father is dark, too, but my mother and sister are light. He said he'd join us at the church today."

"Good."

"Will you hold my hand?"

"Ah, Michelle, you are a jewel. Of course I will, if that's what you need. Father, may Your Spirit fill Michelle with Your overwhelming love for this father who has already missed too much of her life."

Michelle blew her nose into a tissue she had crumpled in her hand. When they turned on the street, she saw a beautiful brick church loom before them. She pointed to a burgundy BMW. "That's my mother's car. I'm glad she came."

Michelle got out of the car, and her mother scurried to her. Giving her a hug, she whispered, "Thank you. Your father is frightened. He feels guilty, I think."

As he should. Pausing, looking at the cross on the steeple before her, Michelle bowed her head. *Father God, help me. Jesus, go before me. Holy Spirit, give me words.*

Father Manny was introducing himself to Michelle's father, who was making the appropriate responses but was staring at his daughter.

"Michelle, look at you! You are beautiful. What happened to your..." He pointed to his eyes.

"Herman, I told you she had surgery in Ohio."

"Oh, yes. But she is trim and graceful."

"I got over the clumsy stage. May I have a hug, Father?"

He held out awkward arms, and she stepped into them. They weren't Marcus's papa's arms, but it was a start.

Father Manny escorted them into the church. Doctor Mondalah hastened down the aisle, saying. "Good morning, Manny." He shook his hand. "So, this is the wedding party? Welcome!"

"Part of it. Dr. Mansour wasn't able to get away from the hospital, but this is his bride, Michelle, and her father and mother, Herman and Louise Logan."

After pleasantries were exchanged, the pastor took them around the magnificent historical building, showing them where the wedding party would gather, where the bride would dress, and where the groom and his ushers would stand. After everything was arranged and Michelle had Dr. Mondalah's contact information, her father asked if Father Manny would join them for lunch. He took them to a crowded restaurant on K Street and introduced them—especially his daughter, Dr. Logan, who was doing a fellowship at Johns Hopkins—to many people.

During the ride home, Michelle was quiet.

"Thoughts?" the priest asked.

"How do you do that? Act as though fourteen years never happened?"

"It's called denial. Shame perhaps? Sadness for lost years?"

"It's called mental."

Father Manny's generous belly jiggled. "Marcus has gotten himself a treasure."

"Kind of a lost treasure, I'd say."

"But our Lord came to seek and save the lost, and He's carried His precious sheep a long way home."

"He has." She looked over at the priest. "Thank you for Cassie's service. You made heaven so real."

"Maybe too much so. Her brother asked if he could visit her in the jasper walls. I was explaining to him that he couldn't go to heaven until he completed his mission here. God has a job for him. Fortunately, her mother walked up when he asked what Cassie's mission had been. Mrs. Stewart told him Cassie's mission had been to lead her family to their eternal home."

"Cassie was a special child. Marcus called her a 'heart thief.' He said his papa called special children that. I can't wait for you to meet him."

During the rest of the trip, she read from her personality inventory, noting the strengths and differences between the two of them.

"You will make a good match, a good balance, but you will have to sort out these areas and work on them. For a rejected child, you have become a strong woman."

"I'm a competent pediatrician, and knowledge is power."

"You're right, but he is a powerful man, too." He pulled up in front of the hospital. "Is this the right entrance?"

She leaned over and kissed his cheek. "This is good, thanks."

Because she had texted ahead, Marcus was there to greet them. He thanked the priest and waved as he pulled off. Kissing her cheek, he asked her how it went.

"Not bad, I guess. Like something out of the twilight zone."

"I have to sign off on a few things, but thanks for leaving your car here this morning so we have it."

She followed him through the familiar hallways. She walked behind him, seeing his strong shoulders and watching the muscles in his long legs as they ate up the space. Sometimes she still couldn't believe this magnificent man was her betrothed.

Chapter Eight

AND WE ARE ONE

Marcus knew from listening to phone conversations and hearing Michelle talk that the Hope House girls were close, but when he arrived at her apartment, he could hear the din before he knocked. The talking and laughter were at a fever pitch. After introductions and hugs, he stood to the side and watched. Sandy and Pat seemed to be in awe of a petite Native American woman who must've been the famous Christian singer but acted like the girl next door. Her companion, the therapist, joined in with them, and they acted like fast friends. Already, the women weren't strangers. He watched his bride, the competent and controlled professional, giggle like a schoolgirl, and he enjoyed it.

When they paused for breath, he asked, "All right, ladies, are we back to the Four Seasons for dinner?"

"We have reservations at Philippe's. Is that all right?"

"I'm along for the ride." Marcus held the door for the gaggle of women, wondering what he had gotten himself into. "Perhaps this is a hen party?"

Missy hung on to his arm. She was so tiny that he thought she'd dangle, but she must've been used to large men, because she slipped into his rhythm. "You aren't getting away. Cathy and I are here to make sure you are good enough for our girl. Right, Cathy?"

"You're too late. She is so far stuck on this guy that we'd never get them apart."

"I hope not!" Marcus pointed to the Audi at the curb.

Pat and Sandy followed them to the harbor. Marcus waited for the interrogation that never came as they enjoyed a comfortable, relaxed evening. The mothers told child stories and showed pictures. Marcus knew the backgrounds of both of Michelle's friends, but they showed no signs of fragility. Both of these women, victims of rape in their teenage years, had recovered from their traumas and matured into happy, healthy, married women who were loving wives. Like his beloved would soon be. The water in the harbor sparkled in the setting sun, and sailboats drifted offshore. Michelle looked up at him as she slipped her arm in his, and he remembered the first time they came here. Now they belonged to one another. They had never taken the tourist boat. Something to look forward to doing together as man and wife. He leaned to steal a quick kiss.

"I saw that!" Missy teased.

"I can do better," Marcus said, taking Michelle into his arms.

She shoved him. "Too many observers, big guy. Catch you later."

"Oooh," the girls all echoed.

"Shall we eat, ladies?" Marcus waved them ahead. He wouldn't have minded if Michelle had surged forward with them, but he was proud that she seemed to want to show him off, instead staying beside him.

When they broke away later, Cathy and Missy remained at the hotel. Pat and Sandy drove home, and Michelle took him to his apartment, where they shared a nice kiss before they parted.

Marcus had to work until 3:00 p.m. the next day—the day of the rehearsal. His parents had arrived the night before, but they were sleeping. Michelle had taken four days off. Tomorrow was the rehearsal, and the next day was the wedding. Mr. Logan had not only paid for the reception at the Willard, but he had also reserved two nights for them in the bridal suite. Marcus told

Michelle her father was trying, though he knew throwing money her way at this point was too late. They would need to seek to repair the damages in the years ahead.

* * *

After Michelle dropped him off in the morning, she met his parents at the Four Seasons. Beaming, Papa wrapped his arms around her, introducing her to his wife, announcing in his booming voice that this daughter God had chosen was easy to love. Alicia rolled her eyes at her husband and took her new daughter into her arms. Michelle loved her groom's mother, as she'd known she would. Seeing Missy and Cathy come into the dining room, she waved them over, making introductions, and they joined them for brunch.

"I can't believe you're so calm, girl," her friends said. "Where's Marcus?"

"He had to work this morning. Father Manny is bringing him. Marcus convinced me this was God's idea," she replied, "so how can I be nervous?"

"I've set us up for manicures and pedicures at the spa," Missy informed her, and that's how they spent the afternoon.

Alicia joined them while Harry went upstairs and worked online. They discussed the rehearsal. Cathy and Missy were her attendants. Since Marcus's brother, Dennis, couldn't come, Michelle's brother, Herman Junior, as well as a friend from his office filled in. Her father must have twisted a lot of arms. She had been *persona non grata* for over a decade. Tonight's rehearsal would continue the twilight zone. God help her. Thankfully, Harry would serve as his son's best man the next day. She could keep her eyes focused on her father-in-law and feel his love. Everyone put on a smile that night, greeting each other as if fourteen years hadn't passed. Bizarre.

At the wedding, Missy sang, holding everyone in thrall. How such power could come out of that little body! Even Marcus had tears in his eyes as he turned to take his bride's hands and clearly repeat his vows.

Michelle had been right. Her father displayed her to Washington, but Marcus kept her close. They had a formal sit-down luncheon but no dancing.

Because of the busy season, a morning wedding worked better, and the couple wanted the earlier time because they only had the Christmas weekend off. Missy took Cathy to the airport and drove on to West Virginia that afternoon.

They would be home by Christmas Eve. Harry and Alicia took the hotel shuttle to Dulles later in the night, and they were flying to London to see Dennis and his family. The couple left the reception as soon as it was polite, after bidding everyone farewell.

The moment Marcus had long awaited arrived. Sweeping her into his arms, he carried his wife into the bridal suite. "Come away with me, my bride, my fair one," he quoted.

She believed him, but just in case, he convinced her all night long. Never had she felt so loved. Never had she been so chosen. She let out a long breath after the first time they came together.

"Are you all right? Did I hurt you?"

"You are glorious. Magnificent. And I love you."

Marcus propped himself above her and touched her forehead with his. "I had a dream, but the reality is far better. I love you, and I always will." He stretched out beside her, keeping her in his arms until they began again.

When the sun slanted across their bridal chamber, Marcus looked across at his new wife. His heart was full. He ran his fingers down her cheek, and she stirred, looking up at him. She was tangled in the sheets, and he unwrapped her. Her body was bare, and he felt his body respond to her beauty. How could this wonder happen again? He asked permission with his eyes, and with a slow smile, she pulled him down until they were one. "My body belongs to you," she whispered.

"And mine to you."

They had brunch delivered to the room. "Your father gave us a nice two days."

Her brow furrowed. "Can we not talk about my father?"

"I'd rather talk about you. How beautiful you are. How I was surrounded by your love. I never imagined being pulled into someone, the way your body pulled me in. It was magical."

Michelle put one of the hotel bathrobes on to be decently covered when the waiter delivered their food. Marcus pulled her into his lap and put his hand inside. She was making nice little welcoming sounds when a knock came at the door.

"Housekeeping."

"Didn't we put out the sign? Get rid of her!" Michelle hissed, fleeing to the bathroom.

Chuckling, clad only in his pajama bottoms, Marcus answered the door, explaining they did not need any service, thank you very much. He inserted the *Do Not Disturb* sign into the key slide and went to look for his bride. He found her in the bathroom, brushing her teeth. She rinsed her mouth and turned to kiss him. He lifted her up on the counter, wanting to hear again those little noises that told him she was ready, working until he did, and when they came, he filled her. They were both sweating and naked when he lifted her down.

Michelle put her hands over her face.

"What's wrong? Am I hurting you?"

"I can't believe I'm acting this way."

"It's fine with me." He kissed the side of her long neck. "I love the way you're acting."

She moved her hands to the sides of his face. "You make me positively wanton." She looked at him, all of him. "You have a magnificent body, and you do wonderful things to me."

"I hope so. Words fail to tell you the pleasure, the joy, you have given me."

"I thought I'd be embarrassed to be naked with you."

"Please don't be. I don't want us to ever feel shame with each other's nakedness. Always remember, my body belongs to you." He leaned his forehead against hers again.

"And mine to you," she whispered. "Do we ever have to leave here?"

"We do have to go to work Monday, but Father Manny said we only have two days and that he didn't want to see us in church tomorrow."

"God bless Father Manny."

"God bless him for giving us those books!"

"They were helpful. How does he do it, this marriage thing? Not being married himself."

"His wife died three years ago. Drunk driver."

"How sad for him. Does he have children?"

"No, she had childhood leukemia, and the treatments left her infertile. He said her love was enough, but he is thinking of adopting."

"From Africa?"

"Maybe, but he's also thinking about the poor black children right here in Baltimore and Washington. He is challenging the congregation to take in foster children."

"Maybe we can do that someday."

They got dressed and walked hand-in hand down the street, looking at the holiday decorations and picking out a few Christmas gifts. The cold drove them inside before long, but Christmas music was playing in the lobby, and they sat to listen. Marcus enjoyed when she was excited and chattered, but he also liked the easy, comfortable silences they shared. She leaned her head on his shoulder, and he kissed her brow. He put his hand behind her waist as they stood, and steered her over to the restaurant. In a cocoon of warmth, love fulfilled, they ate a delightful meal, although Marcus couldn't have said what they ate, as sawdust would have been nectar from the gods this day.

They returned to their room, looking around the untouched living area of the suite. Tugging him by the hand, Michelle brought him over to the large sofa. She sat, patting her lap, and he dropped beside her and put his head there. She stroked his head with the lightest touch. No wonder the frightened children were calmed.

"You have been a wonderful husband to me." She smiled down at his beautiful face.

"You like married life, do you?"

She leaned her head back while a smile played on her face.

He rolled to kiss her belly and straightened with a chuckle. "When Dennis and I were young, about nine and six, we took Mama away for part of her recovery. Come to think of it, the doctors had probably given them the all clear to resume their relations. I remember that Papa was rather mellow, and now I understand that, being rather mellow myself. We had gone swimming, and when we returned to the locker room to change, my brother told me to look at Papa. Our eyes got wide. Dennis pulled me behind our little curtain, exclaiming over Papa's size and whispering his concern, checking himself out. 'Mine is little bitty,' he mourned. Not kidding you. He mourned. Mine was none too big, I agreed. 'We have teeny weeny wienies,' he said. We stared at ourselves for a few minutes before pulling our clothes on. Papa had a big smile on his face when we came out, and he rubbed our heads with his big hands, pulling us close. Mama was waiting for us, and I remember he kissed her on the lips.

"By the time we drove home, it was late, so we had our family devotions, and he sent us to bed. We were whispering and giggling like hyenas when they walked by. He sent Mama to their bedroom and sat on the edge of our bed. "Boys, don't worry about your bodies. Every part of you will grow—your legs, your shoulders, and yes, even your penises. God will make you a man.' Of course, we giggled again. He leaned to kiss us both. 'My fine little boys will grow up to be big men.'

"He walked down the hall and closed their bedroom door. I heard the rumble of their voices and Mama's sweet laugh. When I was in residency, he came to visit me in Pretoria. His hotel had a sauna, and after a swim, we sat together. I had a towel wrapped around my neck. I was embarrassed and wanted to drape it across my lap. He read my mind, because he said, 'Not so teeny weeny anymore, is it, son?'"

"He got that right!" his bride replied.

He draped his arm around her. "You like it?" he teased.

"It's magnificent, and it fills me."

Marcus grinned and went to the minibar. "Want a Coke?"

She placed her hand on her neck. "My throat is a little dry."

He poured two glasses and brought one to her, setting it on the table. After a few sips, he pulled her head down into his lap. "My turn."

"I love your Papa," she murmured. "You told me he was tender with your mother. The day after Cassie died, the nurses on the floor told me how fortunate I am because you were so tender with me."

Marcus ran his fingers across her high cheekbones. "You were broken."

"I thought then that your father taught you well. He showed you how to be tender with a woman."

"My wife. Do you know what I think when I look at you?" She didn't answer. "You came into the bedroom with that slinky blue gown, and I envisioned you as an Egyptian princess stepping out of the bathing pool at the Nile, your serving girls drying you with linen towels and slipping that gown over your head. You are so gorgeous." When he saw she was about to protest, he put a finger over her lips and began to describe her attributes—her large dark eyes, her arched brows, her high cheekbones, her regal neck, and her delightful breasts. He began to unbutton her blouse to reach in and play with them. "I like this bra with the front fastener." He pushed it aside, and she swelled under his touch "Ah, you are easy to please."

"Are you calling me easy?"

"No, or else I would have had you in my bed months ago. Far from easy. But passionate, responsive." His fingers touched her lips, and she drew one into her mouth and sucked it. His breath caught. "Let's move this to the other room." And he led her to their chamber of delights.

Although their second night had marvelous and repeated interruptions, they slept more than their first night together. They had a late check-out, leaving mid-afternoon, and they looked forward to christening the big king-size bed his father had bought for him.

All too soon, their world crashed in. Michelle had to pull several double shifts to make up for the time she took off for their wedding. Still, they found married life natural and easy, although they missed the languorous days of love they had shared. Rarely did they have the slow hours of pleasure, but they found joy in the moments of passion they stole. Marcus felt anticipation climb every time he turned the key to their apartment, and if she was sound asleep, he fell into bed bedside her. Even when she didn't stir, his world was put together. And sometimes they had mornings! Later, hearing her moving in the kitchen, smelling the coffee, he greeted five o'clock with undiluted happiness and wondered how he ever lived without her.

Chapter Nine

BRINGING THE FAMILY TOGETHER

They were on their way to their first family gathering, and Marcus was remembering one evening a while back when they were meeting Louise for dinner. While they waited for Michelle to change, she expressed her fervent desire for the family to be restored. That's what mothers did, after all. Women worked on relationships.

"I know Herman hurt Michelle deeply," she had said, "but someday I want her to know his childhood wounds, and she'll understand. Please help me."

"I'll make sure he gets an invitation to the wedding," he had said then, "but the rest is up to him."

"Thank you." She had looked up at her daughter coming through the door. "You look lovely, dear."

"You're good for my ego, Mother."

"Me and this guy here." She jerked her thumb at Marcus. "He melts when he looks at you, and you have softened in his love, too. Your eyes glow when you take his hand."

"Where are we going? Oh man, who makes my eyes glow?"

"I have an early day today, so the little café around the corner will have to do."

That was the extent of the conversation that day, but Marcus knew his mother-in-law was doing her part. He also knew that since the wedding, Michelle's parents had been attending Dr. Mondalah's church. God was working on this family, bringing down their walls—less dramatically than Jericho, but just as divinely.

They were joining the Logan family at HJ's for the senior Herman's birthday dinner, and Marcus knew Michelle's mother had worked overtime to make it happen. Both Michelle and he had to work 7:00-3:00, and the drive to Washington took an hour, so they didn't take time to change. HJ's wife had complained about waiting that late for dinner, but "Mother Logan" was planning to bring a brunch spread and play games at their home.

HJ opened the door, and the older boy was chasing the younger, who didn't seem into the game. They were screeching in the living room. "They're hungry," HJ informed them. "It's been a long time since brunch." He reached out to take the hand extended to him. "Marcus," he said with a nod, but then he dropped his hand and looked at his sister. Marcus had his other arm around Michelle, and he gave her a little shove toward her brother, who was forced to give her an awkward embrace.

"Come in. Beatrice has everything ready. The folks are here."

Nothing folksy about this family, Marcus thought as he followed HJ to the dining room. His wife, Beatrice, had seated and calmed the boys, who were eyeing the food before them. The older one was banging his spoon on the table, and his father snapped at him. Father Logan and Mother Logan, as Beatrice called them—which was super weird to Marcus—were standing behind their chairs. Everything seemed designed to make them feel late, like they were an inconvenience.

Marcus wanted to make sure they understood it was an inconvenience for them, too. "We haven't eaten since before early service. It was frantic in the hospital today. Usually, Sundays are slower, but not today. We didn't take time to change." He'd much rather be kicked back in his living room with no shoes on than sitting here in his scrubs at a fancy dinner table.

Food was passed around and served, and forks clinked, but no blessing was said before the eating began.

Michelle found his hand under the table, and they bowed their heads. *It is the celebration of their father's birth, and still no blessing? No thanksgiving to God for this bounty? No watchcare for the head of the family?* The couple prayed silently. Marcus gave his wife's hand a quick squeeze and looked up to see the rest of the table averting their eyes. *Are they embarrassed? Convicted? Angry?* To fill the uncomfortable silence, he reached for the platter of ham and served himself and Michelle, saying, "This smells delicious!" And eating resumed. Only the children remained unaware.

"Father Logan"—Marcus would never call Michelle's father that—told them about how they had attended Dr. Mondalah's service and enjoyed it very much.

"I liked him," Michelle said.

"It's a beautiful church," Louise added. "An exquisite setting for the wedding."

Everyone complimented Beatrice on the meal, but Marcus saw that Michelle had been watching Andrew, the younger boy, throughout the meal as he pushed his food around the plate, showing no interest in the food. His eyes looked dull, too, and Marcus saw her pediatrician radar picking up signals.

After they ate, they moved into the living room for coffee. Beatrice apologized because she had given the help the day off and she had to clean up—it was Sunday, after all. Louise helped her, urging the two doctors to sit because they had worked.

Marcus asked Michelle if she wanted to change, then went to the car to get their clothes. He went to the bathroom to put on some jeans, but she wanted to get her hands on Andrew. She squatted to his level, asking him about the games they had played and whether his grandmother had brought him any toys. Before long, he was on her lap with a new book, and Marcus smiled when he sat beside her. What child could resist her?

Beatrice entered the room and told Andrew to quit hanging all over Aunt Michelle.

Michelle tightened her arms. "If I didn't love children, I wouldn't be a pediatrician. He's fine." Beatrice's eyes narrowed, and her lips pursed, but she didn't say anything. However, Michelle noticed the boy's eyes when they flicked over to his mother. She unobtrusively pulled his lower lid down and elbowed Marcus. "Look," she whispered.

Marcus leaned to tickle the boy's tummy, and he giggled. Michelle pulled his lid down again. Her husband glanced up at her. He'd seen it, too. Jaundiced.

"He seems to be a bit warm," Michelle said.

"He's been having a fever off and on for five to six weeks now, but nothing's wrong. We've taken him to the pediatrician. Nothing," HJ said. "His ears are fine, and his throat."

"Maybe you should get a second opinion," Marcus suggested. "Have they done any blood work?"

Beatrice bristled. "We go to an excellent pediatrician. He's on staff at Children's Hospital. I know you're a pediatrician, but he knows our child. He has attended him since birth."

Marcus looked at Michelle's mother. Surely, she would respond to the condescension toward her daughter. It crawled all over him. But she remained silent, uneasy. Michelle gave her husband a pleading look. She didn't know the child well, but this was her nephew. Marcus caught HJ's eye, saw him observing them, and waved him over. "Perhaps he didn't notice this." Gently, he tugged the child's lower eyelid down. "Do you notice the color? It's hard to spot it when you have dark skin and eyes as we do. He's jaundiced."

Marcus saw that HJ could tell they were concerned. "What could it be?" the boy's father asked.

"It's worth taking a look," Marcus told him. "Would you like me to set something up for you in the morning?"

"I am presenting oral arguments in the morning. Maybe later next week?"

"It might be something where days, and certainly weeks, would make a big difference," Marcus stated in a quiet but firm voice. "Can someone else in your office cover for you? I could get some blood work and an MRI in the morning."

"An MRI?" Beatrice echoed.

"I would urge sooner rather than later."

A hush fell over the room. Herman took his son's arm. "Get someone, HJ. Marcus knows what he's talking about. Better safe than sorry, anyway, right, Marcus?"

"Yes, sir."

Michelle's mother stood behind her and, in a small voice, asked her if she would pray. "I'm trying to learn, but I'm not very good at it."

"Prayer is something you don't get 'good' at, Mother. You simply talk to God or cry out to Him." But she did just that, asking for God's help and direction, along with a "word of knowledge" or a "word of wisdom," though no one but she and Marcus had a clue about what that was. "Jesus, Great Physician, You took the little children in Your arms and welcomed them. Welcome Andrew into your presence, Lord, and grant him healing." Filled with compassion, she looked down at the boy still in her lap, gently kissing his brow.

Marcus had never felt the presence of God as he did that moment. He blinked before he looked up, and then he noticed that Herman and HJ appeared to be strangely moved, as well.

"If you are that concerned, doc, I'll have him there," HJ said.

"Seven-thirty. I'll meet you outside the east door." Marcus reached for his hand but instead pulled him to his chest. If this was what he thought it was, his brother-in-law would need lots of hugs.

"I'd better get these boys to bed if I'm leaving at six in the morning." HJ looked around for the sister he scarcely knew. "You'll be there?"

"I will."

He gave a curt nod. "See you then."

"We'll walk them to the door," Herman Senior said, but he walked them to their car. "What are you thinking?" He took Marcus by the elbow.

"We know nothing yet," Marcus answered.

"But jaundice has to do with the liver, and the boy is not an alcoholic. What could cause it?"

"Let's not jump to any conclusions, Herman."

"Cancer?"

"Could be."

"God!"

"He'll be the one to see us through this."

Michelle took her mother in her arms. "Marcus is the best, Mother."

As the older couple moved off, Marcus seated his wife. He cranked the car. "What are you thinking?"

"Hepatoblastoma."

"Usually, it manifests in toddlers. How old is he?"

"He's five."

"Was he premature?"

"I think so, but I wasn't in the family then."

"Dear God. I prayed for an entrance into the family, but not this way." He glanced over at Michelle. "Why do you think that?"

"We lost one at Cleveland Clinic. We treated him for everything else, and when we finally diagnosed it, we were too late. I studied it upside down and backward. I vowed we'd never lose another. His side is sensitive. When I palpated it, he shrunk back. He has no appetite. I noticed that at the wedding, but he's even more lethargic today."

"If this is what we've got, you did a good job picking that up, Dr. Logan."

"I wish I hadn't," she choked.

"Sooner is better," he said. "I felt the presence of God in that place. Maybe Andrew is already healed."

Faith dropped into Michelle's heart. "Maybe he is."

Chapter Ten

A LITTLE CHILD SHALL LEAD THEM

Michelle felt her husband's tender lips on hers the next morning. "We have to meet your brother in an hour. Sorry about that. This was the first time you could sleep in a long time. I hated to wake you."

She pushed herself up. "I'm on it."

When they got to the hospital, the little boy was all eyes as he walked toward them, clinging to his daddy's hand. Marcus squatted to be eye level. "Hey, tiger, did you come to see where your aunt Michelle works?"

"Daddy says you're my uncle."

"I married well, buddy, and I'm proud to be your uncle. I'm going to help you do some things that might be a bit scary, but they are going to tell us how to make you better." Taking the boy's hand, Marcus led him into the hospital and up to an examination room, then lifted him up on a table. "How long have you been feeling bad, Andrew?"

"Thanksgiving. I threw up after dinner, and Mama thought I ate too much."

"Threw up, did you?" His father added that he'd done a lot of that lately, but they thought it was stress from first grade.

"Do you hurt anywhere, Andrew?"

"Yes, sir, here."

"Here?" The child shrugged. "How does this feel?" Marcus touched him, and he winced. "Not so good?" Andrew agreed. "We can't see your boo-boo because it's inside, but we have a big machine that can look all the way through and see where you hurt. Then we can know how to help you. You need to lie down on a big table that moves into a cave. Will you do that?"

"Aunt Michelle?" She came to stand beside him. "Will you go with me?"

"I'll hold your hand. First, we need to put you in hospital clothes." She gently tugged his polo shirt over his head, trying not to wince at his thin body, and slipped a pediatric gown around him. "I'm going to pull your pants down, too. Is that okay? You can leave your underoos on. Batman, I see." The boy grinned. "I brought you a little drink." She set him down, and he dutifully swallowed. Within minutes, he was drowsy. She held his hand as Marcus rolled the stretcher to the MRI and lifted him over to the table.

"You can take a little rest, Batman. This machine makes a loud noise, but you're a tough guy. It won't hurt, I promise, and it won't take long. Aunt Michelle has a toy for you."

Michelle tucked a small plush toy into his hand, but it drifted out of his fingers. The little figure disappeared into the machine.

"He looks so small," HJ whispered.

Michelle and Marcus walked to a screen scrolling an image, and her brother followed. Simultaneously, they pointed.

"What is it?" He looked from one face to another. "Is it cancer? That spot there?"

"It could be benign," Marcus said.

Michelle took her brother's arm.

"But you don't think so?" he asked them.

Marcus shook his head. "But it's small. We caught it early."

"Michelle caught it," HJ said.

"She's an excellent diagnostician. One of the best." Marcus took HJ's other arm and led him to a consultation room. "Michelle gave Andrew a sedative. We're getting blood work now, and I'd like to admit him."

"Listen, I'm sorry about Beatrice last night. She called our pediatric group after you left, and the guy on call said that if you could get an MRI this quick, go for it. He said Johns Hopkins has excellent pediatric oncology. Is that where he'll go?"

"Marcus is an oncologist, HJ," Michelle told him.

HJ searched his brother-in-law's face. "I guess we are in your hands, then. I feel like such a fool. I didn't realize you... Can you help my little boy?" His voice cracked.

"I'll do everything in my power, and we'll keep praying." Marcus rested his hand on HJ's shoulder for a moment before leaving him with Michelle, walking out of the room to input the information into the computer.

"He's good, HJ. He's the best."

"He was good with Andrew. You, too. Thanks."

"It's what we do."

"How could we not know?"

Michelle figured her brother was unaware of the tears streaming down his cheeks. He'd been away at school her entire life, and she'd only seen him on holidays, but he was her brother. She kissed his cheek, and his arms came around her as he sobbed.

Marcus came in quietly. "He's in room eight hundred and four. You'll want to be there when he wakes. Any questions?"

"What's the next step?" HJ pulled himself together.

Marcus looked over at Michelle. "Chemo?"

"Let's shrink it first, to excise it more easily."

"I think so, too," he agreed.

"When?" the junior Herman asked.

"Chemo starts this afternoon."

HJ put his hands over his face for a moment. Pulling them down and bracing himself, he faced them. "All right. Let's do this."

"I'll show you where to go," Michelle said, leading him to the elevator. When they reached the eighth floor, they had to don gowns and scrub their hands up to the elbows. "Patients undergoing chemo have their immune systems compromised. We have to be careful about bringing germs in."

"I've got a lot to learn." He stopped. "I need to call Mother and Father. And Beatrice."

"Let's get in the room. I don't want him to wake without you. You'll have some forms to sign."

The senior Logans were at the hospital with HJ before Beatrice was out of class, but Michelle had already spoken to her, assuring her she'd send the MRI to their pediatrician. While Andrew was sedated, an IV had been put into his arm, and now Louise sat on his other side, cuddling him and reading a book.

Marcus entered the room, greeting everyone.

"Where's Aunt Michelle, Uncle Marcus?" The child looked at his grand-father. "Did you know he's my uncle and he's a doctor?"

"I did, and right now I think that's a pretty good thing."

Marcus tussled the boy's black curls. Beautiful, but he would soon be bald. "Aunt Michelle is with her patients."

"But I'm her patient."

"You are one of them." He leaned to whisper, "Probably her favorite, but don't tell." Andrew beamed. "I'm going to put some medicine in this line. No needles in you. You might not want to watch."

"Can I?"

"Sure, you can." Marcus stepped to the side while Andrew watched him. "It may burn when it gets into your arm, bud." The boy's eyes widened. "You okay?"

He nodded. "But it hurts."

"I'm sorry." He sat on the edge of the bed. "Forgive me?"

"Will it make me better?"

"Yeah, but sometimes it gets worse first. I'll give it to you straight, Andrew. You can ask me whatever you want, and I'll tell you."

"Will this make him sick?" HJ wanted to know.

Marcus grimaced. "Depends. Sometimes. Usually. We'll see how effective it is to determine how much we have to give him." He patted Andrew and winked at him.

Beatrice crept into the room. "How are you, Andrew? I see everyone is here."

"Not Aunt Michelle."

Louise Logan stood. "I'd better go get Peter."

"I've put him in aftercare. Herman and I should tell him together."

"We need to let you talk to Marcus." Herman Senior said.

Beatrice swiveled around. "I...um...I owe you an apology."

"No need."

"I went by our pediatrician's office. They showed me the MRI and said you were doing everything right, and then they told me they'd looked up your credentials. What a fine reputation you have, and all the training and everything. I'm sorry."

"When Michelle told me this morning, I was shocked, too. I asked her how we could not know," her husband said.

"Father, forgive us, for we didn't know," Louise murmured.

"We didn't exactly crucify them, Mother Logan."

"Didn't we, Beatrice?" Herman Senior asked. "I certainly did."

"Regretfully, God has brought us together for such a time as this," Marcus said, and then he turned to Beatrice. "Was Andrew premature?"

"Yes, he came at seven months. He was in the NICU for weeks, but he's been healthy. He caught up with his growth and weight by the time he was three."

"What does he normally weigh?"

"Right at forty-three pounds at his last checkup, before school started," she replied.

"He weighed thirty-eight and a half this morning. He's down about ten percent."

Beatrice teared up. "He's lost that much?" She turned to her husband.

Louise put her arms around Marcus. "You said regretfully. I regret this circumstance, but I have no regret that you and Michelle are here."

"I want to see Aunt Michelle," Andrew whined.

"Your wish is my command!" Michelle swung open the door. "Ta-da. And I've brought Ginger Ale for the boy." She handed him a glass with a bent straw and glanced at the IV. She cut her eyes over to her husband, and he spoke to her without words. "I can't stay, big boy, but I see Uncle Marcus is doing his job. I'll be back."

"Uncle Marcus told me you have other patients but that I'm your favorite."

She tossed him a brilliant smile. "Don't tell, okay, Batman?" In that brief moment, she bolstered him.

Marcus followed her out of the room, and the grandparents trailed behind. He led them to a consultation room. "HJ has given them disclosure and asked me to fill them in," he told his wife. He flipped the MRI on the screen and, with a pointer, outlined the dot on Andrew's liver. "This is a small tumor on his liver—very small, thank God. I hoped it was benign, but the blood work indicates it's not. Michelle and I want to shrink it, and then we'll do surgery. That's why I told HJ it depends on how effective the medicine is."

"You will operate?"

"Yes, sir. We have to excise it and pray for clean edges."

"If the edges are clean, he's done with chemo?"

"No. We'll give him more for good measure. We want to destroy every cancer cell that might be in there."

"What are his chances?" Louise asked.

"We caught this very early. His chances are better than most. Thank God that Michelle picked up on the jaundice. His side is tender. She checked it yesterday."

When Louise started to cry, Herman took her in his arms. "Let's get all our crying done out here, Mama."

Tears pricked Michelle's eyes. She'd never heard her father call her mother "Mama." She hugged her mother before she left. "Sorry, I have to go." She gave Marcus a finger wave and hustled away.

When she returned to the room later, her mother and father were there.

"They've gone to get Peter at school and tell him." Louise glanced over at Andrew, who was dozing. "We said we'd stay until one of them got back. How long do you think he'll be in the hospital?"

"Hard to say. If the tumor doesn't shrink at this dosage, we'll have to up it. That could take up to two weeks. Once it does, we can operate. After he recovers from surgery, and after a few treatments, he can do the rest of his chemotherapy outpatient. Maybe four weeks. Maybe five. If all goes well."

Herman looked stricken. "Michelle, I don't... What can I say? I-I'm sorry. Terribly sorry. You have accomplished...you've become, without any support at all." He jerked his head toward his wife. "Except Mama, over my objections." Tears crept down his face, and he roughly swiped them away. "Please forgive me."

"I already have, Father. But just so you know, I forgive you."

"Thank you."

"And I'm sorry for the mistakes I made. You raised me better."

"We didn't. We sent you away. I don't know who made you the woman you are."

"Hope House was a wonderful place. We had the sweetest housemother and excellent counselors. I found a personal relationship with God there. Remember the gal who sang at my wedding? Missy? She prayed with me to receive Christ. And I lived with a lovely couple from my church while I was in college. God has blessed me with amazing people in my life."

"And now Marcus."

"Yes, ma'am. Now Marcus and his family. But God's giving me my own family back! My cup is full and running over. I wish it didn't have to come at this cost to Andrew."

"A little child shall lead them," her father said.

"If you guys want to go, Marcus and I will stay until Beatrice or HJ gets back."

At that moment, Marcus pushed open the door with a tray. "How's he doing?"

Michelle hastened to the bed, lifting Andrew as he threw up. He cried. "It's okay, honey. It happens."

"I threw up on you, Aunt Michelle."

"I'll remember that and return the favor someday." He giggled, which was her intent, and she took the wet cloth Marcus handed her to wipe her nephew. "There, that's better. Uncle Marcus shouldn't have brought that smelly food in here."

"Sorry, buddy," Marcus said.

"'S okay." Andrew closed his eyes, and Michelle lowered him and pulled the cotton blanket over him.

"I'm going to run and change," she told them.

"This is the chemo?" Herman asked. "Making him sick?"

Marcus raised his eyebrows and took a deep breath. "Yeah. Hopefully, it's a sign that it's having the effect we need."

Herman shook his head and moved toward his son-in-law, who took him in his arms. The older man hung on for a minute, then stood back. "I've never hugged a man before, but I needed that."

"My papa hugs me all the time. He's a champion hugger."

Herman gave him a strange look, then offered his wife a hand. "I guess we should be on our way. You'll let us know...?"

"If anything changes, yes." Marcus clapped him on the shoulder. "You got it."

When Michelle got back, she was wearing surgical scrubs. Probably a man's size, solid blue, but they were unisex. She pulled up to the tray and lifted the lid. He blessed it, and they dug in. "Not too bad."

"I've had worse at home."

"Watch it!" She peered over her fork. "My father apologized. He asked my forgiveness."

"Well, he hugged me."

"You're kidding!"

"He apologized, though, and said he'd never hugged a man before."

She snorted. "I've never seen him hug my mother. I heard him call her 'Mama' today. Never heard that before. What's this world coming to? Maybe the mountains will quake and the tides will roll back."

Marcus had to laugh. "I told him I was used to it and that my father is a champion hugger. He looked at me kind of strange. He said a little child shall lead them." They glanced over to the boy lying on the bed and joined hands and hearts as they said a prayer. They stayed until Beatrice got back, and got home around 9:30 p.m.

The next morning, Marcus went into Andrew's room while Beatrice was in the cafeteria. The nurse had bathed him, and he told her to take a break.

"You doing all right, partner?"

Solemn eyes held his own. "Uncle Marcus?"

"Yep."

"You said you'd tell me straight."

"I did."

"This is bad, isn't it?"

Marcus thought those words sounded strange coming out of that little piping voice. "It's serious, but we're on it."

"Is it cancer?"

"What do you know about cancer?"

"My teacher died of it last year."

"Some people do, but lots more don't, especially children."

"So it's cancer?"

"You are too young to be so smart, buddy. Yes, it is. I wouldn't be making you so sick if I had any other choice. Did you keep your breakfast down?"

"Uh huh."

"Well, there's always lunch." He winked and held up the syringe.

"Will I get well?"

This kid is five? God, give me a hand here. "I certainly think so. We're going to give it our best shot. Are you with me?"

"I have to get well. Mom wouldn't do too well without me."

"That's not the way it's supposed to work. Kids need to be around for their moms."

"Have you seen kids die?"

Marcus didn't want to say it, but he had, and not that long ago. "Yes. But I don't think you will, Andrew. I really don't."

Beatrice gasped.

Marcus turned and saw her fist in her mouth. "I promised him I'd always tell him the truth, Beatrice, but I honestly think he's going to be fine." He walked over to her and led her to the bedside. He winked at Andrew. "You tell your mom you're going to be fine."

"Uncle Marcus is going to help me get well, Mom."

Marcus slid a chair under her, and Beatrice sat. She gathered her son into her arms. "That's good. We'll do everything he says, okay? Dr. Ross says he's the best doctor ever for what you need."

"He says he has to make me sick to kill the cancer."

"I didn't tell him that."

"You told me you wouldn't make me so sick if you didn't have to."

"He's too smart for his own good. Listen, I'm going to hold off on this a little while so you and your mom can have a talk." He held up the syringe.

"Okay," Andrew said. "See you later."

"Love you, kiddo."

"I love you, too, Uncle Marcus."

Marcus was sitting at the doctors' desk, inputting information into the computer. He felt his wife's presence before he felt her light touch on his shoulder. He growled, low and sexy. "I might haul you into the linen closet and have my way with you, woman."

"Why, Dr. Mansour, that would be sexual harassment."

"You bet it would. More than harassment, and you'd enjoy every moment of it."

"I wish. Look, I only have a few moments. Have you given Andrew his chemo?"

"Not yet. He's in there confronting his mortality with his mother. You're the pediatrician. Isn't he too young for that? He's really a bright kid."

"Of course, he's got my genes. And his father's. And his grandfather's. Harvard Law. I'll pop in and tell him 'hi,' then scoot. But hold that thought."

He craned his neck to see her walk away. She was graceful, and he loved to watch her move, although he regretted it was away from him. God knew he loved that woman.

* * *

Michelle peeped in the door. "How's everything going? It's a beautiful day outside. Spring is definitely coming."

"Uncle Marcus hasn't given me my shot yet." Michelle examined the IV site. It was puffy but not infiltrated. "He has to make me sick so I can get well."

She looked at him. "You know he's sorry, don't you?"

"Yeah. He loves me lots. I can tell."

"He's wonderful with him. Your husband is a wonderful man."

This, from Beatrice? "Don't I know it? I have to pinch myself every day to believe God gave him to me."

"No, seriously. Both of you. I don't know what we would've done without you. Dr. Reed said it was a miracle you caught it so early."

"God's in the miracle-working business." She dropped a kiss on her nephew's cheek. "And He's obviously got plans for this one here. I can't stay, buddy. I've got clinic today. Love you."

"Love you, too, Aunt 'Chelle." As she walked out the door, she heard him say, "I've got lots more people who love me, Mom."

Chapter Eleven

ANDREW HAS SURGERY

HJ learned that another scan on Monday revealed the tumor had shrunk, so they would take Andrew to surgery on Tuesday at seven in the morning. Beatrice and Herman were with him, but Louise took Peter to school. They asked if Michelle could wait with them, but Marcus explained she would be his assistant. Before Louise arrived, the surgery was completed. Marcus walked out of the operating room, his mask pulled down, a big smile on his face. "Looks good," he proclaimed.

"Were the edges clean?" HJ wanted to know.

"We'll get a lab report in a couple of days. Have to have those back before we can let him go."

"Where's Michelle?"

"She's getting a spinal tap on a kid she suspects has meningitis. She's probably right. We came in around five."

"Do you guys ever sleep?"

"Some, but the sex is pretty sparse at times." He winked at HJ, who almost choked, and walked off.

HJ couldn't look at his father, but when he heard him chuckle, he peeked.

"That guy is going to shake this family up good and plenty. And for the best, I might add. Mama told me I'd like him. He's quite a guy."

HJ had never heard his father refer to his mother as "Mama," nor had he ever heard him laugh about sex. He'd often wondered if he and his sisters had sprung out of their mother's forehead like the gods. He glanced at his wife, who was trying to hold her merriment in check. She held it until tears escaped her eyes.

She shook her head. "He is the most amazing man I've ever met. He talked to Andrew about dying, so gentle and wise, and yet imbuing hope. I felt stronger and more confident, even when the poor kid was puking all over the place later."

HJ saw the gurney rolling out of the recovery room, took his wife's hand, and waved his father forward. They followed the boy to his room. When they learned he was sedated, the senior Herman called his wife and told her to stay home and pick up Peter after school. She was thrilled the surgery was already over, and he said he would go back to the office.

Beatrice and HJ took turns spooning ice into their boy, and he was allowed to have Jell-O. HJ noticed his son becoming increasingly agitated, and he looked up with relief when his sister came into the room.

"When did he have his last pain meds?"

They looked at each other. "In the recovery room, I guess," HJ said, watching her march down the hall. He heard her talking to the nurses in no uncertain terms. She came into the room, nodded him out of the big chair, scooped Andrew into her arms, and, ducking him under the IV lines, sat with him in her arms, cradling him. He rested his hand on her bosom, and she sang some hymns HJ had heard at one time or another, but he didn't know the spiritual songs. Andrew's dark lashes brushed his cheeks as the nurse came bustling in with a shot.

Michelle leaned her face over his, kissing him softy. "A little sting, baby, but it'll make it feel better soon." The child hardly stirred.

HJ took his wife's hand, tears blinding his gaze. Marcus was beside him. How could such a big man could move so quietly? How long had he been there?

"How's he doing?" Marcus whispered, watching Michelle.

She glared up at him. "They hadn't given him any pain medicine since he left recovery."

"Oh." He looked at HJ. "Guess it hit the fan, right?"

"Something like that. But she already had...I don't know. She picked him up and held him. Then she sang some songs. He was sleeping and peaceful before he ever got the shot."

"She does that, somehow draws the pain into herself. You want me to put him back in bed, honey?" He reached down to gather the boy up and set him in the bed. "I'll go talk to the nurses, and then, if you're okay, I'll take my wife home. She's had a long day."

"Maybe after she rests, you can get some, bro. Go for it."

A wide smile flashed across his ebony face as Marcus left the room. Michelle gave her brother and his wife kisses.

"What is it about those two?" Beatrice asked.

"I don't know, but somehow I think it's got something to do with God. I want to start going to church with the folks." And they watched them walk away.

* * *

Marcus went for carry-out while Michelle napped. He didn't feel like cooking, and he didn't want her to do any work. HJ had planted a seed in his mind, but he figured his wife would sleep through the night. He put the food on the counter when he came in and went back to peek at his wife.

She was sitting there, awake. "What smells so good?"

"Lasagna from Murial's."

"You wonderful man. I'm starving!" She hustled to the bathroom.

"Thank you, Jesus, for the food." He set two places at the counter. *Thank you, Jesus!* He poured some tea and helped her onto the stool. "Did you get anything to eat today?"

87

"I grabbed a granola bar around one. Mmm, this is delicious!" She waved her fork. "Eat up."

Although he was hungrier for something other than food, Marcus dove in, figuring he'd need his strength if his wishes came to pass. He really loved this woman God had given him!

After she had devoured most of her dinner, she asked, "What did my brother mean about getting some? Was he talking about carry out? This was thoughtful. Thanks."

"Uh. Well, I sort of made a joke."

"Yes?" She turned her head and raised her eyebrows.

"I explained that you'd been in the hospital since five. You know, about the meningitis case."

"That wasn't funny."

"Uh, he asked me if we ever slept." She waited. "I told him some but that the sex was pretty sparse at times."

Her fork clanged on her plate. "When did you tell him this?"

"After surgery. He and your father wanted to know where you were."

"You said *that* in front of my *father*?"

"Yeah. It kind of slipped out."

"Like their teeth?"

"I don't know. When I turned the corner, I saw both Hermans laughing."

Michelle buried her face in her hands. "How can I ever look at either of them again?"

"I'm sorry, baby. It's been too long, and I..." He shrugged. "Eat up."

She laughed. She put her head down on her arms and laughed some more, and he thanked God. She pushed her half-eaten dinner away, took his hand, and led him to the bedroom. If they had to throw away the plates, he figured he wouldn't say a word. Besides, he was too busy pulling off her clothes to worry about the stupid dishes.

Later, she put her hand over her head on the pillow. "'Go for it, bro.' My brother!"

"Wasn't that a great idea?" He rolled over and grabbed her. "'Fess up. It was a good idea? Wasn't it?"

She giggled. "It was the best idea we've had in a long time. But really, we've had the idea, just not so much the opportunity."

"You got that right. I think about you and me doing this all the time."

"Good." Then she rolled over and promptly fell asleep.

Neither of them had to be in until seven the next evening, however, so they enjoyed more of the same the next morning. Marcus did manage to run to the kitchen and soak the dishes before dashing back to bed.

He followed his wife into Andrew's room around ten.

"Where have you been, Aunt Michelle?"

HJ gave Marcus a sly look.

"This was the first day we've both had evening shift together in a long time," Michelle said, "so he took your advice, dear brother. I have to check on a patient real quick."

"What does that mean?" Andrew asked.

"It means we slept in, buddy." Marcus winked at HJ.

"I guess that's good."

"Where's your mom?" Marcus asked.

"She went over to the university," HJ explained. "She has grades and exams coming up."

"You feeling better, bud?" Marcus asked.

"Yeah, unless I move wrong."

"Let's take a look at where I cut you." Marcus gently pulled back the dressing. HJ turned away, but Marcus and Michelle thought it looked good. He re-taped it and asked the father if he'd needed more pain medicine last night.

"He needed some around eight, and then more sometime after midnight, but none since."

"You're a tough guy, aren't you?"

Andrew grinned. "I'm going to get well!"

"Atta boy." Marcus held his fist out, and they bumped fists.

"Father likes you, Marcus. He said you were shaking this family up 'good and plenty,' and for the best." He grinned. "He laughed, you know. He's so strait-laced! I didn't know what to do until I heard him laugh. Beatrice and I used to say we kids had to have sprung out of Mother's forehead, like the gods."

"Daddy, you had to grow in Grandmother's tummy."

"Right, buddy. Where did Daddy get a silly idea like that? But it is an old story ancient people used to tell."

"They were dumb, Uncle Marcus. They weren't doctors like you."

"You got any questions, Dad? Although I can't give you any more answers until the labs come back."

"My father laughed, and he called Mother. When we get all this behind us, we'll have more than Andrew's life to thank you for."

Marcus shrugged. "For such a time as this."

"What does that mean? You said something like that before."

"God arranges circumstances," his sister said. "Nothing is by chance. Divine appointments."

"She's right. Read the book of Esther." Seeing HJ's puzzled face, Marcus said, "It's in the Bible, before Psalms. You'll find a Gideon Bible in the drawer." He waved, took Michelle's arm, and went into the hall.

* * *

"I don't want to hang around here. Why don't we drive over to D.C.?" They drove to Arlington Cemetery and hopped a tour trolley. Michelle leaned her head on Marcus's shoulder, and he pulled her close. They huddled together in their parkas. The skies were a brilliant blue, and white clouds floated above them. The January day was spring-like, despite the cold. He pointed to an eagle flying over the Potomac. He breathed in the sweet scent of fresh air. It was good to get out of the hospital. All too soon they had to get on the beltway and drive back to Baltimore.

In the car, Marcus cleared his throat. "I was thinking this morning."

"About?"

"I know we have to get through this year, and I'm glad the doctor had you on the pill to straighten out your periods, but when do you want to start trying to have a baby?"

"I guess maybe Easter. If I got pregnant then, I could finish my fellowship. Are you going to sign on for a second year?"

"I'm praying about it, and so far, my inclination is to do one more year."

"If I get pregnant, I'll take some time off. I've never taken time off. I could volunteer in some clinics."

"That's your idea of taking time off? But that'd be good."

"I won't renew the prescription after March."

Marcus smiled and reached for her hand. "You'll have beautiful babies, sweetheart."

"You're a gorgeous man, and you'll be a wonderful papa. And no one will ever think our babies sprung out of my forehead."

"Poor, deprived gods. They missed all the fun."

* * *

The lab report came back with clear margins. Marcus called their pediatrician, Dr. Ross, and suggested they could supervise the follow-up chemo there, if he preferred, and save the family the drive. But their pediatrician said they'd built their trust with him, and he preferred they remain there. For the next week, Andrew had chemo three times, and then for three months he came as an outpatient. Beatrice and HJ were confident enough to take him home, and they swapped off for traveling, a basin in the car. Michelle advised them to not wear perfume or aftershave and to avoid strong fragrances in the home. They waved as they pulled out the last afternoon.

"God has used this to bring the family closer, and the two of them seem...I don't know...more devoted."

"I saw him pat her on the bottom this afternoon."

She craned her neck up at him. "That's your fault."

"What do you mean it's my fault?"

"Your behavior is quite contagious."

He dropped his hand down and squeezed. "I can't help it. You have such a beautiful bottom. It cries out to be touched."

"If anyone sees you touch my bottom—" She was cut off by his kiss.

"Ready to go home?" He leaned and whispered, "Maybe I'll kiss it."

She walked ahead of him to the car, swaying her hips.

"You're asking for it, lady."

Chapter Twelve

NEW LIFE

On Easter Sunday, Marcus and Michelle headed over to Michelle's parents' for dinner after attending early service at their own church. Herman and Louise went to early service at Dr. Mondalah's church. They had attended regularly since the wedding, and even more so since Andrew's treatment. He'd been home for three months and had been done with chemo for three weeks. By some miracle and a bit of conniving, Michelle and Marcus were both free for the day and were pulling the 7:00–11:00 shift that night. As they turned into the driveway, the door flung open, and Andrew raced down the sidewalk, tackling Marcus, who caught him and threw him in the air.

"You're a bit heftier, buddy. Feeling good?"

"I love you, Uncle Marcus."

Herman Junior followed his son, beaming. "Welcome. You're too late to find any eggs in the yard, but we have basketfuls of candy. Mother says Michelle needs to help her make egg salad." He leaned to kiss his sister's cheek.

With Andrew perched on his shoulders, Marcus put his arm around his wife and followed his brother-in-law into the house, ducking under the doorway.

Beatrice greeted him with a hug, glancing up at her son. "Pretty high up there, aren't you?"

Marcus swung him down and hugged his sister-in-law. "How was the service?"

"Lovely. It was beautiful! He is risen."

"He is risen indeed. Hallelujah." Marcus winked at his wife. She had prayed for her family since she was fifteen years old, when she found Christ at Hope House. After her diagnosis and Andrew's treatment, the family had been restored, and now the Logans were attending the church where the couple had married. Andrew's older brother, Trey—Herman Logan the third—was studying to be a junior acolyte, and the entire family was taking catechism classes.

"Uncle Marcus?"

The big man squatted to be eye-to-eye with the earnest little boy. "What, Andrew?"

"I'm old enough to be confirmed, aren't I? I know all the answers."

"I was a bit older than you when I was confirmed."

Andrew huffed. "I figure if I almost went to heaven, I'm old enough."

"You've got a point there, buddy, but we're glad you put off going to heaven for a while." He stood. "What does Dr. Mondalah say, and the bishop?" Herman pulled his son close. "Dr. Mondalah says Andrew has a unique grasp for his age, but we're waiting for the bishop's verdict. Try to get off. It's next month, and we'd love to have you come since you were responsible for all of us being there."

"I'd say that was God's doing."

"God had a lot of help from you two. But He lives in you, right?"

Marcus put his arm around his brother-in-law. "And in you."

"I read yesterday where John the Baptist said, 'He must increase, and I must decrease.' Someday I pray to have as much of God in my life as you. How long have you been listening to the voice of God?"

"When you lived in my home, you heard it twenty-four-seven. Don't despise these little ones. They respond more quickly than we do. Papa said that when I was two, I told him my aunt had died two hours before he got the call."

"Fascinating. Do you think some people are naturally gifted, then?"

"No. We all can hear God, and the more of His Word we get into us, the more we recognize His voice. But children are not paralyzed by reason and diluted by the world, so they respond more readily. Have you read the story of the child Samuel?"

"Where is that?"

"In the book of Samuel. First Samuel."

"Logical. Must be in the Old Testament."

"Right after Judges. First the Pentateuch: Genesis, Exodus, Leviticus, Numbers, Deuteronomy, and then Joshua and Judges, followed by First and Second Samuel."

Herman fell silent. "You know your Bible." He scratched his head. "I haven't gotten into the Old Testament yet. I like reading about Christ."

"Jesus is in every page. He is the Word, remember? 'In the beginning was the Word, and the Word was with God, and the Word was God. And the Word became flesh and dwelt among us.' The Old Testament speaks about Him, paints pictures of Him. The author of Hebrews says the characters warn us against unbelief and turning back. The Israelites turned back again and again and paid the price." Marcus rested his big hand on Herman's shoulder. "Enough of a Sunday school lesson. Let's go fellowship with the children. Their angels constantly behold the face of the Father. I like hanging around kids."

"When I first woke up, after you cut the cancer out of me, I saw a big angel by my bed. He was standing at the foot of it, and I felt warm. He was big and fierce, but I wasn't afraid. At first, he didn't know I could see him. When he did, he smiled at me."

Marcus looked down at Andrew and placed his big hand on his head. "We have a good team on our side. That's what Elijah said when he saw the angel armies of the Lord around the city. We have more for us than against us. Don't ever forget that, even when you don't see them."

"I didn't think anyone would believe me. Was I dreaming?"

"I believe you. God lets us see into the spirit world sometimes. It's a gift of the Holy Spirit called 'discerning of spirits.' Your angel probably was with me in the operating room and helped me. You are here with us on this glorious morning when we celebrate the Resurrection of our Lord." The faith, love, and joy Marcus felt radiated from his face.

Michelle stood at the door, holding it open. "I've been sent to ask if you guys are coming in or if you are going to stand out here and palaver all day." They followed her inside.

Louise bustled in the room. "Can't you even let them sit?" She reached for Marcus, who took her in his arms and gave her an affectionate kiss on the cheek. "Michelle, come help me peel these eggs. We'll send you home with enough egg salad for sandwiches for a week." The three ladies went to the kitchen.

Herman Senior followed them with coffee orders and returned with cream and sugar for Marcus, cream for his son, and black for himself. Marcus looked around the antique-filled room in the old Georgetown home. Although the drapes were open and sunlight flooded in, he found it felt formal and staid. He looked around for a chair his bulk would not break and finally settled on a Duncan Phyfe sofa, placing his cup on a delicate table beside him. No wonder the boys were sent to the playroom. After discussing Andrew's weight gain and his rapid advance in school—he studied along with his class in the hospital and returned to school even when finishing up his chemo—the men went over the sermons they had heard. Herman Junior began by discussing the angels at the empty tomb, God's messengers proclaiming the good news, and the shepherds appearing at His birth.

Marcus heard his wife's voice in the dining room. They had been married less than six months ago, and their time off was limited, so he rose to find her and helped her set the table. "Sure is different than the dinner for your father's birthday meal."

She agreed. "I was so scared! And when I realized Andrew was sick, I thought they might argue and ignore the symptoms. I didn't know what I would do."

"Through faith and patience, you inherited the promises. Listen to them in there talking about the sermon."

Michelle moved to pull open the drapes in the dining room. "This place is elegant, but I always thought it was so dark. I want to take you to Hope House. It's an old historic mansion, but it's bright and warm. The light and love of God filled it, and it's filling this place, as well."

Louise herded the family into the dining room, Beatrice lifted the pitcher from the sideboard and filled the glasses, and the husbands held chairs for their wives.

Before anyone sat, the elder Herman lifted his voice and they joined his song. "'Praise God from whom all blessings flow. Praise God, His creatures here below. Praise God above, ye heavenly host. Praise Father, Son, and Holy Ghost.'" He bowed his head. "Dear God, we thank You for the many blessings You have poured out on us this day. Thank You for family. Thank You for health. Thank You for Your goodness to bring us all into Your Kingdom. We lift up those who are not with us. Our daughter and her family, Harry and Alicia. Bring us all together in one place sometime. We ask in the name of Your Son, our Lord, Jesus Christ." He glanced up. "I forgot your brother's name, Marcus. I'm sorry."

"Dennis and Marie, and their boys, Luke and John."

"God bless them, as well. He's a priest, isn't he? Studying in London?"

"Yes, sir. At Westcott in Cambridge, where Dr. Mondalah got his doctorate."

"So the Mansours will have two doctors in the family, one for the body and one for the soul," he joked. "Although you have been very good for our souls. Both of you."

"God has been good to all of us this spring." Marcus picked up his wife's hand and kissed her fingers. He reached for the bread. "These hot cross buns are wonderful, Beatrice. We have a little bakery in Cape Town that makes them every Easter."

"Herman gave me a bread-maker, but I dare not use it too often, or we would regret the pounds."

Andrew slipped out of his chair, and when his father asked if he needed to be excused, he said he didn't. He wanted to sit on Uncle Marcus's lap. Marcus opened his arms, and the lad climbed up and leaned his head on his chest. The family had been to sunrise service, and the sleepy boy dropped off to sleep. When they moved onto the patio, Marcus sat on the chaise, the child in his arms. The sun kissed the short, dark curls beginning to reappear. Remembering his baldness, Marcus dropped a kiss on his little patient's head. Last week, all the reports had come back clean, but he would be examined again in three months. He liked it when children survived. It's what he lived to accomplish. Looking over the boy, he caught Michelle watching them.

Her eyes were brimming with thankful tears. "Happy Easter, love."

Watching the pair, Andrew's father said, "You've taught me many things, Marcus. You demonstrated the love of God to all of us, especially Christ's love for my son. You exemplified how to love my wife, but most of all I thank God you showed me that tenderness is manly."

"Marcus is tender," Michelle agreed. "When we lost a little patient, I was broken, and he was precious to me. All the nurses said I'm blessed to have a tender man. He's like his father."

"I really think she fell in love with my father and married me because I was the closest she could get." Marcus gazed at his wife, his glance filled with affection.

"I don't think so." Herman looked at his sister. "You seem to like this guy."

She grinned.

"Trey, tell me about being an acolyte." Marcus turned to the older boy. "Do you like it?"

"Were you an acolyte, Uncle Marcus?"

"My brother and I both were. It's a big responsibility."

"Sometimes I'm scared, and once I forgot what I needed to do, but Dr. Mondalah whispered to me."

"I forgot lots of times, but after a while it's second nature."

"I only help in smaller services, but when I get good, I can help in the big services."

"Scripture says to never despise the day of small beginnings. God is preparing us for big things."

"How long did you help in surgeries before you did one yourself?" Trey questioned.

"I did little stuff first, but it was a couple of years before I did a major surgery alone. A more senior guy would watch and help when I started."

"I wouldn't mind being a doctor, but being a surgeon looks scary."

"It is. The body is the temple of the Holy Spirit, and I never dare to cut anyone open without first asking God's help and direction."

"Did you pray before you did Andrew's surgery?"

"You betcha! And I was glad your Aunt Michelle was with me, because I knew she'd be praying the whole time. We all serve God in some way. I bet your dad and grandfather pray when they go into the courtroom or advise a client."

The Logan men looked at each other, realizing they had a lot to learn about this Christian walk.

Herman Senior cleared his throat. "I will now. I've leaned on my own understanding for too many years, and I hurt a lot of people in the process." He reached across to pick up Michelle's hand from the arm of the Adirondack chair where she sat. "I acted like I was God." She covered his hand with her own.

Andrew stirred and struggled to sit. He rubbed his eyes.

"Did you have a nice little rest, son?" Beatrice asked. "Ready to play?"

With a bit of help, the boys set up a croquet set, and soon the mallets knocked against the balls with a loud crack. The younger Herman and Marcus soon engaged in a hot rivalry with hearty laughter.

Marcus missed an easy shot. "I haven't played this in a thousand years. I wonder if we even have one in the shed at home. I spend too much time indoors, looking at screens." He held out his arm. "I'm going to lose my tan."

The boys looked down at their own black arms. "Huh?"

"Uncle Marcus is being silly. God made you perfect, boys." Michelle shook her head. "With that remark, it's time to go home!"

"Aww, don't go yet."

"I have to work tonight, Andrew, and so does Uncle Marcus, and we need to change our clothes first."

"I love you, Aunt Michelle." Andrew threw his arms around her.

She lifted him. "Ugh, you keep gaining weight, and I won't be able to do this!"

The entire family waved as they pulled away.

* * *

After that night, Michelle and Marcus worked different shifts for two weeks until they finally both pulled a 7:00–3:00 and came home together. They had exchanged suggestive plans throughout the day whenever their paths crossed, and now they chased each other up the stairs to their apartment.

Marcus kicked the door closed while seizing her in his arms. "I've missed your sweet loving, baby."

He kept her lips occupied as he backed her down the hall to their bedroom. Her knees hit the bed, and she fell into the softness. He fell on top of her, still managing to remove her clothes. She tugged on the strings of his scrub pants, and he kicked them aside. It was almost six before they left the bed. After their initial frenzied coming together, they took time to please one another in a slow, thorough fashion.

They lay, dozing in one another's arms, until hunger drove them to explore the refrigerator. Michelle sniffed and threw out several containers. Marcus teased about their lab experiments, noting that several were fuzzy. Eventually, she pulled a bagged frozen meal out of the freezer and dumped it into a frying pan.

After dinner, Marcus said he needed to get on his iPad and make some clinical notes, but he decided that could wait until tomorrow, instead pulling his wife into his lap.

"Haven't you had enough?"

"Never enough of you. This has been a long stretch. We haven't had time off together since Easter."

"And we spent it at my parent's house."

"It was a good day, though. Your brother sent me an email. The confirmation is scheduled for two weeks from Sunday. I'm trying to juggle our schedules."

* * *

Managing to have the same day off, the pair left for Washington while the fog still hung over the Potomac, heading for the old church where they had gotten married. They parked and hurried around the block, only to see the youngsters lining up to walk in the building. Scooting around the front of the line, Marcus touched Andrew on his way by and gave him a wink. The younger Herman picked up the jackets he set on the pew to save their spaces, and they sat together, leaning to wave to Herman Senior and Louise.

"Where's Beatrice?"

"She's helping lead them in," Herman told his sister.

The music started, and the congregation rose to greet the procession. Each youngster who was presented to the congregation up front responded to a question, and Andrew handled a difficult one with aplomb. The bishop laid hands on them one by one, pausing when Andrew tugged his sleeve to whisper something. The group knelt together and received their first communion. Beatrice and two other adults answered questions, and Louise and both Hermans, who had been baptized and confirmed Roman Catholics, were welcomed into the church. The bishop introduced each new member of the congregation, and everyone joined in a joyful song.

Stifling her tears, Michelle clung to her husband's arm. "Your suffering has its reward," he whispered. She swiped her nose against her sleeve. He wiped it with a handkerchief he'd remembered to stick in his pocket earlier, knowing she'd be emotional this day. She looked up at him, and their hearts joined without a word.

The sun broke through the beautiful stained-glass windows, streaming down upon the procession as the newly confirmed made their way down the aisle.

Gathering in the fellowship hall downstairs, each one sought out family members and friends. The Logans and Mansours grouped together. Dr. Mondalah and the bishop approached the family.

"Bishop, this is Michelle and Marcus Mansour. They were married here on December twenty-third of last year."

The bishop took Marcus by the elbow. "This is the couple who saved the life of a very special boy."

"God did, sir," Michelle replied.

"But He had two faithful instruments who brought not only natural life to their family, but also life everlasting, and I'm proud to meet you."

"What did Andrew say to you up there?"

The bishop looked in her eyes. "He said he felt God touch him, and I told him I did, too. He has a special anointing, and I felt it. He's a unique child, old for his age. I came intending to deny his request, thinking he was too young, but in his interview I felt as confounded as the priests must have felt when the boy Jesus was in their midst. He's not just bright, although he certainly is; he is also sensitive to the Spirit of God."

"Did he tell you he saw an angel after his surgery?"

"He did, and he tells me I must hear how God led you two together."

Marcus laughed and shared his miraculous discovery in the cafeteria at Johns Hopkins, where he came face to face with the woman God had shown him in a dream in South Africa.

"Perhaps he learned to hear the voice of God from his uncle?"

Marcus shrugged. "Like you, sir, I feel privileged to be a part of Andrew's life. He's special. But we must hide these things in our hearts until it is time."

The bishop studied Marcus. "Indeed. You two are in Father Manny's congregation in Baltimore?" At their acknowledgement, he added, "I hope to see you there," and the servant of God moved to speak to other families.

The day turned warm and sunny, and after service and the reception, the families strolled around the Jefferson Memorial, stopping to eat together before Michelle and Marcus left for Baltimore.

* * *

The next evening the couple shared, Michelle worked 7:00-3:00, and Marcus came in after 7:00 in the evening. "It smells wonderful in here. What are you cooking?" Noticing the dining table was set with special silverware and plates and an arrangement of roses, Marcus racked his brain. Had he forgotten her birthday? His own? It wasn't the anniversary of the day they met. "What are we celebrating?"

Without answering, Michelle put the plates on the table. Roast chicken, hot rolls, rice, broccoli, and salad. She urged him to sit, and when he did, she reached for his hand to say the blessing.

He felt something in his hand and saw a test strip there. He looked at it and then up at her smiling face. "You're pregnant." He came around to her chair and helped her stand. Placing his hands on either side of her face, he kissed her. He would have moved the celebration down the hall, but he realized she had worked to make this special meal, so he sat, blessed the food, and savored every bite. After the main course, however, when she would have brought his favorite lemon pie, he asked if they could defer it until later. Knowing his heart's desire, she took his hand and led him to the bedroom. The spread was turned back, the sheets were clean, and fragrant candles revealed her intention. Keeping his gaze on her, he moved about the room and lit them. One. Two. Three.

"One for Mama, one for Papa, and baby makes three."

"My heart is full with love for my beautiful wife. You'll have such beautiful babies."

"I married a beautiful man." She stood before him, tall and proud, and unashamed. His Nile princess.

Chapter Thirteen

TAKING HIS WIFE HOME

They went to the hospital together the next day. Marcus couldn't stop smiling as he looked at his wife across the car. He was sure she had a glow. She touched his leg.

"Don't get that thing all worked up again. We'll be late."

She giggled. "Surely, it is exhausted."

"Don't count on it." He turned into the garage, and as soon as he parked, he drew her into his arms and kissed her deeply. "I love you."

"I know. Love you, too." She pulled on the door handle, and they met behind the car to walk to the elevator. As they stood waiting, he cupped her bottom in his big hand.

"Quit that!" She glanced around the garage. "You are incorrigible."

Looking innocent, he greeted those stepping out and led her inside. She moved away from him, backing into the corner. "Nervous?" His black eyes twinkled.

"Stay back." She held her hand in front of her. "I'm warning you."

He kept his hands to himself. She left at floor five, and he continued to eight. When he got out, the nurse told him Dr. Campbell wanted to see him in his office. Pausing only to check one patient, he walked to his boss's office and tapped on the door. Responding to the invitation, he stepped inside.

"You wanted to see me, sir?"

Dr. Campbell waved him over. "Have a seat, Marcus. I noticed you signed up for another year, but Michelle hasn't. Is she returning to Cleveland? They've called about her." He appeared concerned.

Knowing the good doctor's affection for his wife, Marcus answered, "No, sir, we planned to start our family. She's going to take some time off, but she's looking into volunteering in some free clinics, which is her idea of taking time off."

"That's our Michelle. Then you may be interested in a proposition I have to offer." Marcus leaned forward. "I have been asked to work in Portugal's medical school for a year. My wife is from there, and she's eager to return home. I would like you to be acting director here next year. If Michelle isn't working, the extra salary would be a help."

"That's quite an honor. Do you think I could do it?"

"If I didn't, I wouldn't have asked. Do you want to talk it over with her?"

"What would you do if I didn't take the position?"

"I'd turn down the offer. It takes time to fill this kind of a job. I don't want to leave permanently; I only want to take a sabbatical. Has your wife ever been to South Africa?"

Marcus shook his head. "I hope to take her when I finish here."

"Take a month and take her home. Paid vacation. We'll leave when you return."

"That's a generous offer, sir. I'd like that."

"Think about it tonight, see what she thinks, and we'll talk again in the morning."

With visions of taking his beloved home dancing in his head, Marcus had to focus to get his work done. As always, he felt her before she spoke.

"Got time for coffee?"

He swiveled around after closing his screen. "Yep. Let's go down to the cafeteria. Got time?" Since they usually ducked into the doctors' lounge, she was puzzled, but she followed him. "Feel like walking?" To get exercise, they had a habit of using the staircase. She was game.

They didn't say a word the entire decent. "Is something up?"

Pulling the door open for her, he said, "My boss surprised me this morning." And he told her about Dr. Campbell's request and offer.

"A month to go to South Africa? To see your family? Will Dennis be there?"

"They get home in May. You won't be done till June. He's thinking July. It's winter at home, but it's not like winter here. Rainy, but rarely below fifty. The coast is sunny much of the time. We live at Hout Bay, a coastal suburb of Cape Town. Remember, I showed you pictures on the net of feeding the seals there?"

Michelle stopped walking. "Are you serious? You aren't joking? How can we afford the tickets?"

"Papa has promised to send tickets anytime we could come. A month off! We've never had a honeymoon."

"We'd be staying with your parents, wouldn't we?"

"We could take some time. What do you say, honey?" She threw her arms around him. He was startled because they tried to be professional in the hospital, but since they were still in the stairwell, he kissed her. "I take it that's a yes?"

That afternoon he gave Dr. Campbell his answer, and the older man teased him about returning pregnant. When Marcus told him it was a fait accompli, he offered his congratulations.

Fortunately, Michelle didn't get sick. She continued to work every day, but she was tired. The staff made her rest, insisting she put her feet up throughout the day, and they had a baby shower for her. Many of them were finishing up, and they wanted to share their love before the end of the term. Marcus teased her about all the baby things she had to put away before they packed.

Michelle didn't get much sleep on the plane. She made frequent trips to the lavatory, which was located conveniently beside their seats. God bless

Papa for first class tickets! Marcus slept, although he frequently checked her blanket or adjusted her pillow. Michelle's longest flight had been from Ohio to Baltimore, which was nothing like this. Sixteen hours. She didn't want to turn on the reading light and disturb anyone around her, all of whom seemed to be sleeping soundly. One man roused and glared at her the third time she used the lavatory. She almost asked him if he'd like being pregnant, but she restrained herself. She collapsed on her seat.

"You okay, honey?"

"Fine. I had to go to the bathroom."

"How many trips is that?"

Without answering, she turned her back and closed her eyes. Ages went by. Centuries. Eons. Marcus reached under her blanket and caressed her breast. She looked over her shoulder. He wasn't even awake! She stared around the quiet cabin, fighting the urge to pee again. Finally, she dozed off, but soon the overhead lights came on, and the attendants moved about the cabin, handing out warm cloths for their faces.

"Did you have a nice sleep?"

Michelle glared at him. "Not as nice as yours."

"Need to use the restroom?"

The man in the seat across the aisle spoke. "She must have used the lavatory twenty times last night."

Marcus raised his seat and leaned over her. "She's pregnant."

"That explains it." Their fellow passenger gave her a forgiving smile.

"Sorry." Michelle raised her seat, and Marcus lowered their trays before their breakfast arrived. As usual, she was starved. She finished hers and looked at his. "Are you going to eat your fruit?"

"You can have it." He exchanged his fruit bowl for her empty one. "Want me to ask for more?"

"No, thanks. Excuse me again." She went to the lavatory, overhearing him explain to the man across the aisle. "She doesn't get sick, but she's grumpy sometimes, and weepy all the time."

She sat. "Do you have to tell strangers about my pregnancy foibles?"

Looking chagrinned, Marcus mumbled, "Sorry."

"Me, too. I'm sorry for my behavior."

As soon as their trays were removed, he drew her to his chest. "Won't be long now, sweetie." He raised the window screen, and sunlight flooded in. The captain announced it was 11:45 in Cape Town, and the weather was thirteen degrees Celsius.

Michelle looked at him. "About fifty-five Fahrenheit. Did you put your liner in your raincoat?"

"Yeah." Her husband pointed to the seatbelt sign, and they both buckled up. She felt the tires touch down with a bump, squealing.

Chapter Fourteen

HOME TO SOUTH AFRICA

Because Marcus was a citizen and Michelle was traveling with him, they went through the expedited customs for nationals. Pulling their luggage, they made their way into the main terminal and spotted his parents.

Harry lifted Michelle off her feet. He put her down and looked her over. "Harry, she's not even twelve weeks yet! How was the flight?"

"Great!" said Marcus.

"Long," said Michelle.

Alicia tucked her arm under Michelle's. "You look tired, honey. Let's get you home."

As much as she wanted to see everything, almost immediately after they began driving, Michelle leaned her head on her husband's shoulder and fell asleep. Alicia noticed and asked Marcus if they should stop for dinner. He told them they'd had breakfast on the plane, and they drove straight to the house.

His papa stopped in front of the old guest house, which had been used for play and storage when he was a boy. "Knowing you never had a honeymoon, we decided to prepare a love nest for you. You're spending your only vacation with family, and we're grateful. Come see what Mama did."

Marcus nudged his wife. "We're home." She only mumbled. He helped her out of the car and led her through the door. Alicia scurried ahead and turned down the comforter on the new bed in the new bedroom. He lowered Michelle, and she mumbled something about "Sorry" and "Thanks" as she sunk into the pillow.

"Is she all right?" Harry fretted.

"She didn't sleep on the plane. The man across from us said she must have gone to the bathroom thirty times. She doesn't get sick, but she's tired." He waved them out of the bedroom and lowered his voice. "And she gets a bit grumpy at times." He looked around at the lovely sitting room where they were standing. "This is nice, Mama. You turned the old dump into a magical place."

"There's a master bath off the bedroom." His father pointed through the bedroom. "Cost me a pretty penny, this love nest of yours."

"We appreciate it. You're right. Michelle and I haven't had time off. I don't know how we'd have made it without that nice apartment you found us." He followed them into the main house. "When's Dennis coming?"

"We told them to hold off until tomorrow. They'll be here all next week, and the boys are talking about nothing else. You wouldn't have a moment to yourselves in the big house."

"You're very thoughtful, Mama, but do me a favor and explain that to Michelle. She's been rejected her whole life, and she's super emotional these days."

"We thought the family was restored after her nephew's ordeal." Harry took his son's arm. "Haven't they been going to church?"

"They've all come a long way, and she's been gracious to forgive, but she still thinks of herself as unattractive."

"Why, Marcus? She is beautiful!"

"Don't I know, Mama? But her self-image is marred. She's self-conscious about being a large woman. Apparently, she attained her height at an early age, which made her awkward. Her father had strange notions about beauty and projected them onto her. Louise says we'll understand more when we learn about his childhood."

While the two men stood talking in the kitchen, Alicia scurried around, preparing supper. "Will she want to eat?" They decided she needed to sleep more, so she wrapped a plate and set it aside, telling Marcus they had a microwave in the cottage.

The parents enjoyed having their son to themselves, although they looked forward to getting to know the new daughter he brought them. He shared many stories of their working together, including Cassie's death, which ended in his proposal. He lauded her expertise, telling them, "She's the finest diagnostician I've ever known," but it was the stories about her gentleness with children, especially Cassie and Andrew, that moved them to tears. He described the family's journey to wholeness, giving God the glory for all He had done.

"I'm glad you waited on the Lord, son. He brought you the perfect wife."

"Amen, Papa. I got ahead of Him, or we would've married sooner." He stood. "I'll head over there now and turn in."

His mother pressed the plate into his hand. "You'll find a small refrigerator beside the sink." She lifted her arms for a hug. "I love you, son."

"Love you, too, Mama. Papa."

* * *

In the shower, he realized Michelle had been up and had showered. Her clothes were on the floor, and she'd fallen back to sleep wearing the blue gown he loved. He tried not to disturb her when he slipped into bed, but her eyes opened.

"Marcus, do you love me?"

He lost himself in her eyes, sinking into their dark pools of love, and propped up on his elbow. "Do I love you? Does the sun come up every morning, and does the moon reign over the night skies? Do the stars sing above us? Does the tide roll out and wash back over the sandy shore? Does spring follow winter, and does summer return? Do I stand at heaven's gate when you kiss me and enter in when you love me? Do I love you?"

She reached up her arms. "Yes," she whispered, smiling. "Welcome to heaven." And they entered in together.

Chapter Fifteen

FAMILY

They were lying in bed when Michelle heard Dennis's vehicle pull in. She got up and pulled on some jeans and a shirt. Marcus did the same. After brushing their teeth, they joined the others in the big house. The brothers greeted one another with effusive hugs and loud exclamations, pounding each other's backs, while little boys shouted and danced around them. Harry took his daughter-in-law in his arms, asking if she slept well. She loved this family and mouthed a silent prayer that she and Marcus could rear their children in an atmosphere of love like this.

Dennis broke away and took his new sister's hands. "Michelle, we love you already. Papa never stops talking about you, and the folks were thrilled you came. Papa was afraid no one would take Marcus off our hands." He kissed her cheek, then pulled his wife forward. "My wife, Marie, who's also the better and more beautiful half, and our boys, Luke and Mark."

Michelle reached behind her and brought forward a canvas tote. "We brought something for you boys."

The boys stormed the bag.

"What do you say, boys?"

"We don't even know what it is, Mama," Luke protested, shrugging his slender shoulders and raising his hands in a gesture of confused helplessness.

"If you don't appreciate a gift, we don't have to open it," Dennis warned.

"Yes, sir." John approached his new aunt. "Thank you, Aunt Michelle."

"Open it so we can see if you like it. Uncle Marcus and I picked it out for you."

With her permission, John tore into the wrapping. His eyes opened wide as he saw the box. "Oh, wow! I've wanted a globe forever. Now I can see where Uncle Marcus is. And Grand-Papa when he travels."

Michelle slid another box toward Luke. The younger boy was a timid child, and he grabbed her heart. He was a heart thief. But his dancing eyes revealed his excitement.

Dennis pointed to Michelle. "Tell your aunt 'thank you.'"

His head dropped, and he stared at the floor, but he mumbled, "Thank you."

Cupping her hand under his chin, she brought his face up and kissed his cheek. "You're most welcome, Luke." She picked up the big box and placed it in his outstretched hands.

Luke took care unwrapping his package, soothing the folded paper and setting it aside. Seeing the picture on the box, he asked, "Is it a boat?"

Marcus squatted beside him. "We brought batteries, so we can run it when we go to Hout Bay." He opened the box and lifted it out. Winking at John, he added, "We may have another for you to play with if you can make the globe a family gift." John flung his arms around his uncle's neck before standing before his aunt.

Michelle put her arm around his shoulder. "I'm glad to meet my new nephews."

Because of her good sleep, Michelle was eager to see the sights she missed coming home the night before. First, the family gathered around the breakfast table. After the boys sang a blessing, serving bowls moved from hand to hand. Michelle scooped out eggs, bacon, sausage, and rolls, then lathered rolls with jam.

Marie looked at her. "Aren't you pregnant? Dennis told me you were pregnant."

Marcus explained that his wife didn't get sick but that she was weepy all the time. He glanced at her and lowered his voice, leaning forward. "And sometimes she gets grumpy."

Marie laughed. "You're fortunate. I hardly had my head out of the commode for three months!"

Michelle explained that her only complaint was that she was tired all the time, and the women cleared the table while the men drifted to the living room.

"Before we go anywhere, Michelle, you must see Mama's garden. Did you like the guest house? She worked so hard in there."

Alicia put her arm around Michelle. "We knew the boys would give you no privacy, and you had no honeymoon, so I wanted to create a honeymoon cottage. Papa calls it a love nest. You're our daughter, and this house is your home." She waved around the big house. "But you chose to come here on your only vacation, and we were determined to give you your own space." Michelle cried, and Alicia pulled her into an embrace. "Welcome home, daughter."

"She is weepy, isn't she?" Marie observed. Marcus had told his brother about Michelle's rejection as a child, so her sister-in-law was aware of how much the warmth of her husband's family meant to her. She took her arm and led her outside into the sunshine.

Taking a deep breath, Michelle breathed in the fragrances surrounding her, and Marie pointed them out. The Lambode Aloe and the Kranz Aloe, both used to treat stomach disorder. The beautiful Leopard Lilly, and the Impala Lilly, with its yellow and purplish brown stripes. "Over there is a sprawling bed of Morning Glory, but it doesn't bloom in winter," Marie said. "Mama had brought some of these down from the mountains, and they survive under her tender care."

Michelle almost didn't see a small flower close to the ground. "This is a shy one," she observed, kneeling to see its lovely white flowers.

"That's a Pajama flower." Pointing beyond them, away from the walk, Marie cautioned, "The so-called Lucky Bean Creeper isn't lucky. Those red pods are poison."

"But they're pretty. Like Lucifer, they are a beautiful but deadly temptation." Michelle felt overwhelmed at the profusion around her. "This is winter?"

Marie laughed. "Come in summer next time. By the shore today, we'll show you more." She looped her arm in Michelle's. "I'm glad to have a sister. Marcus is a wonderful brother, and now he's brought me a sister. I was an only child."

"I was a late-in-life baby, and my brother and sister were off to school by the time I came along. Almost like being an only child."

"We're excited to get to know you, and we're curious about the dream woman. Papa loves you, and Mama was thrilled when she met you. She regretted that she didn't have more time, but it was the holidays."

"Marcus overwhelmed me at first. He blurted out his dream and expected me to believe him. I told him I didn't have a dream, and I insisted we had to get to know each other. I made him afraid to propose! When I told him I was more than ready, he rushed me to the altar."

The women giggled. "The Mansour men are very tender and loving. Dennis and Marcus have a good father, who demonstrated how a husband should love his wife. We're blessed women, Michelle."

"The first time I met Papa, he took me in his arms. I had worked a double shift that day, and I was exhausted. When he hugged me, I was overwhelmed and cried like a baby. My father and I were estranged at the time, but in my entire life he had never held me like that. Mother wants me to know about his childhood, but ours was nothing like your boys have. I saw the way the brothers hugged this morning and prayed God would give us a family like this one."

"He will. The Mansour children are planted in the rich soil of love, and they grow like ground cover, profligate in affection."

"What a nice image, Marie. 'Profligate in affection.' Marcus and I lost a little cancer patient, a precious girl, and Cassie's death, though inevitable, crushed me. I was sitting in her dark room after they took her out, and he found me there. I don't know how long I cried, but he simply held me. I begged him to take me to his place, and he did. That night I asked him why he hadn't proposed, and he reminded me I had warned him to give me time." Michelle swiped her eyes. "By that time, we'd been together for months, and I had tons of respect for him. He's an excellent doctor, tender with his patients and kind to the staff. The day Cassie was admitted, she was held in the pediatric unit until we had a bed in oncology. He came into the room and swooped her up. Her mother said he was like a mighty angel. In the hospital we have protocol about moving patients, but he said, 'Rules are made to be broken,' and carried her in his arms to the elevator. By the time her mother and I got through the hygiene station upstairs, we found him cradling her in his arms. 'We needed a bit of a cuddle,' he said before he tucked her into bed. How could I not love a man like that? I am a most blessed woman. God had to call a man from another continent to make me whole."

"Papa made Mama whole, too. You'll have to get her to share her story while you are here."

The two women wove around the profusion of color among the fragrant flowers. They fell silent, hearing only the tinkle of fountains and the trickles of water beside the path. Michelle felt comfortable with her new friend. Her husband's family provided her not only exuberant joy but also peaceful serenity. She saw Marcus approach.

"Mama sent me looking for you. Did you have a nice visit?"

"She is wonderful, your wife!" His sister-in-law took Michelle's hand.

"She is the missing part of me. I looked a long time to find her." He took her other hand. "Mama has packed a picnic lunch for us."

They drove to a white sandy beach. Harry helped Alicia spread two blankets, and their sons carried the two hampers. Marcus pretended to groan under the weight and asked if she had rocks in them. Marie and Michelle cleaned their hands with sanitary wipes and attended to the boys. Dennis suggested they say a blessing before unwrapping the sandwiches.

"Grand-Mama put fried chicken in there, Papa. I saw her!"

Marcus swung John onto his shoulders. "Too bad you won't be able to reach it. I'm going to eat it all up."

"You're teasing, Uncle Marcus."

"I am. Bow your head so we can eat."

After they spent time walking along the beach and playing in the water lapping on the shore, they picked up their picnic and drove back in the flaming sunset over the Atlantic coast. The shore birds squawked, dancing and diving as they swooped to pick off their dinner. Harry fetched a jacket from the van and wrapped it around Michelle. When they arrived home, they talked about what they would do in the coming days. The next day was Saturday, but Dennis had an associate who would do the service on Sunday, so they could attend church with their parents. After church, Alicia had a staff party to introduce Michelle and so everyone could see Marcus. They set up a huge tent and lavish foods. Of course, Marcus's mama wanted to take Michelle to see her schools, and Harry insisted she couldn't visit South Africa without seeing the diamond mines. They would fly to Pretoria and visit the hospital where he did his residency, and Marcus was eager for his grandfather in Soweto to get to know his wife. His grandfather had the most faith in his dream.

Michelle turned her head from one person to another as the ideas flew. Since she was rarely silent about their plans, Marcus checked himself. "What do you want to do, honey?"

"Will we have time to go to Table Mountain? You showed me on the computer. You said we could ride the cableway."

Marcus pulled her close. "That is a day trip for the two of us. The tour books say sunsets over the bay are ideal for a bit of romance."

Michelle patted her tummy. "Too late for that, dear."

Everyone joined in the happy laughter, but Dennis put his arm around Marie. "Never too late for romance."

"Indeed not!" Harry agreed, gazing fondly at Alicia.

"You men are all alike," Alicia protested.

"Just the way you like us." Harry winked at his boys. "After all, the Good Book commands, 'Husbands, love your wives,' and I try to be obedient."

Marcus spoke over the din of merriment. "God made that command-ment easy for us by giving each of us such beautiful, good wives."

"Amen," chorused Dennis and Harry.

"And on that note, we shall adjourn to our appointed marital cham-bers." Harry stood and offered a hand to his wife.

"Harry!" Alicia exclaimed, but he pulled Alicia to himself and gave her a resounding kiss, which his boys applauded.

For once, Marcus was too tired when Michelle nestled up to him. "I love you."

"Love you, too," she responded, and then his regular breathing was all she heard.

* * *

The next morning, Michelle lowered the window in their bedroom. Yes-terday's pleasant breeze had turned chilly. Michelle saw Marcus open one eye and watch her disappear into the bathroom. She did her morning ablutions, but she didn't carry any clothes in there.

He followed her so he could complete his own morning chores and brush his teeth. "Don't bother to dress."

"I won't. I like you in the mornings."

He growled. "I love you anytime. Morning, nighttime, and you were pretty good in the middle of the night if I remember correctly."

"Hurry."

And he did.

They were late getting to the kitchen, but the family still sat around the table, plotting routes for their excursions.

Alicia waved her hand. "Food's under the warmer, and coffee's in the pot."

Marie jumped up. "The teapot is hot. What kind do you want?" She pushed the selection toward Michelle but handed her ginger tea.

"Why did you sleep so late?" John demanded.

Dennis choked on his coffee.

"Jet lag," Harry told the boys. "When you fly over the ocean, it takes a few days to adjust."

Carrying her tea to the table, Michelle scooted next to the younger boy. "Everyone has a plan. Are you in?" The boy bobbed his head.

Marcus brought her a plate of eggs, English muffins, orange marmalade, and Canadian bacon.

"Yum." She reached for it.

"I can't believe you!" Marie fussed.

Dennis took her hand. "Marcus says she's carrying a girl. Let's try for a girl, and maybe you won't be sick."

"If Marcus says it's a girl, it is. Can you guarantee us one, brother?" Marie looked across the table at her brother-in-law.

"I don't do guarantees, but sometimes God shows me things."

"Like me," Michelle piped in a happy voice.

"Took you long enough to believe it," he grumbled.

"I'd never met anybody like you before." She turned to the others. "Let me tell you about the day he stopped the rain."

"I did no such thing!"

But she described their run in the downpour, how their umbrella turned inside out in the wind, how he hollered at the heavens and the rain stopped, the wind died, and the sun came out. "I became a believer that day, but I'd already fallen for him."

"You'd already fallen for my father."

Michelle reached to cover Harry's hand with her own. "Yep. He's pretty irresistible."

"Who could not love you?" Harry looked at her with fondness.

"Uh, my dad? And my brother."

"They never knew you, baby. But they do now." And Marcus boasted about her diagnosis of her nephew and their subsequent treatment. "They stand in awe now."

"Hardly. You're the hero." Michelle gathered their plates.

"We make a good team. What am I going to do without you next year?"

"You'd better not harass any other doctors!"

"I only have eyes for you." Marcus tugged her hand and pulled her down for a kiss.

"Ugh, Uncle Marcus."

He pointed to John. "I'll talk to you in six years." He stood. "Who's ready to go?"

And the scramble began as they did bathroom chores, collected towels, finished the picnic baskets, and went out the door. They drove from their neighborhood down to the harbor. When they got to the bay, Michelle couldn't believe the seals crowding up to the dock. Harry had to go for another bucket of fish. John held the bait until the seals took it out of his hand, but Luke threw them, and the seals swam after them, sometimes fussing a bit as they fought over a tidbit.

Michelle laughed before she stood, looking around for a bathroom. Alicia took her to the nearest one. She came back to the dock, and Marcus pulled her down beside him. "That's the other symptom, but it's mostly an inconvenience."

"Says you. Thank God our seats in the plane were right beside the lavatory!"

"I couldn't eat for two, but I certainly peed for two." Marie pulled John close.

"What about the next three months?" Dennis recalled. "You ate like a fisherman then." She shoved him, but he clung to her. Michelle held her breath, thinking they were both headed for the bay, but Marcus grabbed his brother's hand and tugged them both to their feet.

Michelle thought she'd never had this much fun in her life as she looked around at the Mansour family. Her family. Her eyes filled.

"I really don't know how you have any water left to pee. You lose so much from your eyes," her husband teased. They sat side by side, kicking their legs off the side of the dock.

He put his arm around her, and she rested against him, looking over the bay, which was crowded with boats of all kinds. A seal brushed against her leg, acting pathetic. "You beggar!" She reached for another fish and teased the seal a bit before rubbing her hand on its smooth side as she gave it to her.

"I see these kids feeding them out of their hand and remember that God gave us dominion. It's a foretaste of the restoration of all things," Dennis mused.

"I'm hungry, Papa," John complained.

Dennis shoved himself up and lifted his son. "Grand-Mama has lunch packed. Let's find a picnic table."

The family moved to the van. Luke wanted Aunt Michelle to sit by him. They climbed out of the van and spread a picnic.

"This is pretty weather for winter," Michelle said.

"Our coastline has sunshine over three hundred and twenty days a year." Marcus patted his lap, and she put her head on his strong leg. He fingered her short curls.

"Michelle isn't hungry?"

"She's tired," Marcus told his brother.

"Didn't get much sleep last night," Dennis teased.

"Didn't you hear? The flight got to him. He went right to sleep," Michelle mumbled.

"She likes me in the morning." Michelle slapped his leg, but she giggled.

Dennis laughed. "They all like us in the morning, bro." And the two men laughed together.

With a smile on her lips and contentment in her heart, Michelle dozed.

Harry asked him if she'd eat, and Marcus assured him that after a twenty-minute nap, she'd be fine. Dennis and Marie ran around with the boys and their Frisbees, and by the time the boys were ready for seconds, Michelle was awake and "absolutely starving." After they ate, the women packed up the hampers and stowed them in the van. The three couples walked along the beach, hand in hand, boys scampering out front. Michelle pulled her jacket closer.

"Cold?" Marcus put his arm around her shoulder. "It's about thirteen degrees Celsius."

"That would be what in Fahrenheit?" Alicia wanted to know.

"About fifty-five or fifty-six," Harry offered.

"Not bad for winter. Last year in Baltimore, we had twenty inches of snow and temperatures below freezing. That's zero degrees Celsius. Even I know that."

"She's used to it." Marcus nodded toward his wife. "The temperatures in the U.S. are much more extreme. In the summer, which is now, it's hot! If hell's any hotter than July in Washington D.C., I don't want to go."

"You liked fall. It's beautiful in the fall. We drove down the Shenandoah Valley, and Marcus was amazed at the colors. The leaves are glorious in autumn. Red, orange, burgundy, and yellow. God's palette. The Shenandoah Valley is one of the most beautiful spots in the world, but this is magnificent!"

"Let's turn back if you're cold." Marcus took her hand, and the troupe reversed their steps, the boys running ahead as they approached the van.

Holding her shoes, Michelle toed the sand. "It's so white. It looks like someone bleached it," she said. The gentle waves lapped the shore, breaking white against the turquoise waters farther out, pushing them inland. She leaned her head back, looking up at the clear, brilliant blue sky above and the coastline curling around them. This was the most perfect day of her life.

Marcus pointed out the window as they drove, showing her the sights, identifying the coastal flowers, pointing out Sprawling Dunewood and Sea Pumpkin with its yellow daisy-like flowers. He explained how those plants stabilized the sand. "That's Hottentot Fig. It was the base of your jam this morning."

"Thanks for bringing the church van, son," Harry said to Dennis, who was driving while he rode shotgun. "It's comfortable and fun to be all together in here. Makes for a better visit."

Seeing Michelle in the bosom of his family, laughing and chatting, Marcus rejoiced. He was home, and his soulmate was beside him. He wondered where life would take them. He knew she loved Cleveland, and most of her friends lived in nearby Columbus, but he longed to return here. *God, give her a love for my home. But don't let my will be done; let thy will be done.* He loved his wife more than any place, and their home would be together. If God sent him to the United States to find her and kept him there, he'd be content.

They got home, raiding the hampers for supper, and chatted around the table. Michelle helped Marie put the boys to bed, but after their mother left, she sat with her arm around Luke, reading from the new books she and Marcus brought them. The beautifully illustrated volumes about Jesus held them captive, and they wanted to read more and more.

Dennis poked his head in the door. "You boys will have Aunt Michelle reading to you till midnight. Let's pray and go to sleep." Michelle joined the boys on their knees beside their father as they said their prayers.

"Now, into bed, both of you." Dennis kissed first John and then Luke, tucking them under the covers.

Michelle kissed Luke, and John wanted his, too. She followed Dennis down the hall, but he turned to her before they got to the family room, saying, "We're glad to have you in the family, Michelle. Papa adores you. We wanted to come to the wedding."

"I know you had examinations, but Marcus was rather in a hurry."

He laughed. "He waited for you a long time. He searched, waiting for God's best. When I first heard about the dream, I thought perhaps he'd gone over the edge. Papa said he wanted a woman so much that he made one up. But Marcus always heard God's voice. Welcome home, my sister."

The ever-present tears mounted.

Dennis drew her into his arms. "Thanks for making my brother happy. I can see you have completed him." Taking her by the hand, he led her to where the family waited. "Your wife has my boys eating out of her hand."

"I should have warned you. Children can't resist her. She has some sort of magic. I'm rather spellbound myself." Marcus patted the couch beside him, and she sat and leaned on his shoulder.

"Sleepy?"

"I'm okay. How long did I nap today?"

"About a half hour, or maybe forty-five minutes."

They talked about what they would do in the coming days, and Dennis proposed the family crash the romantic getaway to Table Mountain because the boys loved the cableway. Alicia grabbed a notebook, and Harry teased her about making her schedules, pronouncing it like the British do: "shedu-als." Alicia wasn't in the classroom as much these days, to her regret, but she was a gifted administrator, as well, and had the school running with top efficiency and performing with excellence.

* * *

It was a packed week! Michelle couldn't believe how much they had done. Table Mountain one day, and the boys did love the cableway! Michelle clung to Marcus but was thrilled at the magnificent view, and they walked Boulders National Park.

Another day they spent in downtown Cape Town, visiting Harry's office complex, where twenty-two assayers worked. The Mansour complex was large and busy, phones rang and faxes whirled, and secretaries and runners scurried in constant motion. Here, she realized how wealthy her husband's family was. She learned Harry was world renowned, and the British royals insisted he appraise their jewelry. They wouldn't acquire a new piece without his approval. Saudi princes shopped in the Private Collection, a membership store. They lived in a modest house compared to those surrounding them, although the gardens were exquisite, and they themselves were not pretentious, but this place astounded her. It was not only large; it was bright and beautiful, open, with lots of glass walls and windows.

One day they enjoyed High tea at The Princess Anne Hotel after Dennis stopped by his church and the exclusive school where his mother worked. He wanted to check in with his new assistant, hired because he would cut his pastoral duties when he added teaching at the seminary to his responsibilities. Alicia toured Michelle around the school, which was closed for midwinter holiday. She showed her the administrative office, the library, the cafeteria, and the grounds.

"Ready to go, Mama?" Dennis came after them. "Marcus and I went here when we were boys. Mama was a teacher then. We hated to be in her class because she was tough on us! She didn't want anyone to accuse her of playing favorites." He put his arm around his mother's shoulder. "But she's a great teacher, and she's proud of this place, as she should be. It always had a fine reputation, but she's brought it a long way. The board is reviewing plans for a boarding facility because we are getting requests from all over South Africa and out of country."

"We need to rescue Marie and the men from the boys." Dennis pulled the door open for Alicia and Michelle. "And then we can be off to the Princess Anne. I hope they didn't get too dirty at the playground."

Today was a rest day, as designated by the schedule. Marie had to pick up a few things for the boys before school started again. Michelle and Alicia sat under the porch, listening to the rain tap on the roof. They sipped tea, looking out over the vast garden.

"While Marie and I were walking in the garden, I told her how Marcus healed me, and she said I should ask you how Papa healed you."

A smile played around Alicia's lovely mouth. Her mother-in-law was the color of creamed coffee and had taffy brown eyes. Although tall, she was slender, and she walked like a dancer. "Marcus is a lot like his father, but Harry couldn't have waited. As you know by now, the Mansour men are passionate. Dennis married while in college. Harry was barely twenty, and I was seventeen when we met. I wasn't rejected like you." She lifted her daughter-in-law's hand and covered it with two of her own. "I was an only child, petted and pampered by my indulgent parents. I lived at home but went to private schools. When my mother died, I was twelve, and my father became obsessive in his protection. He took me to a diamond mine when he was considering an investment. I'm sure when we go to Johannesburg, Harry will take us to the nearby Cullinan Diamond Works, where everyone knows him by name and speaks with deference. I met him there. He was a miner, and quite filthy when I first saw him, but immediately I knew he was God's choice. He was young but was a foreman. I began to sneak out to meet him when he got off, and when my father found out, I was put under house arrest. He took my car keys and forbade me to see him. No miners for his daughter! Then he said I wouldn't go to college. I was to marry well and keep a nice home. I had two passions: to become a teacher and to marry God's choice. And I knew that was Harry. I found a servant who agreed to carry a note, so we exchanged notes and planned how we would do this. I graduated and turned eighteen the same week. Borrowing money from a friend, I got transportation to Soweto, where Harry lived with his grandfather. We eloped that weekend." Tears glistened as she remembered, and she gave a little chuckle. "Harry said he'd never kissed me, and we needed to consummate the marriage so it couldn't be annulled."

"You'd never kissed?"

"Our courtship, such as it was, was by notes we exchanged and the few times I'd snuck away before I was caught." She glanced over at Michelle, her eyes dancing. "I said, 'I guess we'd better get right on it, then.' And we did. His grandfather stayed with a cousin that weekend. I didn't mind living with the old man. He's a dear soul. Harry was determined I would fulfill my dream and become a teacher. He worked overtime at two jobs, and I worked until we saved enough for the first term. My father found us, of course, only to inform me I was disinherited and that he had no child. Once I enrolled in the first term, I earned scholarships and teaching assistantships. I worked in the library, and we survived. My love for Harry grew deeper. He was careful that I wouldn't conceive, although I wouldn't have minded. He knew I'd leave school, and he wasn't going to be the cause of the death of my dream. I completed university in three years, and he took off a day to attend my ceremony. I sent Father an invitation, but he made sure I didn't see him, though I learned later he did attend. I had a different path to rejection. My own willfulness and my father's stubbornness. But I understand your pain."

"Did you and your father ever reconcile?"

"We did. He attended Marcus's christening. By that time, Harry's unusual gift, his knowledge of diamonds, had advanced him. He was no longer 'a miner.' He can recognize a diamond's quality by eye perhaps better than any man alive, but he will explain that better than I. He became an assayer, and men more trained soon came to him for assistance. Because he was so able, he was in demand, well paid, and even renowned within the profession. He would sort through the rejected diamonds, buy them, and take them to a friend who was an excellent cutter. The two of them began the business. They could cut and produce saleable diamonds, sometimes smaller but still within the reach of less wealthy patrons. Young assayers wanted to apprentice under him. He worked hard to give me my dream, and when he bought this house for me, he apologized because it wasn't the mansion where I spent my childhood. I told him this is the home where I would be loved and set free. He told me it was the home where I would always be loved and free. 'Free birds sing,' he said."

"You have a lovely voice," Michelle said. "Is your father still living?"

"He died when Dennis was four, before...did Marcus tell you?

"About your injuries? He did. He thought he was losing both parents because Papa fasted until he was emaciated."

"He would remember." Almost to herself, Alicia added, "We have a grand passion, Harry and I. It took almost a year for me to recover, and it was my great sorrow that I couldn't have more children. But you are the daughter God gave to me." She opened her arms, and Michelle went to them, resting her head like a weaned child on Alicia's bosom. Marcus brought my father into God's family. He was an unusual child, always sensitive to God's Spirit. My father loved him. When he had a stroke and no one could understand him, we made plans to put him in a nursing home. Marcus was only three, but he begged us to bring him there, insisting he could understand him. We took him to the hospital to show him that his grandfather couldn't speak, but he understood every word. He even knew his IV was hurting and made us get someone to help him. That stubborn little boy insisted Grandfather would get better, so we hired some help and brought him here. I was expecting Dennis at the time, and Father would sit with the baby in his arms and Marcus at his knee. I had maternity leave, which gave me a precious time to love my father. A stroke has a way of removing all arrogance and control from a man. One day he clung to my hand, trying to communicate. I called Marcus to interpret.

"'He says he's sorry, Mama, and thanks you for your love.' My father nodded with such enthusiasm, grabbing Marcus's hand, and his smile pulled down on the paralyzed side of his face. 'What's Grandfather got to be sorry for, Mama? He loves us. Aren't you glad he lives here? I am.' And he kissed the old man's cheek before he ran off to play. It wasn't long after that he passed away in his sleep. I worried about Marcus because he truly loved my father, but he smiled, patted the cold hand, and said, 'Everyone can understand Grandfather now.' And when he was confirmed years later, he insisted he felt my father's spirit."

Michelle told Alicia about her nephew seeing an angel. "Marcus says not to despise the little ones because they see into the spirit world more easily than we do."

"But Marcus retained the heart of a child. Dennis says he finds God with his intellect, but Marcus finds him with his heart. He often calls him when he has a spiritual struggle. So does Harry."

Michelle linked her hand with Alicia. "Aren't we blessed to have him in our lives?"

"I feared for him because I thought he'd never find a woman who could understand."

"I confess that when he told me he saw me in a dream and God told him I was to be his wife, I was a bit nonplussed."

"He told us he'd messed up and blurted it out when he first met you. That must have been a shock. Even Harry and I, who have known him all his life, thought he'd gone too far when he told us. When Harry found out what he had done, he said, 'He's like Joseph the Dreamer, and he couldn't keep his fool mouth shut!'"

"I listen to him now, believe me! I don't want one of those lightning bolts to strike me."

The two women fell silent, breathing in the fragrance of the garden. The rain had eased, and a soft breeze blew. Alicia began to sing, "'Now thank we all our God—'"

And Michelle joined her. "'—with heart and hands and vices, who wondrous thing hath done, in whom this world rejoices; who from our mothers' arms, has blessed us on our way, with countless gifts of love, and still is ours today. O may this bounteous God through all our life be near us, with ever joyful hearts and blessed peace to cheer us, to keep us in his grace, and guide us when perplexed, and free us from all ills of this world in the next. All praise and thanks to God the Father now be given, the Son and Spirit blessed, who reign in highest heaven the one eternal God, whom heaven and earth adore; for this it was, is now, and shall be evermore.'" [Psalter Hymnal (Gray), 1987]

* * *

As Marcus and Harry were walking across the kitchen, Harry lifted his hand and put his finger on his lips. They froze, listening to the sweet blend of the voices they loved. Harry pulled back the curtain and watched the two of them. "Mama wanted a daughter. I buried the baby we lost, and when she could go to the graveside, she wept. 'I wanted a girl to sing beside me through life.' Now she has one."

"We're hearing heaven's choir. Perhaps my sister is singing along, eh?"

"My son, you have always heard heaven's voice."

"Michelle's brother asked me when I first heard the voice of God, and I told him, 'When you lived in my home, you heard it twenty-four-seven.' You were God's heart and hand and voice to me, Papa, and I'm forever grateful."

Harry took his big man-child in his arms. "I'm glad you came home, son, and even more so because you brought her with you."

"Me, too, Papa." Marcus pulled open the door, and as they stepped out, the sun broke through the clouds. "I bet we'll see a rainbow." He offered his wife his hand, and they stepped out into the garden. His parents followed, and the four of them stood breathless at the promise of God.

Chapter Sixteen

SOWETO

Michelle had never seen Marcus so excited. They were flying to Johannesburg, and she would meet his beloved paternal grandfather, who lived in nearby Soweto. Harry and Marcus were going home, not to a place but to a man—a man who centered their lives, who loved them with God's own love, and who led them into manhood. Harry's mother died in the uprising in 1976, when he was ten, and his papa had been Mother and Father to him and his older sister and brother. When Harry brought his teen bride home, his father loved her as his own daughter. Alicia had told her of her own father's rejection, but she had added that her husband's father's amazing acceptance surrounded her with the confidence and self-esteem to complete college in three years. Although he had counseled Harry not to marry without her father's consent, the day she walked into his little home, he declared they were ordained of God to be one flesh. He said he saw in the Spirit that they were joined, and when the doctors said she would die, he never wavered in his faith that she would be raised up.

The heritage of faith was deep-rooted in the Mansour family, and she looked forward to meeting this patriarch. Perhaps she would understand her own husband better if she met yet another father in the faith. When they reached the hotel in Johannesburg, Harry ordered a car to immediately drive to Soweto. Marcus urged her to sleep on the ride. He didn't want to delay presenting her to his grandfather, but he knew she tired easily.

She wasn't disappointed. His grandfather's first words to her were, "Do you believe the dream now, my daughter?" His eyes twinkled down at her from the vast height that he shared with his son and grandsons. He carried his age with pride and stood erect. He held his arms wide, and she stepped into his embrace as readily as she did the other Mansour men.

"Yes, sir, he has convinced me, and I'm honored God led him across the ocean to find me. His love has made me whole."

He held her back. "God led him to you to be complete, Michelle. Without you, he would never become what God intends him to be."

"Amen, Grandfather," Marcus proclaimed, reaching for his own hug.

The old man looked into his grandson's soul and smiled. "You have done well, Marcus. This woman is a handmaiden of the Lord, a helpmate fit for you. Already she has delivered you from many mistakes, am I right?"

"Yes, sir. I'm grateful."

"As you should be. Listen to her." And he slapped him on the back.

When Marcus's papa stepped forward for his embrace, Michelle thought she could almost see the flow of the Holy Spirit from man to man, through three generations. She bowed her head, whispering a prayer of thanks that she would bring her children into this legacy.

"Come, come. I have food prepared for you after your journey. Are you weary from your travels, daughter? I hear you are with child."

"Yes, sir, I am. A little weary, but not as much as I was."

The family trailed behind him as he pulled out a tray of cheeses and meats, breads and crackers. The house was small, and Harry joked about living here with his brother and sister, then later with his wife. Michelle remembered Alicia telling her about how she didn't mind the crowded conditions because the older man made her so welcome after her father's cold rejection, and she reached for Harry's hand.

He put his arm around her. "What are you thinking?"

"I'm thinking you did for me what your father did for your wife."

He beamed. "I saw you as God's choice for my son, as well." She turned aside, blinking back tears, but Papa cupped her chin. "We're blessed that you are a part of our family. Did you hear my father? You are the completion of my son, just as Alicia was the completion of me."

"And I am so grateful."

Michelle learned in the conversations that followed that Marcus had talked to his grandfather about her and how they had worked together. The Mansour men had no secrets among them, sharing their vulnerabilities with an innocence that charmed her, but then they had no fear of rejection, no need to hide. Once again, she reached out to embrace this quality for the family she would build with her husband. Marcus caught her eye and beamed with pride—pride for her and pride for his family—noting her hand held firmly in his father's.

All too soon, Harry stood, reminding them he had to meet with the hotel about a meeting he was organizing later in the fall. Seeing her disappointment, he assured Michelle she and Marcus would return tomorrow because Marcus wanted to visit with friends here in Soweto at Baragwanath Hospital, the largest hospital in the world. Marcus's grandfather urged her to spend the day with him.

"I'm not good company in the afternoons," she explained. "I usually nap."

He winked at her. "So do I." And it was settled.

Marcus took her by the hospital, and she was breathless at the vastness of the complex. She wanted to know how he kept from being lost. He laughed and told her he had been lost many times but that after several rotations here, he learned his way around. He took her to his grandfather's home, promising to be back later that afternoon.

"Welcome, daughter," the old man said, descending the front stairs and taking her hand. With a waving motion, he sent Marcus back to the car. Leading her into the house, he offered her refreshments, noting her healthy appetite, and she explained she was always hungry and never nauseated, only tired. "Understandable, with the burden you carry. A joyous burden, to be sure, but a burden nonetheless."

"I am thrilled. I never thought I would have children."

"Why is that?"

"I thought I was unattractive. My father convinced me I was too dark and too large. I wore thick glasses as a child, and my rapid growth made me clumsy. I didn't date much."

"That is why God has given you a double portion. Marcus told me he thought you a goddess."

She ducked her head. "He makes me feel beautiful."

"Because you are." She started to protest, but he lifted her chin. He was like his son and grandson, bringing her eyes up to look in his. "The correct response, my daughter, is 'Thank you, Grandfather.' Can you say that?"

"Thank you, Grandfather." Her eyes shone with unshed tears, and he kissed her.

"When my grandson told me about his dream, he said he couldn't believe someone so beautiful would love him, but God told him you would be his wife. When he found you, he said you were more beautiful than his dream. Harry and Dennis teased him, saying he'd been alone too long, that he'd waited too long, but I had a witness in my spirit, and I knew it would come to pass. And here you are, with the daughters he has longed to have— daughters to share their mother's beauty." He paused. "Did you have enough fruit? And the scone, was it acceptable?"

"Delicious! Thank you for the tea, as well. May I see your garden? Alicia tells me it is lovely."

Edward Mansour gave her his hand and led her to the small backyard. As he steered her around the built-up plots, she recognized some of the plants she had seen in Alicia's garden in Cape Hout, and when she commented on them, he affirmed that Alicia took the cuttings. They talked about her garden and the peace and beauty she had created. The old man loved his son's wife and shared how happy he was to share his little home with them when they were newlyweds. "Alicia reminded me of my wife. She was a special gift to me. They were so much in love. The house, as you see, is small, and though they tried to be quiet, I could hear the love they shared, and it made me happy." He placed a long, lean finger on her lips. "Don't you tell them. I always pretended to be asleep!" He chuckled. "It is our secret."

This precious secret, she could share and hold close to her heart.

"Now we will take a tour around Soweto. I will show you Nelson Mandela's home, and Desmond Tutu's, as well. We will see the Hector Peterson Memorial. Hector was a good friend of Elaina's. I begged her not to go with him that day. Hector was our first martyr in the uprising. Elaina was the second. She continued his funeral procession, and although she urged peace and calm, it got out of hand. The police were jumpy, and the people were angry and began to throw stones. When tear gas did not stop them, the bullets flew. My wife stepped in front of a youngster and never got up again."

Michelle laid her head against the old man's shoulder, seeing the grief that even now ravaged his countenance.

"I look forward to the day we meet again, and you will love her. Harry was her favorite, although parents shouldn't have favorites, but she saw his sensitivity toward God. And you see it in Marcus, too."

"I do, and I have learned to honor it and respect it. Alicia says he was always sensitive to God and that he sees him with his heart and Dennis sees him with his intellect."

"Both men of God, and I'm proud to be their grandfather."

"They love you very much, and yesterday I thanked God that my children would have such a godly heritage."

"I will live to see your children. Do you think you and Marcus will live in Johannesburg or Cape Town when you return?"

Michelle stopped and looked at him. "Uh, we haven't discussed where we'll live."

"I spoke out of turn, and I apologize. It is your decision. Come. The taxi will be here, and you might wish to refresh yourself."

While she used the bathroom, Edward gathered an armful of fresh flowers, and during their tour he stopped the taxi and laid them in the middle of a broad road, in the spot where his beloved fell. They ate lunch in a Victorian tearoom, and by the time they arrived back at the house, they were both ready for a late nap. She felt a cool hand on her forehead, but no one was in the room. She heard Marcus greeting his father, and he peeked into the bedroom.

"Did I wake you?" He leaned over and gathered her into his arms. "I missed you. I don't know how I'll go to work without you when we return to Baltimore."

Michelle noticed he didn't say return home. Funny, she never realized he didn't refer to Baltimore as home. Did he want to return to South Africa? Could she make this lovely country her own home? She would ponder these things in her heart, pray about them, and ask him in time.

He ran his finger down the furrow in her brow, as he often did when he wormed her thoughts out of her. She drew him in for a long and lingering kiss, hoping to divert him, and she succeeded.

"I hope you had a good nap today. I have plans for later."

She placed her hand on his face. "I sincerely hope they include me."

"We have a big suite, and our bedroom is far from Mama and Papa. We haven't made use of the privacy, and I intend to remedy that waste tonight."

"That suite is bigger than this house. Can you imagine your mother and father as newlyweds here?"

"Good thing we didn't have to. You get a bit noisy sometimes."

She pushed him away. "It's your fault!"

"I certainly hope so." He gave her another brief kiss and helped her stand.

Although she did not want to leave Marcus's grandfather, Marcus told her his mother had plans that included him the next day, so she kissed his dear cheek and promised to be back. They drove in silence, Marcus thinking about the needs of his country, Michelle turning over his grandfather's words. She paused over the double portion and the "daughters" her husband longed to have. She sat straight, pushing herself off his shoulder.

"Marcus, Grandfather is like you, isn't he?"

"Yes, he is a big man and a one-woman man, like all the Mansour men. His libido died with his Elaina. He never wanted another." He leaned to nibble her lips. "My libido rested until I found you. Now it's out of control!"

"No, I don't mean that. I mean about seeing things from God."

"Yes, he knew God gave Mama to Papa, even as young as they were. And though he saw how badly injured Mama was that night, and though all the doctors said she would die, he declared she would live, never doubting."

"And he believed your dream." She was pensive. "When you go to the hospital, do you think we could get a sonogram?"

Marcus looked alarmed. "Are you worried about something?"

Her slender fingers curved around his face. "No fears, just something your grandfather said. I do believe we have a girl." She didn't mention two girls.

Marcus beamed. "Out of the mouth of two witnesses, a thing shall be established." He pulled the shade behind the driver and took her into his arms for a long and passionate kiss, running his hands over her body until she pushed him back, breathless.

"Can we save this for the hotel?"

"Maybe, if he steps on it." He laid his forehead on hers, and they giggled, but when she trailed her hand down his leg, he frowned. "Watch yourself, woman!"

She giggled again, and he remembered the solemn Michelle before, who never giggled, never played, and he rested his head on hers with a contented sigh.

Michelle raised her head to look out the window. The traffic was horrific, and she commented that it was as bad as the Beltway. He responded that if he lived here, he would choose to ride the Blue Train to work and live outside the city. Another thing to ponder in her heart.

They arrived at the boutique hotel and took the stairs to the second floor. Michelle said she hated to step on the luxurious oriental carpet, so Marcus pushed open the door and swept her into his arms to carry her to their room on the east side of the suite. His parents weren't in, thank

God, because the couple let the door shut behind them and reached for one another. Clothes flew, and by the time Marcus lowered her on the bed, nothing was between them. Already beside herself from his fondling in the limo, Michelle sought to make him as crazy for her, and it never took long.

Only pausing to ask again if she felt well, Marcus looked deep into her eyes before he lowered his mouth to hers. She whimpered. He growled low in his throat.

When he was able to speak, Marcus said, "I wasn't jealous of Grandfather, because I want him to know you and love you as I do, but I missed you all day."

"I understand you better now that I know your family, and I'm proud our children will share this heritage."

"Mama said she prayed all my life that God would give me a wife who understood, and He answered her prayers. Sure took long enough, though."

"I had to be refined in the fire first."

"You came out pure gold." He ran his fingers down her face, and lower.

"I hear your parents." She scrambled to get out of bed and fled to their bathroom while he pulled on his trousers.

He stuck his head out the door and hailed his father, who wondered if they were ready to eat. He raised his eyebrows and grinned. "Looks like you may have worked up an appetite." Alicia swatted at him and told him to hush.

"Give me a time, Papa."

"Oh, about half an hour?" He gave his wife a hard look. "Make that an hour."

Marcus laughed as his mother spun into their bedroom, throwing a come-hither glance over her shoulder. Still chuckling, he opened their door only to see Michelle standing in the middle of the bedroom, still naked, and he let the door close behind him. His dark eyes got darker. "You might be the death of me, but what a way to go."

"Soon I will be big and fat, so I'm going to store up, if you think you are up for it."

He held her back. "No, you will not! You will blossom with our love and be even more beautiful than you are now."

Thinking of the puzzle of her double portion, Michelle continued her plan to store up, and they returned to the bed. He was up for it, which seemed impossible after they were so fulfilled, but when Marcus explained his father's intentions, they took the time to pleasure one another yet again.

They fell into a lazy doze but roused when they heard movement in the living room. They dressed and joined Alicia and Harry. Harry made reservations, and the rain let up, so they went up to the rooftop for dining. Michelle looked out over the twinkling city. They were above the noise and hustle, though they could hear horns honking below. Marcus took her hand, pointing to Mandela Park and the hospital in the distance, where they would go tomorrow.

"She doesn't have to go to the hospital with you. I was planning to take Michelle somewhere tomorrow," Alicia complained.

"Would the next day do? Or maybe in the afternoon?"

Alicia frowned but said it would have to do. When Marcus pressured her about her plan, she was reluctant to give the details, and their orders arrived.

As usual, Michelle dove into her food, and Harry said she figured she must be eating for three. She studied him, wondering if he was teasing or serious.

"We're going to try to get a sonogram in the morning," Marcus said, "so we'll see this baby."

Alicia's eyes brightened. "Oh, super! Can I...?"

Michelle covered her hand. "Would you go with us? I'd like that."

"Tomorrow, do what you want, but we are taking the Blue Train to Pretoria on Thursday. I have arranged a tour of Cullian." Harry informed them.

"The diamond mine?" Michelle asked.

"Where I worked when we were first married," he confirmed. "I have only booked the walking tour above ground. The underground tour would be too difficult for you and Mama."

"Do they know you're coming with your family?" Alicia asked. When he nodded, she turned and winked. "It will be a good tour. Everyone at Cullian loves Harry."

"I want to show off my fine son and his excellent wife."

"Let's walk around Mandela Park," Marcus suggested. "It's started raining again, but they have slickers at the door." He took Michelle by the hand and led her to the front of the hotel.

The park was well lit, and many people were ambling around the park in the gentle rain. Michelle, who had always held Nelson Mandela in awe, along with America's Dr. Martin Luther King, was surprised at how much she learned about South Africa's hero and the influence he had on American politics. He was a follower of Dr. King, also urging non-violence. They sat on a bench, talking about the debt they owed the leaders who carved a way for them and their children to be full citizens of free countries. And then they mediated on the heroes of faith who preserved Christianity through the Dark Ages—the Irish monks who spent their lives hidden in caves faithfully transcribing the Scriptures and preserving them, along with Wycliffe and others who paid the price to translate God's Word into their native languages.

"I'd like to go to Ireland one day," she mused. "We are debtors to those who have gone before."

"And to those who come behind. We must leave a legacy of faith and discovery. I want to eradicate cancer! Cassie must not die in vain."

They fell silent, listening to the pattering rain and thinking about the little girl they loved. When the wind picked up, Marcus urged her to hurry before the rain got heavier. They semi-jogged back to the hotel hand in hand. Hotel personnel met them at the door with towels, easing the slickers off their shoulders. "Not too cold, sir, but you just got here in time." The rain began a furious drumming, and water filled the streets from curb to curb. Other walkers, less aware, came tearing to shelter, and the bar was filled to overflowing. Good-natured shouts and laughter filled the lobby.

Marcus grinned. "Tourists aren't aware of how fast the rain can gather. Aren't you glad you are with a native?"

She laid her gentle hand on his cheek. "I am always grateful for you, my love."

He covered her hand with his own. "You have healing in your touch. I love to watch you with your patients, and I'm so glad you're my wife. My children will have the most wonderful mother."

Michelle's hand dropped to her tummy, and she rubbed circles. "I'm excited to see tomorrow."

"Me, too."

Chapter Seventeen

AND THEN THEY WERE THREE

They had barely stepped through the hospital doors when the announcement came over the P.A: "Dr. Mansour, Dr. Marcus Mansour, report to the conference room on the second floor." Michelle looked at her husband, who shrugged and led the way. Banners fluttered over the doorway, saying *Welcome home, Marcus,* and a shout erupted. "He's here." Laughter and hugs, claps on the back and embraces, and so much confusion. Michelle tried to step back, but his arm was firm around her as he waved for silence.

"Look at the prize I brought home from the United States. My beautiful wife, Dr. Michelle Logan Mansour."

And the greetings began again. Some already knew, and a few looked disappointed, but everyone was kind. Coffee, juices, and sweets were set around, and everyone helped themselves. Alicia and Harry were beaming and greeting those they knew. Michelle missed Marcus hovering beside her and saw him draw a woman to his side, who nodded and looked at her. The party broke up; everyone had work to do, and they drifted away.

Marcus introduced her to Susan Porter, who took her by the arm, explaining she was chief of OB and that she'd take her to get a sonogram, inquiring about her symptoms and her due date. Before long, she was lying on a table, covered by a sheet, agreeing that Harry and Alicia could come in. Marcus perched on a stool beside the table and took her hand, turning his eyes to the screen.

By this time, Michelle had absorbed Marcus's grandfather's words and knew she was carrying twins, so she kept her eyes on her husband's face, eager to see his response. She felt the wand move and watched him lean in, surprised joy springing tears to his eyes. He searched her face. "You want to see our beautiful daughters, Mommy?" Only then did she turn to the screen with a smile as she clung to his hand.

"Two? You have two?" Alicia exclaimed.

"Definitely two," confirmed the resident as she moved the wand. "That appears to be all. Good size, and close in size to one another. I'd say we have two viable babies here. Congratulations, Dr. Mansour, Mrs. Mansour."

"I said you were eating for three! We need to call Dennis and Marie. You weren't surprised, Michelle. Did you suspect something?" "Grandfather talked about 'Marcus's beautiful daughters' and my 'double blessing' yesterday, so I asked for a sonogram. I'm getting used to the Mansour men who hear God's voice." She reached up to touch her husband's face. "Good job, Daddy." He leaned to kiss her lips. "Can you tell if they are identical?" She raised her head to stare at the babies.

"They have separate sacs. Fraternal twins, and both look good," the resident said. "I'll print this out for you. I'll see if Dr. Porter can take a minute to check this out."

Dr. Porter did pop in, and she checked the screen, offering her confirmation of a healthy pregnancy, adding that she didn't foresee anything but the natural difficulties of a twin birth, as they often came before term, and she encouraged Michelle to eat well, get enough sleep, and take it easy. When she learned she planned to take this year off work, she encouraged her to rest on her laurels and enjoy gestating these babies.

Marcus escorted everyone out of the room, then drew his wife to himself.

"Are you surprised?" she asked him.

"I wondered why I had two names, and neither seemed to wait for the next baby. Two little girls! My cup runs over."

"You have two names? What about me? Do I have a say in this?"

"Of course, but you will like them." He held her blouse for her to slip on and picked up her slacks to hand to her, setting her on the chair.

"Okay. Let me have the names."

"Michellena Marie. We can call her Lena. And Cassie Grace. Do you like them?"

"I'm guessing you won't budge on Michellena Marie."

"The only thing better than one Michelle Mansour is two, and I know you won't argue about Cassie Grace."

"I won't, except to say we need to ask Cassie's family."

"When we ask them to be her godparents."

"Marcus, would you pray?"

Those outside waited while the new parents spent time thanking and praising God, asking Him to hover over these babies and make them healthy and strong. After concluding their prayers, the couple stood, holding one another until they heard a knock.

"Are you guys coming? Dennis wants to talk to you."

Marcus's papa stood, holding out his phone, which Marcus took. He had a huge grin on his face as he listened to his brother's exclamations of joy. When things calmed down, the family broke apart. Marcus was staying at the hospital and meeting with colleagues. Harry was returning to the hotel to work on plans for the upcoming conference. And Alicia was whisking Michelle to her mysterious appointment. Agreeing to meet at the hotel for dinner, they parted. The hired car dropped Harry at the hotel and continued to Soweto.

Alicia was thrilled about her new granddaughters, promising to come help when they were born, but Michelle told her she needed to include her mother, as she was hoping to build the newly developing relationships with her family. Alicia understood but asked if she could come, as well, and Michelle welcomed her.

The now familiar streets of Soweto surrounded them, and Michelle asked how long Marcus's grandfather planned to stay by himself in his little house. Alicia explained that he wanted to remain independent but that they were feeling some concern since he was in his eighties.

"He could move into the carriage house. He would have his own space there."

"Harry and I talked about that. We have room in the house for guests. He could even fix his own meals. We'll have him down for a visit and mention it."

"Will we see him later? When are you going to tell me where we are going?"

"I told him we'd be at his place for tea. We are going here." She pointed to a sign that read *Orlando Children's Home*. The car stopped in front, and the ladies arranged for the driver to meet them later before they walked up the stairs and into the bright, cheerful building. "I'm on the board here, and I wanted to have your opinion of the place." Alicia looked up into the smiling face of the social worker and extended her hand. "I brought Marcus's wife to see the facility, as I'm hoping to capture her interest and support. This is Michelle Mansour. She's a pediatrician. Michelle, this is Cecile Miller, our social worker."

"Welcome to both Mrs. Mansours. May I show you around?"

They followed her through the main building, which housed classrooms and offices, and then she led them to the dormitories. She explained that they had space for sixty children, and they needed more. Michelle asked about adoptions, and Cecile agreed that was the ideal choice, asking if she and Dr. Mansour were interested in adopting. Michelle laughed, telling her they learned only this morning that were expecting twins, so not at this time, but she told her she had a friend in the States who was considering adoption, saying that he was a single man whose wife had died three years ago.

"Do you know him well?"

"Yes. He's our pastor, and he married us last December. His wife was killed in a traffic accident. She was infertile because of childhood cancer, and they had planned to adopt. He is a loving man and totally charmed my nephews. He also visited a little girl Marcus and I were treating. She was terminal, and he prepared her for her death. She told me it would be a 'great adventure,' and as she was dying, she told her mother she saw Jesus coming for her."

The social worker placed her hand over her heart. Her eyes were brimming, and she replied, "He sounds like a lovely man."

"He's amazing. I didn't know he had lost his wife. He's a cheerful soul. Do you allow single parents to adopt?"

"Sometimes, and you give a glowing recommendation. Let's go meet some of the children. The younger ones will be having their lunch now. We feed them first so they can go to their naps, and when they wake, we give them a healthy snack." She led the way, and they heard the happy sound of children's laughter. She led them to a boy around eighteen months old, who was sitting in a high chair, waving his spoon. "This is Timothy," she said, placing her hand on his dark curls. "His parents died two months ago, and his brother, Paul, keeps a close eye on him." She turned to a three-year-old sitting beside him. "Don't you, Paul?"

Paul's large brown eyes fastened upon Michelle. "Miss Cecile is looking for a mother and father for us. Would you like to be my mommy?"

Michelle squatted down beside him, taking him in her arms. "I'd be proud to be your mommy, and I'm sure God has a perfect plan for you. Let us ask Him to bring you to your new home." And she bowed her head and prayed. Then she asked him if she could take his picture, and she snapped several on her cell phone, including individual ones of him and his brother as well as an adorable shot of the two of them together.

They spent time visiting with the children before leaving the lunchroom to sit in Cecile's office. Her husband, Theodore, the principal of the school, joined them and asked them if they would like to join him for lunch. Getting permission from Cecile to send the pictures to Father Manny, Michelle did, asking him if he would pray about the boys and if she should proceed with sending the paperwork. As they walked back to the lunchroom, she told them Father Manny had taken them to the airport and said, "Perhaps you could bring home a child for me."

"I don't think he meant children this young, though. He is a busy pastor and can't stay home with them."

"Does he have sufficient income to bring two children into his home?" asked Theodore.

"He comes from a wealthy family. His parents are dead, and from what I gather, he was the only son. He said he owed a debt, and he planned to adopt. The church is growing, and I know he has health insurance from the Diocese. He is an Anglican, second generation American."

They waited for the older children to be seated, and the principal stood to bless the food. He called the children by name, hugging many who came by for attention.

Michelle's phone dinged, and she saw the incoming text: These boys grab my heart, but how can I care for them during the day? I can't put them in our daycare anytime soon because of the disruption in their little lives. Tell me more. I am praying for what is best for them.

She showed the text to Cecile, and Theodore read over her shoulder. The couple looked over to a young woman with the children and then back to Michelle.

"This is your pastor?"

"Yes. He married us, but we had to borrow another church because we couldn't handle the numbers in our little sanctuary. We married in his friend's church in Washington."

"Would that be Otiano Mondalah?" Theodore asked. "He is an Anglican priest in D.C."

"Yes! Such a lovely man, and a good friend of Father Manny's."

"When Otiano was here, speaking at our Diocese, he mentioned this man. In fact, he said Manny wanted to adopt. Didn't his wife die in an automobile crash?"

"We have two excellent references from Marcus and Michelle and Otiano, Theo. What do you think? Shall we pursue this?" Cecile cocked her head up and looked at her husband. "Marcus and Michelle could take them when they go back to the United States."

With texts, they arranged a Skype conference. It was night in Baltimore, so they set it up within the hour. Michelle had a peace about this "serendipitous" meeting, and when they spoke, all the pieces fit, although it would take the hand of God to organize everything before their departure in two weeks. They would ask the young lady in the cafeteria if she would agree to nanny the boys until they adjusted to their new home, and if things didn't work out, she could bring them back. Theodore would call the authorities in the State Department, but between him and Harry Mansour, he thought the visas and permits could be arranged. The skype conference went well, and Cecile immediately attached the application to an email and asked about bringing the boys in the next day to talk to Father Manny.

When Alicia and Michelle got in the car, Michelle was beside herself. They stopped by Marcus's grandfather's to pick him up for dinner in town, and on the way, she showed him the sonogram phono.

He beamed, embracing Michelle. "God is turning your mourning into dancing, my daughter. As a pediatrician, you will facilitate many more joyous families. Will you work with Orlando when you return home?"

Michelle turned to her mother-in-law. "Do you think Marcus wants to return to South Africa to live?"

Alicia caught Edward's eye. "That's not our decision, Michelle. You and Marcus must choose. You know we would love it, but you have family and friends in America."

"Do you know, Grandfather?"

He put his hand around her shoulder. "I would not say. Alicia is right. This is your decision. You and Marcus must choose your life together."

"I never thought about coming here. I have an offer at Cleveland Clinic, where I did my residency, and Marcus would be welcomed on staff at Johns Hopkins or Cleveland. I've never had to include anyone in my decisions before, but the idea of living here has been growing in my heart."

The car slid to a stop, and the driver came around to help them out of the vehicle. Alicia must have notified the men of their arrival, because Harry and Marcus were waiting at the door.

"Are you tired?" Marcus asked. "You haven't had a rest today. Mother hasn't exhausted you, has she?" He gave his mother a chiding look, but Michelle was bouncing.

"Wait till you hear what we're doing!" She took Harry's arm. "Can we eat?"

And the three of them laughed and chorused, "I'm starving!"

"Absolutely!" Michelle confirmed, laughing with them. "I'm not as tired now that I'm in the second trimester."

"Papa has ordered appetizers for us." Marcus led her into the dining room. "What is all this excitement?"

Throughout the dinner, the ladies shared about the two little boys for Father Manny, and when Marcus explained he thought their pastor was looking for older children, they insisted these boys were God's choice.

"God will have to move mountains, though, so it is up to Him to open doors."

"Why?" asked Marcus, and Michelle explained they'd be taking them back to Baltimore if all worked out.

"That's a great plan, isn't it?"

"A baby and a three-year old?" He chuckled. "You are out of your mind." Michelle pouted, and he kissed her cheek. "God help us!"

"If He opens these doors, we know it's His will, and He will help us."

After she was "stuffed," Michelle wanted to go upstairs, and as soon as they arrived at their suite, she was ready to go into their bedroom. Marcus left her soaking in the tub and returned to talk to his mother and father.

Chapter Eighteen

CHOICES

Marcus returned and found Michelle dozing in the tub. "Ready to get out?"

She opened her eyes. "I fell asleep."

"I'm glad I checked on you." He grabbed a towel and held out his hand. He wrapped her up and kissed the back of her neck. "Mmm, you taste sweet."

"Have you been out there?"

"I've been talking to my folks in the living room."

"I mean to Orlando, to the children's home."

"Sure, my family was big into organizing the Soweto community's takeover when the Johannesburg child welfare couldn't maintain it. Grandfather got Mama on the board, and Papa spearheaded the fundraising. It's a fabulous little orphanage. God knows we need it." He led her to the bedroom and toweled her dry. He set her on the bed and pulled a gown over her head. "I got a text from Father Manny. He's excited about the boys, says he's going to talk to them tomorrow."

"They are adorable! You should see the older boy look after his baby brother. It's the cutest thing."

"You want to lie down?"

"What do you want to do?"

"What do you need me to do?" He tugged her down and put his arm around her.

"We need to talk."

"Will it be a mood killer? Are you upset about something?"

"No, but I'm wondering." She propped up on her elbow. "Do you want to live in South Africa?"

"I've been offered a position on staff here and thought we'd pray about it. What do you think? You're doing well with your family now, and I don't want you to lose that."

"South Africa is your home. I don't know why I assumed you'd live in America."

Marcus drew her down to claim her lips. "My home is wherever you are."

She snuggled close to his side. "Wherever we are together is paradise."

"Did you get a little rest in the tub? Can we go to heaven together?"

She reached down and stroked him, feeling him respond to her touch. "Can we ditch these slacks?"

Marcus unbuckled his belt and threw the offending garment on the floor. "Your wish is my command." He kissed her again and felt her smile against his mouth. "What?"

"I thought I wasn't very good at this, but you never fail to prove me wrong."

"Good? Baby, you are fantastic. I couldn't ask for a better wife."

"It's because I have such a good lover for a husband."

He began to address himself to her needs, and when she whimpered, he chuckled. He cut off her cries with a kiss, and they entered into the joy that was theirs.

Breathless, they fell apart. "No wonder we're having two. Do you remember your first ovulation, when you stopped the pills?"

She giggled. "We did go after each other like rabbits, didn't we?"

"And a good time was had by all."

"You always make it good for me, Marcus."

"I love you. You are so responsive, so generous." He cupped her breast. "Getting kind of big there, Mommy."

"I'll be big as a country barn carrying twins."

"And I will love every inch of you."

She closed her eyes, and her head fell back on the pillow. "We didn't come to any conclusions about where we'll live."

"We did. We decided we would live together and be happy."

"I want our son to be born in South Africa."

"Okay. When will this happen?"

"I need to recover from the twins first, but I think you should take that offer. Let's come back when you finish up at Hopkins."

"You don't want to talk to your folks first?"

"This is our decision. That's what Grandfather said."

"It's easy to find household help here. Do you want to go back to work?"

"I do, but I want to have our family, and I don't know what nursing twins will be like. How old were you when your mother went back to work?"

"I can't remember. We had a precious woman who came every day except weekends. I loved her." His fingers idled through her short curls. "You'll be such a good mother."

She rolled over onto her side and laid her head on his chest. "Your mother wants to come help. She figures they'll be born in December, and she can come during the break. I told her I couldn't hurt my mother's feelings, but she'll be sensitive to that. I love your mother."

"She's a good person."

They lay side by side talking until Michelle no longer responded, and Marcus realized she'd fallen asleep. He rested his hand on her belly, praying for the babies growing there, and drew her close.

Chapter Nineteen

LOOKING AHEAD

The family spent the next day at the Cullian Mine, riding up to Pretoria on the Blue Train. Marcus recognized the return of his wife's energy as she noticed the scenery and asked about everything. She was already aware of her father-in-law's fame but felt increased respect when she saw the deference showed to him at the mine. He knew everyone by name, and if they weren't asking him questions, they were showing him improvements. Mining was a serious business, and Harry was knowledgeable He taught her the "four C's of a diamond: color, clarity, cut, and carat weight," then laughingly accepted a challenge to demonstrate his abilities by identifying various diamonds and comparing his hands-on look with the professional appraisal. Invariably, he was correct, and the staff clapped him on the back, exclaiming he was "worth the big bucks."

Michelle did rest her head on her husband's shoulder on the way home, but she popped up every time she heard or saw something interesting. Marcus decided discovering the twins was invigorating her, although he was well aware of the upcoming difficulties she'd face.

For the next few days, while Cecile and Harry worked to cut through red tape and plow through the requirements necessary to take the two boys to the United States, Michelle and Marcus explored real estate in Johannesburg. Each day they dined with friends, often lunching with hospital staff, and she was increasingly convinced their future was in his home country, although telling the Hope House girls her decision wasn't going to be easy!

They went out to Orlando several times, especially as requirements were met, and more and more, they felt they'd be traveling with two little boys and a nanny. Lilly, the young woman, was approaching twenty. She had been at Orlando for sixteen years, completing school and working there. She was a natural with children, and the boys loved her. When all the arrangements were falling together, Marcus and Michelle knew this adoption was God-ordained. Even the travel/work visas went through in rapid fashion.

They flew back to Cape Town to spend a few days with Marie and Dennis but returned to fly out of Johannesburg with their additional travel companions. They put Marcus's Grandfather on the Blue Train to Cape Town, enthusiastically describing the guest house. He was eager to see his great-grandsons there, but he hugged Michelle, telling her he looked forward to seeing the great-granddaughters next year when they returned.

Theo brought Lilly and the boys to the airport, handing Marcus all of the visas and documents they needed to escort them through customs. Michelle opted to take only a few personal possessions with them, assuring them they would get new clothing and toys when they got home. The favorite blankie, the special teddy bears, and precious mementos were carried on the plane with the diaper bag and a change of clothes. Lilly was quiet, overwhelmed with all the changes she faced, but comfortable with Michelle and Marcus, thanks to the time they had invested in getting to know her. Michelle and Lilly swapped off the children, but the boys sat on the ends of the aisle seat and middle row to be next to one another, frequently reaching across to hold hands.

After some time accommodating to their new adventure, and multiple story books, Paul fell asleep watching a movie, and Timothy nodded off against Michelle's breast. Amazing! Marcus knew prayers had to be surrounding them. He tucked the baby into a seat with a belt and looked across the row. Lilly had her eyes closed, and Michelle was drifting. So far, so good. Other than a few trips to the bathroom, Michelle was getting some rest.

The boys were stirring when the lights in the cabin came on. Marcus took Paul to the bathroom, and Lilly changed Timothy's diaper. The flight attendant brought their food first. The boys ate like they'd never seen food before, and Lilly was thankful she'd tucked clean shirts in the diaper bag. Once breakfast was behind them, the ladies were engaged in entertaining the little ones again.

Paul asked how much longer every five minutes, finally asking, "Will my new father be at the airport?" Assuring him Father Manny would pick them up, Michelle showed his picture yet again to the boy. "Do you think he'll like me?" Paul asked.

"I do. He is a man of God, and he says you are in his heart already," Michelle told him.

"I'll be good." Michelle drew him into her lap and sang the second verse of "Jesus Loves Me," and he joined in. "'Jesus loves me when I'm bad, though it makes Him very sad.'"

She smiled and hugged Paul. "We make the ones who love us sad sometimes, but they still love us."

"Like when I spilled the ketchup on you?"

She chuckled. "Like that, and like when I'm not ready when Uncle Marcus wants to leave."

He stuck his head around her, asking Marcus if he ever got sad at Aunt Michelle.

"Only when she's bad," he replied.

"Are grown-ups bad?" Paul was astonished.

"She's a pretty good girl," Marcus assured him. He winked at his wife.

"How much longer?" the boy asked again, and Timothy began to cry as the plane started to descend.

The announcements indicated they should gather their belongings before leaving the plane, and Lilly gave the boys sippy cups so they would swallow. The attendants allowed those with small children to deplane first, so Marcus slung a bag over his shoulder, and Lilly picked up Timothy, leaving Michelle to carry the diaper bag and hold Paul's hand. Processing seemed interminable—gathering bags, going through customs, answering countless questions. Michelle was texting Father Manny throughout, and he told her he had a van and car seats. They finally walked out into the waiting area, and Paul went straight to him.

The poor man almost disintegrated when the boy asked in his piping voice, "Am I to call you 'father'?"

He reached out his arms. "I'd love to be your father. May I hold you?" When Paul opened his arms, Father Manny gathered him up, blinking back tears. "Let's get you home. It's been a long trip." He turned to Lilly and brushed his hand over Timothy's curly head. "Miss Lilly, welcome to America, and thank you for bringing the boys to me." She ducked her head.

Michelle tucked her arm through Lilly's, and Marcus nodded to the bellman, directing him to follow Father Manny. He pulled up to the door in a new nine passenger van with age-appropriate car seats, and they stowed their bags after he fastened the boys into their seats, telling them the social worker from the state told him what to get and helped him learn. He'd practiced until he could do it quickly. Lilly climbed in between the boys, and they put Michelle in the front seat, while Marcus climbed in the far back.

"The seller allowed me to lease the house until the sale is final. It has a nice yard for the boys. The social worker from the state approved of it, and it's not too far from the church. I have five bedrooms, and I hope the two of you can stay until the children are comfortable. Miss Lilly, you're a brave woman to fly across the ocean to a strange place, and a good one to stay and help me with the children."

"Thank you, sir," she murmured.

"Lilly is good with the children," Michelle said.

"I can see that," Father Manny said.

Marcus added, "I built in extra time to adjust to the travel. I start on Monday, but Michelle can stay longer if need be. You've been busy, buying a new vehicle and a new house! How did you pull all this together?"

"I put a real estate agent to work. She sent me listings with a minimum of five bedrooms, and I made an offer in one afternoon. Otiano's wife helped me. She's lovely, by the way. You'll like her. First the house, for the social worker to approve, and then the van. When my parents died, I wondered what I would do with all that money, so I put it in a fund. I haven't even tithed it yet." He pulled up in front of a charming older home. It was brick, with Tudor dormers, and a white picket fence surrounded the front yard.

When they helped the boys out of the car, Paul took his brother's hand. "Look, Timothy, this is our new home. Isn't it pretty?"

"Eat," Timothy said.

Manny chuckled. "We have chicken, mashed potatoes, green beans, and corn, Timothy. Does that sound good?"

Timothy ducked behind his brother, but he nodded. "He likes that, Father, and so do I."

Manny pushed open the front door and showed them into the house, which smelled of fresh paint. "Do you want to eat first or see your room?"

"Oh my, this is lovely," Michelle gushed, but she rubbed her tummy. "Ready to eat, guys?"

Father Manny led the way into the large country kitchen, and a bay window curved in the eating area overlooking the back yard outside. When he went to lift Timothy into the highchair, he reached for Lilly, who took him and set him in it. Manny had a tall chair for Paul, who climbed into it. Michelle appeared with a washcloth to wash their hands, and Marcus and Manny set out the food.

"Say the blessing, and I'll show Miss Lilly the bathroom so she can wash up."

But Paul clutched his crotch and said he had to pee-pee now, clambering down to run after them. Timothy howled, and Michelle gathered him into her lap until Lilly returned and set him back in the highchair.

After they ate, Marcus and Manny took the boys into the back yard, which was surrounded with an eight-foot privacy fence. They tossed around a multi-colored beach ball, laughing when Timothy tried to catch it and rolled end over end. Paul helped him up, brushing the grass clippings off him, but he didn't cry.

"Stoic little lad, isn't he?"

"He has been in an orphanage for six months, Manny. They have sixty children there. Good staff, well-run, but keeping them fed, clean, and educated leaves little time for coddling."

"What's Lilly's story?"

"Michelle knows it better than I, but she was found by a hunter, who heard a child cry. She was able to walk and must have survived on berries and fruit. Her parents were dead in the house, had been dead a while, apparently. She was emaciated and never caught up physically. She didn't talk for two years, but she more than caught up mentally. Cecile and Theo brought her into the orphanage, and she lived there, completing school and working for the orphanage when she got older. She's received a minimal salary for the last few years. She grew up caring for the little ones. She's shy, but she works hard, and she loves those boys."

"I can see that. All this seems miraculous, doesn't it?"

Marcus leaned against a redwood picnic table as he watched the boys explore the yard. "God never ceases to amaze me. You heard Michelle is carrying twin girls, didn't you?"

Manny clapped him on the shoulder. "No! But if anyone deserves a double portion, it's that precious girl."

"My grandfather told her the same thing. God showed him she was carrying the girls and that God was giving her a double portion."

"Your grandfather has prophetic vision, too?"

"I listen to what he says, that's for sure, and Michelle asked for a sonogram because of what he said." Marcus shoved himself away from the table and walked over to look where the boys were pointing up. He hoisted Paul up to look in the bird nest and see the blue eggs. Timothy lifted his arms to Manny for the first time, and the boy peered into the nest.

"We will watch but not touch. The mommy and daddy might not return to their babies if we touch the nest. In a few days, we'll see the babies and watch them feed them." Mother and father robin were screeching above, so they moved away.

Timothy laid his head on Manny's shoulder, and the priest caught his breath, brushing his lips on the child's head. "I'm glad you are here, Timothy. You flew all the way across the ocean to your home." The little boy's hand curved around Manny's collar and held on.

The ladies finished the clean-up and moved into the yard, perching on the bench of the picnic table. As it often does on a summer afternoon in Maryland, the soft rain came down, and they moved into the house.

"We need to make some plans. We have to buy the boys clothes and toys," Michelle said.

"Maybe clothes, but I've bought toys," Manny interrupted. Holding out his hand, he added, "Come see, boys." Paul took the priest's hand, and Timothy took his. They walked down the hall, and Michelle and Lilly trailed after them. The bedroom was robin's egg blue, and the overhead fan swirled overhead. It was furnished with a crib, a twin bed, a long dresser, and two toy boxes, and the room's curtains drifted softly in the breeze from windows.

"I'm trying to get the paint smell out of here. We painted yesterday. I hope it doesn't bother the boys."

Paul broke away and knelt in front of a train table, pushing the wooden trains around a circular pattern. "Come see, Timothy." The littler boy popped his thumb into his mouth.

Lilly knelt beside him. "Look, Timothy, we can push your train over the bridge." And she demonstrated. Looking up at Father Manny, she whispered, "This is nice. Thank you. The boys will love it."

The priest stepped to the door leading to a bathroom. "Your room is beside theirs, through the bathroom. Is that good?" She nodded. "My bedroom is next door, but I have my own bathroom. When the boys are older, they might want their own bedrooms. We have two more, with a bathroom between them."

Leaving the boys with Lilly, Manny showed Marcus and Michelle where they'd stay. The fifth bedroom wasn't furnished. Marcus and Manny hauled their luggage into the guest room and peeked into the boys' bedroom. The toy-boxes were open, and stuffed animals were laying on pillows, but the boys had returned to the train. Lilly sat on the twin bed and watched them.

"I set your suitcase in your room, Lilly," Marcus said. She nodded and whispered her thanks. "Did you see the bookcase?" She smiled.

Manny asked if everything was all right, and she replied in a soft voice. "Perfect, thank you."

Michelle took Manny's arm. "Let's get some tea, shall we?" She tugged him down the hall and put a kettle on the stove.

"I can tell you've been in South Africa a month, serving tea in the afternoons. What did you think of it?"

"It's a beautiful country, Manny. I love it, and Marcus belongs there." She set out a packet of tea and an infuser she'd retrieved from their luggage and set about brewing a fresh pot.

"Tell me about the women you saw there. Did you get a different view of yourself in an African nation?"

"One of the ladies at the orphanage must have been seven feet tall, and many of them were dark as ink. I felt comfortable among them."

"The trip was good, then." Manny took her hand. "I'm glad. Is Lilly all right? She's so quiet. I hope everything is satisfactory."

"She's cautious, and she doesn't require much. Did Marcus tell you about her? She's been at the orphanage sixteen years, after surviving on her own for God knows how long."

"She's a pretty little thing. I hope she'll be happy. Cecile and Theo must be like parents."

"Yes, but they were parents to sixty, and she in lived the dormitory. They estimate she was four or five when she first came. She didn't speak for two years, and one day she began to speak in full sentences. She sat in the classroom for a year, but once she started to talk, they realized she remembered everything." Michelle patted Manny's hand. "This is a big step for her, away from the only life she's known. She'll feel more comfortable when she's cooking and looking after the house. The main thing to be aware of is that she doesn't eat very much at a time. She nibbles throughout the day."

"Let's see if she'd like some tea," Manny said, walking down the hall. Lilly had Timothy on her lap, and they were turning the brightly colored pages of a story book. She looked up when he asked, "Would you like a cup of tea?"

She rose and asked the boys if they wanted juice. Paul shook his head, but Timothy held up his hands. She picked him up, and when they moved out the door, Paul followed.

Michelle had rinsed out the boys' cups and filled them with apple juice. "I found some animal cookies, Manny. Good choice!"

"I loved them as a child. Come, boys, let's have a snack. First, we will thank Jesus for our food." Immediately, the boys bowed their heads and sang a blessing. The good priest was thrilled. He sat, picked up the cookies, and identified the animals. Soon Paul caught on to the game, calling out "giraffe," and "lion." He paused at the bear, and Manny supplied the name.

"Remember the story we read about the three bears?" Lilly hesitated. "That kind of bear?"

"Precisely that kind of bear." Manny smiled to encourage her.

The travelers began to fade, and Lilly took the boys to bathe. Manny showed her the towel racks for each boy and for her. She played with them in the tub but picked Timothy up before long. "He's sleepy." She wrapped him in the towel, and Paul cried to get out.

"Will you let me, Paul?" Manny held out a towel, and they joined Lilly in their bedroom.

"What should I call you?" she asked in a low voice.

"Manny will do."

"Manny, the boys sleep together. Can we push the bed against the wall?"

"I won't need the crib?"

"They will be more secure together."

"You tell me, Miss Lilly. I've never been a father before, and you know the boys."

She handed him Paul's pajamas and diapered and dressed Timothy. When both boys were ready for bed, she started to shove the bed, and he hastened to help her. Together, they tucked the boys into bed and knelt beside it to say prayers. The boys threw their arms around Lilly but submitted to his goodnight kiss with giggles. Manny showed Lilly how to lower the light so they wouldn't be in total darkness. Then he showed Lilly how her door locked on the inside, so she could lock the door to the hall and the door to the bathroom for privacy. She asked if she could leave the bathroom door open to hear the boys, and he promised to knock before he entered their room, but he asked her to please leave their hall door open so he could hear them in the night, too.

Marcus and Michelle settled in their bedroom, and Manny left his bedroom door open, then knelt beside his to offer prayers of gratitude and to ask for help. He asked the Heavenly Father to surround the boys and Lilly with His Holy Spirit so they would feel safe and at home. He praised God for His goodness to bring these precious boys to him, and for Lilly agreeing to be his nanny. He sat and read his Bible for a long time, realizing the quiet was different. He heard occasional sniffles, the sound of breathing, beds creaking when people moved. He had never realized how alone he was before. After he had blessed everyone for making these things happen—Theo and Cecile in Orlando, Harry Mansour for pulling strings, and Michelle and Marcus for bringing them—he finally clicked off the light and lay, listening to the boys' snuffles and the occasional car passing.

Sometime in the wee small hours, a child's cry woke Manny. His first test. Could he handle this? He roused himself and walked to the boys' doorway. Hearing quiet voices, he stopped to listen.

"Shh, Paul, Lilly's here. Everything is fine. You woke up in a strange place. We're in Father Manny's house, your new home. Do you need to go to the bathroom?" He heard the boy's agreement and the sounds of bare feet crossing the floor. He peeked and ducked back, seeing Lilly in her long white gown. She was covered from head to toe in the linen gown, but he wanted to respect her privacy. They returned. The bed creaked twice. It sounded like she had helped him in and sat beside him.

"Lilly, will you stay here beside me?"

"Maybe tonight, until you get used to your room. Let Lilly hold you."

In the glimmer from the night light, Manny saw her leaning against the headboard, her arms around Paul, stroking his head. She looked like a petite Madonna, with the child cradled in her arms, and he thought if he lived to be a hundred, this image would be emblazoned on his heart and mind.

"This is a good home. God has given you a good father."

"Do you think he likes me?"

"I know he does! He is a man of love. Didn't he thank God for you both?"

"I'll be good."

"You're a good boy, a smart boy, and you'll be a good helper to Father Manny. One day you'll be an acolyte."

"I can take out the trash and pick up my toys, and I'll watch after Timothy."

"I know you will. Now, can we go back to sleep? Scoot down and move over."

Father Manny smiled as he listened to them arrange themselves. How blessed he was! When he was convinced they'd settled, he tip-toed back to his room. "God, help me to be a man of love, and help me to guide these boys to be good men." He lay on his back, tears trickling down the sides of his face and pooling in his ears.

He woke up to giggles at his doorway and opened his eyes to see dancing black eyes peeping at him. He rose up on his elbow. "I hear two little boys. Are they happy boys? Well-rested boys? Hungry boys?" He swung his legs out of the bed and grabbed his robe, tying it securely. Hearing them gigging and scampering, he stomped his feet, moving across the floor. "Where are those boys? Can I find them?" More giggles. Scurrying feet. He peeked around the door, and the boys ducked into their room.

"Let me get dressed, and we'll see what's for breakfast."

"We're hungry, Father."

"I'll hurry."

Soon he was dressed in comfortable blue jeans and a shirt. With a shy smile, Lilly asked if he was in civilian clothes.

"I'm home. When I go out, I wear the collar so people know I'm a man of the cloth. Sometimes they come up to me, or in the event of an emergency, they recognize me as someone they can turn to, I hope."

"Lilly says you're a man of love. Is that true?" Paul looked up.

Manny rested his hand on his head. "All Christians should be people of love, son. We love because He first loved us and shed His love abroad in our hearts, right?"

The boy pondered that. "We should be, I guess."

"If we ask God to help us, we can be." He looked at Lilly. She was fully clothed in a long skirt and a white cotton blouse. "Good morning, Miss Lilly. Did you sleep well?"

She ducked her head. "I need to learn where your pots and pans are, and the foodstuffs. I will prepare breakfast."

Manny held out his hand, and Paul slipped his little one into it. Timothy grabbed hold of Lilly's skirt but grinned at him.

Marcus stuck his head out the door to their bedroom. "I hear little boys."

"Where's Aunt Michelle?"

"She's getting dressed. She'll be here in a minute." Marcus followed them down the hall and into the kitchen.

Manny rested his hand on the canisters on the counter. "Flour, sugar, coffee, tea," he recited, "and here's the pantry." He opened both doors of a tall cabinet. "You can go with me and help me shop for the things you like." He opened the refrigerator. "We have eggs, bacon, and sausage, or do you want to make pancakes?"

"Eggs," Lilly said in a firm voice. "They had too much junk yesterday."

"Yes, ma'am," Father Manny teased. She ducked her head. "You take good care of these boys, Miss Lilly. I'm sure I'll benefit from your cooking." He patted his ample belly. Her chin sank lower. Cupping her face, Manny lifted it to look in her eyes. "This is your home, and from now on, you're the boss of the kitchen. Cecile told me you were the manager of the kitchen and supervised all the cooking."

"I hope I won't automatically cook for sixty."

"We can freeze it and use it next week." Manny smiled, trying to ease her anxiety.

"I need a chopping board."

"What for?"

"To cut up vegetables."

"Vegetables?"

"For the omelet."

"Oh. We'll do with scrambled eggs until we shop for a chopping board and vegetables."

Manny browsed through the refrigerator, handing out eggs, bacon, and sausage, which she accepted. He opened the cabinets to show her dishes and plates, and he opened drawers to show her the silverware. Handing up a frying pan from the lower cabinet, he showed her how to turn on the stove. After starting the bacon, she returned to the refrigerator and asked him where the butter was. He reached for a tub and handed it to her. She frowned. He and Marcus set the table. He made some toast and put honey on it to set before the boys while they waited. They began licking off the sticky, and he recognized he had to make a habit of putting a wet washcloth beside the plates.

By the time Michelle entered the dining area, Lilly had plates piled high with food, except her own, which only had bites and spoonfuls. Manny frowned and pointed, but she shook her head. "Too much food makes me sick."

"That's not enough to keep a bird alive!"

"I'll eat more later."

Michelle poured more juice into the glasses that were held up. "Remember, I told you she was starved when she was found, and she still can't eat much at one sitting. She's a grazer, aren't you, Lilly?"

"I eat throughout the day, Manny."

Everyone would need to go the nearby shopping center. Michelle knew Lilly would need her help, the boys wouldn't let her out of their sight, and Manny had to pay for all of it. Marcus went along for the ride, and to help corral the boys. They bought a cutting board, strainers, a steamer, vegetables, and fruit. Manny, who thought he'd shopped well, found himself ringing out almost two hundred dollars!

"What is this?" He pulled out a pot from the various bags and learned it was a rice pot. He didn't eat much rice. Instead of hamburgers for lunch, as he planned, she prepared loaves of chopped beef and vegetables, with rice mixed in. It was good. The boys took a nap right after they ate, tuckered out from their adventure, and the travelers lay on their beds, as well. Manny sat in his study, reading his Bible and jotting notes. He would look up, remembering one incident or another, and smile. He went outside and picked some flowers he had inherited from the previous owner and put them in an old vase. Lilly was the first one up, and he presented the bouquet to her with a little flourish.

Michelle and Marcus wanted to take the boys to the harbor, promising to take them to dinner, so they loaded up the van again. The boys clung to hands, either Michelle's or Lilly's, but tugged eagerly to the water, exclaiming and pointing to the boats.

"They are so good!" Manny was astounded.

"They don't know you yet. Give them time to settle in," Marcus explained. "Paul is a sober little fellow. He looks at books a lot and asks questions constantly, but Timothy is high energy and runs like a rabbit." As if to prove Marcus's words, the little boy took off across the pavement, hurling himself on the railing and leaning over until his feet were waving in the air.

Fearing he would fall in the water, Manny ran as fast as he could to grab him by the shirt collar and haul him to his feet. "You mustn't do that, Timothy. A grown-up must accompany you to the water's edge. We don't want you to fall in!"

Timothy sniffed and rubbed his arm against his nose. Manny knelt beside him, pulling out his hankie and wiping the little nose. He picked the boy up, and before he could reach for Michelle or Lilly, Manny started toward the aquarium, telling him all they could see inside. He held him while Marcus bought the tickets and took Paul's hand. Timothy wiggled down out of Manny's arms. "Hopefully, he's safer inside."

The two boys stood side by side, watching fish swimming by in the huge tank. Timothy put his nose on the tank, but Lilly tugged him back. Paul took his hand, and Marcus pointed out the different fish. They wandered through a few rooms, seeing sting rays, artificial coral reefs, and far more than they could comprehend.

Timothy tugged Marcus' hand and said, "Eat."

Lilly told Manny they had about five minutes before he decompensated, so they hurried to the cafeteria. The men got fish and chips sandwich plates. While waiting at the table, Lilly unpacked a Ziploc bag of apple pieces. Michelle washed their hands with wet ones, and they managed until their fish sandwiches arrived. Lilly took the fish out of the bun and cut it up for them, setting the bread aside. She had eaten a few apple slices and insisted she wasn't hungry, but Manny broke off some of his fish for her.

On the ride back, Lilly and Michelle kept the boys awake by pointing out the sights, then got them in the tub when they got home.

"How long does it take to adjust their hours?" Manny asked. "They were up at four-thirty this morning."

"I've never traveled across the ocean with kids before. It takes me about a day. Michelle was about forty-eight hours, but she was in her first trimester fatigue." Holding out his arms, Marcus caught a wet, slippery Timothy in a flying leap.

Michelle threw him a towel. "He escaped. You dry him off. Here are his pajamas."

Laughing, Marcus tickled him and shoved his squirming body into leg and arm holes. Michelle sat beside them and opened picture books Manny had bought at the aquarium, and they pointed at the fish they had seen. Paul, fully clad, ran in and climbed up beside them, identifying the shark and several others.

Lilly, looking exhausted, collapsed in a nearby chair. "They are beside themselves. Too much excitement."

"Did I do wrong?" Manny asked with a worried look on his face. "I don't know what to do with children this age. I was an only child."

"They're unwinding from the trip, and they're used to a structured life at the orphanage. They're adjusting," Michelle explained.

"They're happy, Manny. I've never heard Paul laugh this much," Lilly reassured him.

He took her hand. "You'll have to help me, Miss Lilly. Tell me if I do the wrong thing."

"How long do you need Michelle to stay?" Marcus asked. "I'll go over to the hospital after church tomorrow and come back here, but I begin work Monday, and I need to go home."

Dropping a kiss on Timothy's head, Michelle entwined her fingers in his.

"Manny and I will put the boys to bed tonight and see how it goes," Lilly said.

Manny chuckled, picking up the younger boy, who was already dead to the world. He carried him to the bedroom, Paul trailing behind them. He tucked Timothy against the wall, and Paul crawled up beside him. Manny dropped to his knees, and they said the Lord's Prayer. Hearing a soft rustle beside him, he felt Lilly drop to her knees. Paul began blessing Cecile, Theo, Michelle, Marcus, Marcus's father, Lilly, and— His voice dropped off. Manny checked, and,] sure enough, the boy was asleep. Offering Lilly his hand, he stood.

"Dear me, they will be up in the middle of the night again." She sighed.

He cupped her chin. "Tired? I heard you up with him last night and the night before. Did you get any sleep?"

"I did, but he was restless in his sleep."

They walked into the living room to visit with Marcus and Michelle. Manny reviewed the schedule for the morning: early service at 8:00,

Sunday school, and then morning service at eleven. Marcus volunteered to run him over at 7:30 and return for the family, but Manny said he could walk.

Lilly tried in vain to keep from yawning, until Manny suggested she turn in. "I hope you get more sleep tonight," he said.

"Can we pray together?" she requested.

Picking up a prayer book from the end table, Manny turned to the evening reading for the day and read aloud. The four of them prayed aloud in a circle, and Manny was surprised to hear Lilly string together several sentences, beseeching God to help her with the boys and to be a blessing to Father Manny. When they stood, the good father kissed her forehead and assured her she was already a blessing. With a quiet smile, she went back to her room and closed her hall door.

After saying goodnight to the Mansours, Manny went back to his bedroom. He left his door open to listen for the boys. He noticed that Lilly continued to keep her bathroom door open between her room and the boys'.

He went to the boys' bed and dropped to his knees, unaware that Lilly heard his prayers of thanksgiving and blessing. He stood and leaned over each one, dropping kisses on their foreheads before he went to his room. Despite his afternoon nap, Manny dropped off to sleep, a smile on his face. His life had changed in a weekend, and he liked it!

Surprised to wake up to delectable aromas emanating from his kitchen, Manny closed his door to pull on his black pants, a shirt, and his white collar. He walked into the kitchen. It was 5:30 a.m..

Lilly turned after pulling a loaf pan out of the oven. "Would you like an omelet?"

"I usually don't eat until after morning Eucharist, but thank you."

"Do you want coffee?"

Seeing she had prepared coffee as well as a bread, Manny felt he should have eaten her offering, so he accepted a cup. God would forgive him. "You didn't need to get up to feed me."

"I am your cook."

Manny was dumbfounded. Yes, she was here on a work visa, to be his nanny and housekeeper, but he didn't see her as a servant.

Manny, the spoiled only son of older parents, couldn't fathom being an orphan, starved and taken in, wordless and dumb for two years, living in an orphanage and working for a living, still unable to eat a full meal. Tears sprung to his eyes. "Here, we will be a family." She stared at him. "Tell Marcus I've walked to the church. It isn't far." He closed the front door behind him, and she watched, looking down the hall from the kitchen.

Manny entered the small sanctuary, looking at the familiar colored panes, and dropped down at the altar rail. After he crossed himself, he looked up at the cross hanging on the wall. "How do I do this, Lord? Bring up two boys and care for the flower you have given me. This beautiful little Lilly. Make her blossom, Lord." He bowed his head, feeling the presence of God, the peace that passes all understanding, flow over him and around him. Gratitude swelled in his heart, and he felt a joyful anticipation, as if God had wonderful, unknown treasures awaiting. He rose to prepare for services, setting out the robes for the season, placing the chalice and tray for the elements. He heard his deacon and his son, the acolyte who would serve today, come in.

"Good morning, Father Manny. Did your family arrive from South Africa?"

"Thursday morning. Thank you. They are settling in nicely."

"Are they coming to services today?"

"Late service."

"You have a very curious congregation, Father Manny. We know you want to let them become used to us, but the ladies are itching to have a welcome party, and the Mrs. wants me to me to ask you about next Sunday night."

"Right now, they're adjusting to the time change, and they go to sleep early. Friday morning, they got me up at four-thirty, but they were still in bed when I left the house around seven today."

"Maybe they'll be adjusted in a week." The two men prepared for the small gathering that came to early service.

Marcus and the family arrived around 10:45, and Paul tackled Manny, who gathered him for a hug. Timothy peeked around Lilly's skirt and grinned. The priest squatted down and gathered them into his arms. He had talked to them yesterday, and they knew he was the priest, so he couldn't sit with them. They had to be good for Miss Lilly, he instructed, and they gave him solemn nods. He ushered them to the first pew, explaining that the entire congregation was eager to see them because they had been praying for them to get home safely.

After the service, Father Manny stood outside greeting people, and he was thrilled that the boys stood beside him. Timothy stood rather behind, holding on to his skirts, but Paul was bold and greeted most people, especially the friendly ones. Several people, women especially, wanted to know where Lilly lived, and a few raised their eyebrows when he assured them he had five bedrooms and she slept adjacent to the boys' room. Only then did he become aware he had a problem of propriety, and Marcus wanted Michelle home as soon as possible, of course. Whatever was he to do?

Chapter Twenty

THE FIRST SUNDAY

Manny was weary when he walked into the house, but the delicious smells that greeted him made his stomach growl. "I have been eager to taste that bread since I woke up! But I smell something else."

"Chicken stew," Lilly said, hurrying to the kitchen to stir the crock pot, which was one of the purchases from Friday. She turned to Michelle. "You are right! This is magic. Perfect."

Manny looked at Michelle. "She's amazed at the crock pot. She makes a lot of stews and chowders. I knew she'd like it."

Lilly set an odd-looking pot on the stove, a pan within a pan. It was another new purchase, a rice pot. While it steamed, she put vegetables in a pot she called a steamer. Was that new?

Manny told the boys they'd set the table, and he doled out forks, spoons, knives, and napkins. He folded the napkins in half and set them under the forks, and Paul tried to imitate him. Marcus and Michelle watched with amusement, standing in the doorway. Timothy was hollering, "Eat!" and pulling people to the table.

While Lilly put the boys down for their naps, he told Marcus and Michelle that he'd become aware some in his congregation were showing concern about propriety with Lilly living in the house. "I know you want Michelle home, and she should be, but please pray with me about how we should solve this problem. I don't want to offend."

Michelle was angry. She thought people should know better!

Manny smiled. "Lilly is a lovely young lady, Michelle."

Michelle raised her eyebrows and shut her mouth. Marcus grinned. "We'll pray. Why don't you call Otiano and see what he thinks? I know he wants to meet your family." He stood, indicating he'd leave but be back that evening. "Where's Lilly?"

"I hope she fell asleep. She was up early and prepared me breakfast. I felt terrible because I don't eat until after the first service. Marcus, when you come back, we need to move the double bed in her room into the boys' room. They sleep together, and she has ended up in there every night. I hope they'll sleep through the night as they adjust, but she's so tiny that the twin bed will be fine for her."

"Sure thing, Manny."

Following his friend's advice, Manny called Otiano and arranged for them to come spend the next day with them. Both priests took Monday off. Manny followed Michelle into the living room, but while she read, he laid his head back and dozed off.

Hearing voices, he opened his eyes. Lilly had fruit and slices of her fresh-baked bread for the boys, and she ate, too, which he was glad to see. He took a slice of bread himself, slathering it with apple butter. He gave the boys a bite, and they were hooked! Lilly had never tasted it, and she liked it, too. When he reached for another slice, his arm brushed her thin one, and he picked it up.

"You're too thin, Miss Lilly. You are petite, but you must put on a little weight to have some reserves for your health. I'll buy some protein powder and make shakes for you." She kept her head down. He cupped her chin and brought her face up. "Would that be all right? We could ask a doctor if you like."

Michelle leaned toward her and took her other hand. "Father Manny's right, Lilly. That's a good idea."

"Are you my doctor, Michelle?"

Michelle laughed. "I am!"

"Okay."

The boys went into the yard with Father Manny, eager to see the bird nest, and they ladies watched through the window as he lifted them up.

"He is good with them," Lilly observed, "but Paul hasn't called him 'Father' once this afternoon. Did you notice?"

"I didn't, but you're right. I wonder why? Ever since we've been here, he's called him 'father' over and over."

The ladies carried lemonade to the patio, and the boys ran over. Timothy sat in Lilly's lap, pointing at the nest and babbling. Father Manny described what they had seen: four blue eggs, the color of their bedroom walls. And Paul told them the birds fussed at them to go away. Timothy slipped off Lilly's lap and ran to some daisies, jerking at the stems.

"Wait, Timothy. Lilly will bring you some scissors to cut them."

Lilly went into the kitchen, pulling open various drawers.

Manny followed her in. "They're in my desk drawer." He retrieved a pair and gave them to her. "He'll pull those poor plants out by the roots if we don't get out there!" When she giggled, he felt like he'd accomplished something huge, and he winked at her. She ducked her head but smiled.

The day was hot, so Manny went into his garage and pulled out a small, round, blue plastic pool. Paul's eyes got big as he watched him pull the hose out and fill it. The boys didn't have swimsuits, which would be another necessary item to purchase, but they played in their shorts. When they began to get rowdy, splashing the ladies, Manny stopped them and made them dry off.

Michelle rose and went into the house, returning with two plastic jars, and showed them how to blow bubbles. Timothy spit more than he blew bubbles, but Paul soon got the hang of it, and even learned to turn in a circle, forming bubbles in the breeze.

They heard the doors open, and Marcus stepped out. He dropped into a chair, took Michelle's hand, and said, "Dr. Campbell's off for Portugal tonight, and he left the call schedule for the month." He brought his wife's hand to his lips and kissed it, saying with a wink, "I missed you. I've gotten used to being around you. It's going to be tough, going to work again."

"I'm positively lazy!"

"You're growing babies. That's work enough." He grinned at her. "Have I told you how beautiful you look growing my babies?"

"I'm already getting a tummy."

"I know." He winked at Manny. "Isn't she cute?"

Timothy pulled on his pant leg. "Bub. Bub."

Delighted, Manny put him on his lap. "That's right, Timothy. Bubbles." And he explained what they had been doing. Paul grabbed a jar off the table and demonstrated. His brother cried and tried to seize it, so Lilly handed him the other jar. He put the wand up in Marcus's face and spit.

"Ugh, you little munchkin!" Marcus swiped his face with his sleeve while everyone laughed.

"Oh! I must fix dinner." Lilly leapt up.

Manny caught her hand. "Not on Sunday. We don't need a big meal on Sunday."

"An omelet?" she suggested.

He chuckled. "You've been trying to make me an omelet since you got here. Yes, that would be lovely." And he followed her into the kitchen.

She got out the cutting board and vegetables: tomato, onion, spinach, and mushrooms. She set cheese beside them, and he handed her the eggs and a mixing bowl. He reached for a knife, but she placed her hand over his. "I'm the cook."

"We are family. I'll help."

She stood, her little hand on her hip, but he didn't move. She shrugged and took another knife. Standing side by side, she showed him how to dice the vegetables.

"Shall we add ham and cheese?" he asked.

She had the cheese, but he reached in the refrigerator and brought out ham. When the omelet was bubbling in the pan, he asked if she wanted him to make toast. She sliced her fresh bread, and he thanked her for letting him help as he popped the slices in the toaster.

"Thank you, Manny."

Michelle popped her head in the door. "Does playing in the pool count for a bath? Shall I put their pajamas on?"

Before Lilly could answer, Manny agreed that the boys were fresh and clean, so Marcus and Michelle readied them for bed while Lilly and Manny set the table. By the time the boys were seated, they were serving dinner. Once again, the boys sang the blessing, and the grown-ups joined their sweet song.

After supper, Manny brought out story books, and Paul sprawled across his lap. Timothy stood beside his leg, pulling on his pants. Manny scooped him up and arranged the little one beside his brother as he began to read.

"You have a lapful of boys there, Manny." Marcus watched his friend.

"I have a lapful of blessings." Manny kissed each shiny cheek.

Michelle sat on the arm of her husband's chair. "Paul, who is this?" She pointed to Manny, but the child shrugged. "Is he your father?" The boy shrugged. "Why don't you call him 'Father'?"

"Everyone calls him father."

Michelle caught Lilly's eye. "So, you want him to belong to you? Just to you?" The boy nodded, tears trembling at his eyes. "Marcus calls his father 'Papa.' Would you like to call your father 'Papa'?

Paul turned in Manny's lap. "Could I call you 'Papa'? Nobody else? You are *my* Papa?"

Manny pulled him close. "I'd like that, Paul, because you are my little boy, and no one else's. We are going to court next week, and the judge will sign papers that will make you and Timothy my boys." He blinked back tears and almost succeeded. Lilly handed him tissues, and he blew his nose.

"You have a wonderful papa, boys. He is a man of love." Manny shook his head, but she said, "It's true, Manny." Lilly handed him the prayer book. "Will you read the evening Scriptures?"

Straightening, Manny took the book from her hand. "If I can." And he did, his voice gaining strength as he read the blessed words.

Chapter Twenty-One

MARRY THE GIRL

M anny was in the study beside his bedroom when he heard when Marcus leave before the household was up. He jotted a few notes in his journal but closed his Bible when Lilly began moving around. He found her in the kitchen.

"Did they boys sleep through the night?"

"They did."

"I'm glad. Did you sleep well?"

"Yes."

Before he realized what he was doing, Manny's hand curved around her sweet face. "Good! Can I help you?"

"No." She paused, looked up, and smiled. "Thank you." Seeing he was dressed, she asked, "Were you studying?"

He nodded, and she told him she would call him for breakfast. He returned to his office until the enticement of smells and little voices brought him into the kitchen.

"I was about to call you."

To his surprise, the table was set, and she had prepared fish for breakfast. The boys clamored for hugs, which he most willingly gave, and he helped

Lilly get them into their chairs. He pulled out her chair, waving for her to sit. She looked at him, surprised.

"Sit, Miss Lilly." She obeyed. "Have you heard from Michelle yet?" As he said the words, she appeared, and he chuckled. "Fine chaperone you are, sleepyhead."

"I told Marcus goodbye and fell back asleep. He tells me Otiano's coming today."

"Yes. They'll be here around ten." Manny rose and held Michelle's chair before returning to his seat.

The ladies cleaned the kitchen while the boys played in their room. Manny heard them pushing the train and hollering "Choo, choo, woo, wooo." Happy sounds. Little boy sounds. He answered the phone, listened to a parishioner report someone in the hospital, and promised to visit. By the time he hung up, he smelled fresh aromas coming from his kitchen.

"What are you cooking up now?" he asked Lilly, coming into the room as she pulled a pan out of the oven.

Her face was flushed from the heat as she set it down. "I made blueberry scones for your guests."

"You didn't have to do that!"

"But you are hosting your friends."

"Give it up, Manny. This is Lilly you're dealing with!"

"Did you help her with this, Michelle?"

"She taught me how to make them. Don't they smell scrumptious?" She turned to Lilly. "Ready to go outside now?" And she explained that they wanted to get the boys out of the house. Calling to them, she went down the hall.

Lilly lifted the scones off the baking pan and placed them on a good china plate. She had coffee ready to make, hot water simmering for tea, and a china tea pot with leaves in an infuser. His eyes swept over her preparations, and he shook his head. Placing his hands on her cheeks, he dropped a kiss on her forehead. Then he drew her into an embrace. "You do too much, Miss Lilly." She shook her head and stepped back. Michelle returned with the boys, and they went into the backyard.

Manny stood at the French doors, looking into the yard, watching the women walking hand in hand with the boys—his boys. "Thank you, Father," he whispered.

Lilly wore a full skirt, and she sat in the grass with it spread around her. Timothy plopped on her lap and patted her face, and she kissed his fingers, nibbling on them until he giggled. Michelle was pointing to something, and Paul watched with fascination.

The doorbell rang, and Manny hastened to it, drawing his friends in with a warm greeting. "Come. Smell what Lilly has prepared! She's a marvelous cook."

"Where are your boys?" Otiano looked around, following his wife inside.

Manny pointed out the door. "They are outside with Michelle and my little flower, Miss Lilly." He pulled open the door. "Come meet them."

"Papa, show me the nest," Paul cried.

"We have robins nesting in the oak tree," Manny explained to his friends, opening his arms wide to the boy. Paul was halfway to him when he noticed the strangers and stopped. Manny waved him forward. "Come meet some friends, Paul. This is Father Mondalah and his wife, Shirley. You may call her Mrs. Mondalah." Paul grabbed Manny's pant leg and ducked his head. Laughing, Manny picked him up and encouraged him to say hello.

"Hello, Father," he said, but he patted Manny. "This is my papa."

Smiling, Michelle walked over to the couple. "Otiano, how nice to see you!"

Putting his arm around his wife, Otiano presented Shirley.

"Manny told me how lovely you are, Shirley. My husband and I were married in your beautiful building."

"You are the doctor, I understand. The Logan daughter?"

"I am. We brought Paul and his brother home with us from South Africa." She beckoned to Lilly, who was holding Timothy.

Manny put his arm around her and leaned into Timothy. "This is Lilly and Timothy." The little one buried his head in Lilly's shoulder but peeped up at the strangers.

"Do you boys want some of Missy Lilly's scones?" He looked at Lilly. "It that all right?" She nodded. "Lilly, this is Dr. and Mrs. Mondalah. Otiano and Shirley. Otiano is from Rwanda, and Shirley is from Jamaica."

"Second generation, Manny. I was born in New York. How nice to meet you, Lilly." Shirley's second-generation accent had a melodious Caribbean sound. Shirley took Lilly's hand in both of hers. "I understand you are from South Africa. Manny tells me you are a fine cook."

Lilly ducked her head. "Thank you," she whispered. "Come." She led the way into the kitchen. "Would you like coffee or tea?" She poured hot water over the infuser and clicked on the coffee pot.

Michelle carried Timothy, and Paul held Manny's hand while the grown-ups chose their drinks, coffee for the men and tea for the ladies. Lilly served the scones, adding whipped cream for those who wanted it. She placed the boys' cups in front of their chairs and split a scone between them, taking a half herself. The boys sang their blessing, charming their guests.

"This is the best whipped cream I've ever tasted!" Shirley exclaimed.

"Made from real cream," Manny boasted. "No canned cream for Lilly."

Lilly took a platter of tea sandwiches, covered with a cloth, off the counter. Noticing she didn't take one, Manny cut one of his in two and put it on her plate. She looked up at him and smiled. She lifted the boys off their chairs and took them to their room to play while the adults moved into the living room with their second cups to chat. For a while they heard the boys playing, but when it got quiet, Manny went to check on them. Lilly followed, and they stood in the doorway together. They returned and told the gathering that the boys had climbed on their bed and fallen asleep.

Manny explained that they slept in the same bed, and he had purchased a crib he didn't need. "Do you need a crib, Michelle?"

"We do. We only bought one." She told the Mondalahs they were expecting twins, and Otiano smiled. "I'm glad to hear it. I thought you were large for five months. It is five months, right?"

They talked about Marcus and his work as acting head of oncology. Otiano asked Michelle if she still planned to do volunteer work. She would do what she could for however long she could, she told them, then discussed their plans to return to South Africa after Marcus finished up at Johns Hopkins.

"Have you told your parents yet?" Shirley asked.

"No. We've talked to them, and we plan to see them as soon as Lilly and the children are settled. Please don't say anything."

"They are looking forward to seeing you," Otiano said. "You'll be surprised how they have grown spiritually."

"Praise God."

"And Andrew has gained weight. He is precious, and so sincere in his faith."

After they had chatted a bit, Lilly heard the boys and rose to tend to them. Manny followed her with his eyes, then turned to look at Otiano. "What do you think I should do, Otiano? I don't want to offend, but I really cannot survive without her here."

Grinning, Otiano slapped his friend's knee. "You should marry the girl, Manny. You're half in love with her already."

Manny stared at him. "I'm much too old for her!"

Otiano looked at Shirley. "How much older am I than you?"

"Fourteen years? Fifteen?"

"You're thirty-one? How old is she, nineteen?"

"She's twenty."

"There you have it. Do it before the adoption, and the two of you can adopt the boys."

"She's so young."

Michelle took his hand. "Manny, she is much older than her years. Ask her."

Lilly walked into the room and looked around. "Ask me what?"

"Are the boys awake?"

"Ask me what?"

"We'll talk later," Manny promised.

"Our job here is done," Otiano said. "Thanks for a lovely lunch, Lilly. You're an excellent cook." He kissed her cheek, winked at Manny, and took his wife's hand. "Since I married Shirley, I feel ten years younger."

When they left, Lilly asked Manny if he needed to study, but he told her Mondays were his day off.

"You gave us so much time last weekend, I thought you might need to spend some time in your office."

Michelle excused herself and walked back to the boys' room, hoping to keep them occupied.

Manny patted the couch beside him. "Come talk to me, Lilly."

She sat, and he took her hand. "What was Dr. Mondalah's job here?"

"That's what we need to talk about. But I need you to be completely honest with me." She held his gaze. "I asked his advice. Some of the congregation questioned your living here, especially after Michelle leaves."

Her eyes got round. "I have to leave?"

"We can make it proper, but I don't want you to do anything you don't want to do."

"I don't want to leave here. I want to stay with you and the boys. But I don't want to do anything that would hurt you."

Lilly had never made such a long speech. Manny sat back, still holding her hand.

"We could get married, Lilly. We don't have to...consummate the marriage. Do you understand?" She nodded. "But it would be proper for us to share the home. I mean, I know I'm a lot older than you are, and you're young."

"Manny, I've never met a nicer person. You are a man of love, and I would find it easy to love you."

"You would?" He tightened his grip, and she squeezed his hand.

"I would, if you are sure."

He chuckled. "Otiano said I'm half in love with you already, and he's right." She smiled, and he leaned to place a gentle kiss on her lips. He put his arm around her, and she laid a slender hand on his chest. "So, you truly are willing?"

"I am. When do we need to do this?"

"I'm going to contact the lawyer. If we marry before the adoption, I want both of us to adopt the boys."

"I would be their mama?" Her eyes filled. He nodded and kissed the tears sliding down her cheeks. She looked up at him. "I would be proud to marry you, and I promise I'll try hard to be a good wife."

"I'll call him now, and then we need to go to the courthouse to apply for a license." He started to stand, then kissed her quickly again. "You're an easy person to love, Lilly." She ducked her head, and he chuckled. "I'll go call him."

Walking by the boys' room, he stuck his head in the door with a triumphant grin. "She agreed! I'm going to call the lawyer."

"Terrific, Manny!"

When he returned, Lilly and Michelle had the boys outside, filling the pool. "The hearing is set for next Monday. He's re-wording the petition. Are you sure, Lilly?"

She walked over to him and took his hands. "I'm very sure. Are you sure?"

"Yes. Michelle, can you watch the boys? We have a license to get." Manny squatted down. "You boys be good for Aunt Michelle. Lilly and I have some business to attend to. Maybe we can buy you some swimsuits, okay?" Both boys' lips quivered, but they were stoic and agreed. Taking Lilly's hand, Manny led her out the door.

When they returned, they had suits and a license, and they had even contacted Otiano, who agreed to marry them Thursday, after Marcus got off work. The petition was changed to include Lilly, and the hearing was still arranged for Monday. The social worker was coming to meet the boys tomorrow, and they agreed they had a few surprises for her!

Chapter Twenty-Two

THE WEDDING

The social worker arrived at 9:00 the next morning, and the boys were dressed in new little outfits. She was good with them, eliciting some conversation from Paul, who told her he loved his papa, and Timothy watched from Manny's lap, leaning heavily against him but observing the lady with large dark eyes.

Manny introduced Lilly to Ms. Baker, and explained she wouldn't be his nanny, but rather his wife and the children's mother. He added that the petition would be amended, and they would secure references for her from Drs. Marcus and Michelle Mansour, Dr./Father Otiano Mondalah, and her supervisors at the orphanage, as well, if she required.

"This is rather sudden, is it not?"

Lilly searched his face, her anxiety reflected on her countenance. He took her hand. "God has arranged this adoption quickly, and He has exceeded all my prayers. The Scriptures say God answers prayer abundantly, above all we can ask or even think. Michelle Mansour is still with us. She and her husband brought the boys and Lilly from South Africa, if you remember, but she needs to go home to her husband."

Ms. Baker asked if she might speak with Lilly in private. He squeezed Lilly's hand. She gave a curt little nod, and he stood, reaching his hands out to the boys.

"Let's go find Aunt Michelle, boys." They scampered after him to their room, and he sat on the floor with them, pushing the trains. Michelle asked how it was going, and they said a prayer for Lilly that God would give her the words.

In about a half an hour, Lilly led the social worker back to the room. "This turned out nicely, Father Manny," she said, looking around the room. "The last time I was here. He was priming it and planning to paint the next day." She turned to the boys. "Do you like your room, boys?"

"Did you see our quilt? Lilly picked it out," Paul said.

Timothy pointed to the trains on it. "Woo, whoo."

She laughed and patted his head. "It's very nice, boys. And who reads all these books to you?"

"Mostly Papa," Paul said.

"He speaks well for his age," she remarked.

He puffed out his chest. "I'll be four soon. I came across the ocean to my papa."

Manny stood, lifting him in his arms. "And Papa is so glad you did."

"It was very nice to meet you, all of you. Congratulations on your marriage, Father. God has certainly given you a family. This young lady said she was drawn to you even when you skyped and that you are easy to love."

"She is, too, Ms. Baker. I'll show you to the door if you have nothing else. Oh, if you give me a fax number, I'll send those references to you quickly." She handed him a card as they walked to the door.

"If I wasn't a believer before, I certainly would be one now," she told him, shaking his hand.

Lilly sank onto the bed. "I guess I passed. I'm glad that's over."

Michelle sat beside her. "Tomorrow we must buy you a dress." When Lilly tried to explain what she had that would do, Michelle told her Marcus and she would buy her a new dress for her wedding, and that was that.

* * *

Thursday evening, they swung by the hospital to pick up Marcus. He got in the front seat because Michelle was in the far back. He hung his suit on the hook, and they drove to Washington. The traffic was congested as usual, but Otiano said not to worry, as they wouldn't start without them.

"My folks are joining us," Michelle told him.

"Good. It'll be good to see them. What about your brother?"

"Not sure."

When they pulled up in front of the gorgeous building, Lilly put her hand over her mouth.

"Pretty, isn't it?" Michelle said. "We were married here, and it worked for us." Marcus helped her out of the van, smiling at her expanding girth. "Don't you say it!" she warned him.

While the others walked ahead, he pulled her into his arms and kissed her long and hard. "You're beautiful."

"I have to dress the bride."

"I like your new dress."

They walked hand in hand. Michelle took Lilly to the room where she dressed for her wedding, and they were ready in no time.

Marcus stuck his head in the door. "Your folks are here. They know about the twins, right?" He offered the two ladies his arms and escorted them to the foyer.

Michelle's mother took her in her arms and hugged her. "You look radiant, dear. How are you feeling?" Before she could answer, Louise turned to Lilly. "You must be Lilly." Lilly all but curtsied. "Otiano and Shirley told us about the lovely luncheon. We want to take you out for a little dinner afterward."

"The boys may not last that long," Lilly explained.

"If they don't, we'll do it another day. This is so exciting! Father Manny's waiting."

"Michelle," Herman gathered her in his arms. "My daughter, having twins. Quite a guy, that Marcus Mansour." He kissed her cheek. "You look beautiful, sweetheart."

"Thank you, Daddy."

"How did you manage those two boys on the plane? They are rascals."

"Lilly is wonderful with them."

"Marcus is signaling to us. We should go." Herman turned to Lilly. "Let them go ahead, and allow me, Lilly." He offered her his elbow. "We'll walk slowly toward your groom so he can see you, a vision in white."

Lilly ducked her head, but she looked at Manny waiting for her at the altar. When she arrived at the front, he reached for her hand, and she stepped forward. Otiano led the couple in their vows and presented them to the gathering. Manny took her in his arms and gave her a gentle kiss, moved by the fluttering of her lips against his. He smiled down at her, and she smiled back.

"This has been quite a week," Marcus said to his wife. "I wanted to give them a night at the hotel, but he told me they didn't think it would be good for the boys. Have they talked to Theo and Cecile?"

"We haven't done that yet. I think a skype is scheduled after the adoption." Michelle squeezed her husband's arm. "Isn't this exciting?"

"If they're married and going home, can we go home?"

The boys were tearing around the front lawn, so Marcus broke away to grab them. Manny apologized to the Logans, begging their indulgence because they needed to take the children home and put them to bed. Louise agreed, so long as they came soon.

Marcus insisted he would crawl in the back so Michelle could sit up front. Only Lilly was tiny enough to squeeze between the two car seats. On their way back to Baltimore, he asked Manny if he would mind drop-ping them off at their place since they were now married.

"I'd say we don't need a chaperone anymore, Marcus. You have been more than gracious to us, and I don't know how to thank you both for all you have done." Marcus directed him to their place, and after they climbed out of the car, he helped Lilly into the front seat. Timothy was sound asleep, but Paul grumbled a bit when he was disturbed.

After the Mansours left the car, Manny reached over to Lilly. "Are you doing okay?"

"I'm fine."

"You are a beautiful bride. Thank you."

"Thank me? For what?"

"For agreeing to marry me."

"I'm honored, Manny."

"I must be the most blessed man in the world."

"Marcus is thinking that himself about now."

Manny flicked on the turn signal and made the turn toward their neighborhood. He didn't know what to say. They drove through the silent evening, hearing the crickets chirping. Lilly had been fascinated with the fireflies ever since they arrived in Maryland, and she mentioned how many were about that night.

"When I was a kid, I'd catch them, and Mom would put them in a jar. She poked holes in the lid, and they'd blink in my room. I always wondered where they went the next day. Finally, my dad told me they released them after I fell asleep."

"We can do that for the boys."

He turned into the driveway and came around the van to help her. He reached in and unbuckled Timothy, placing him in her arms. He carried Paul himself, holding him in one arm to unlock the door. He took him down the hall, asking if he needed to use the bathroom and helping him do that. They decided to let him sleep in his underwear, and Lilly changed Timothy's diaper. Before long, they were back asleep. Manny went to secure the front door. Lilly used the restroom and returned to stand in the doorway of her room, unsure what she should do.

Manny approached her. "Is there anything I can do for you?"

She turned her back. "I need help with my dress."

Unzipping her dress, his eyes lingered on her smooth back. She was tiny but so very perfect. Her skin was dark and smooth. He held his breath. Her dress slid to the floor, and she turned to him, lifting her eyes to look in his face.

"I told you we didn't have to, Lilly." He put his hand on her cheek.

"May I sleep in your room, Manny?"

He lifted her into his arms and carried her, throwing the spread back and sliding her under the sheets. She was wearing an eyelet slip. He went into his bathroom and changed into pajamas, then slipped into bed beside her. She nestled against him, sighing. She put her hand on his chest and felt the rapid beating of his heart.

"I don't want to hurt you, Lilly."

"You won't. You'd never hurt me, Manny."

"Are you sure? The first time for a woman does hurt."

She pulled him down and offered her lips for his kiss, and gently he made her ready for love. Later, as she lay sleeping in the curve of his arm, he remembered his prayer and whispered his thanks to God for helping his Lilly blossom.

Chapter Twenty-Three

HOME AGAIN

Michelle waited while Marcus pulled open the door to the apartment house, said good evening to the doorman, and guided her to the elevator. He decided it would be a while before they raced each other up the stairs and told her as much. They turned left when the elevator slid to a stop on three, and he unlocked their door for her to proceed ahead. She stopped and turned her head from side to side, surveying the place, and then walked forward, running her hands along the back of the black leather couch. Such a man thing, she always thought.

"The kitchen is clean. You've washed the dishes."

"I ate all my meals at the hospital."

She tossed him a grin. "Guess you'll miss Lilly's cooking."

"I've missed you." He took her in his arms and kissed her.

She laid her head on his shoulder, feeling then that she'd truly come home. She went down the hall, stopping to look in the guest room, where they'd put all the baby gifts from the shower. She snapped on the light and wandered from stack to stack, picking up tiny onesies, layettes, toys, and a music box. She saw a screen that hung on the side of a crib and turned it on. Brightly colored fish swam in a blue sea, and a soft tune played.

Marcus stood behind her. "It's cute." He placed his hands on her shoulders and pulled her back against him. He leaned to kiss her cheek.

She was glad he had to lean. She was glad he was so tall, a big man who didn't make her feel big and ugly.

"My beautiful Nile princess. I told your mother once that you were my Valkyrie."

"Weren't they evil Norse goddesses who killed men?"

"They were strong, glorious goddesses who seduced men. Sometimes they led them to death, and sometimes they let them live to breed."

She shuddered. "That's not very pleasant. Why did you say that?"

He chuckled. "You were killing me at the time. I wanted you so badly. I still want you. I will want you till the day we die." She turned in his arms, and they were lost in their kisses. He drew a ragged breath. "I'm going to take a shower. Do you need one?"

"I bathed right before we left for Washington." But she turned and followed him to their bedroom. The bed was unmade, but her side was untouched, the quilt still tucked under her pillows. She kicked off her shoes and rummaged through the drawer. "I should have put my suitcase in the van. I hope I can find something to wear."

Kissing her briefly, he said he didn't think she needed anything, as it wouldn't be on long, anyway, then turned into the bathroom. He turned the shower on, and soon she heard him step in. She slipped on a soft, flowing caftan someone had given her at the shower. It zipped down the front for ease in nursing. She got in bed and hugged his pillow, breathing in the scent of him—hospital smells and his own unique scent. She burrowed into it, feeling her body begin to awaken before he even touched her. It stopped, and she tingled.

Toweling his head, Marcus crossed over to the bed, stark naked and very ready.

She giggled and held out her arms. "We'll have to work out some arrangements in the months ahead."

He gave a low growl as he pulled her close. "Where there's a will, there's a way, baby, and I've got the will. How about you?"

"Always," she murmured. He unzipped her, slid her outfit off her shoulders, and then they were truly home.

All too early, the alarm sounded. Marcus fumbled and turned it off. "Go back to sleep." She didn't argue. He dressed in the dark and left. When he called mid-morning, she didn't answer, but when he called early afternoon and she still didn't pick up, he became concerned. He called the front desk, and a familiar voice answered. "George, have you seen Mrs. Mansour?"

"Yes, sir. She left several hours ago. Said she had nothing to eat in the house, and she was going shopping."

He groaned. "I should have thought of that."

"She looked chipper, but she said she was starving. When's the baby due?"

"Babies. December. She's carrying twins, and she's always starving."

"Do you want me to tell her to call?"

"No. I was checking on her. Thanks."

Michelle came in, eating a bagel with cream cheese. She handed George a bag with a bear claw and a hot caramel coffee. Holding it up, she asked, "Isn't this what you like?"

"That's nice! Thanks, Mrs. Mansour." She waved, munching another bite, and headed for the elevator with her bags. "Do you need help, Ma'am?" he called after her.

"I didn't get much, just some stuff for supper. Thanks, though." And she disappeared.

She had to set the bags down to open the apartment door, holding the last of the bagel between her teeth. She put the groceries away and wondered if she should call Lilly. Deciding to leave them be, she flipped through some recipes on the Internet, trying to decide on something for dinner. Unused to being idle, Michelle checked her email and looked for the list of volunteer clinics she had checked out before she left, wondering how long she'd be able to work.

Realizing she hadn't checked their phone messages, she went through them rapidly, but she stopped when she heard Cassie's mom, urging her to call as soon as they got home. Carrying the phone, she tucked her legs under her, wondering how long she'd be able to do that. Suzanne sounded well and asked how the baby was doing.

"I haven't seen the doctor since we got home. I have an appointment Wednesday. We got home two weeks ago, but we brought Father Manny two adorable boys from an orphanage in South Africa, and a young lady to nanny them, but he married her instead, and they're both adopting the boys Monday."

"Wow! That's a lot of good news."

"That's not all. Marcus and I are having twin girls."

"Michelle, really? How lovely. How do you feel?"

"So far, so good, but I'm on the way to blimp-hood."

Suzanne laughed. "I bet Dr. Mansour is in heaven!"

"He is, and so is Father Manny. You'll have to come meet his family. He told me you are going to a church nearer to where you live."

The two women chatted, Suzanne explaining they wanted to get the children involved in church, and it was so far to Baltimore, but they certainly would come over to meet Father Manny's family.

After a pause, Michelle cleared her throat. She thought maybe she should wait for Marcus, but she charged ahead. "Suzanne, I want you to be honest with me." When Cassie's mother agreed with a puzzled tone, Michelle added, "Marcus wants to name one of the girls after Cassie. Would that bother you?"

In a tear-choked voice, Suzanne replied. "How sweet. What a lovely man. My black angel. I love you guys so much."

"And we want you and your husband to be her godparents, okay?"

"Of course! We'd be proud. When are these babies due? Are they both girls?"

"Both girls, but not identical. Due in December, if I can carry them that long. Twins tend to come early."

"You have to take care of yourself, and I know sitting still is hard for you."

"I'm already fretting."

"We'll come see you. Can you go to the aquarium? I'll bring the kids, and we'll meet you." They made plans for next week and hung up.

Michelle ended up going to the nearby deli because Marcus was late. He arrived home around 9:00. He looked weary, but as soon as he pushed open the door and saw her, he burst into a huge smile. "Coming home to my beautiful wife sure beats walking into a dark apartment!" After they kissed, she asked if he had eaten. "I'm not hungry for food," he said, scooping her up in his arms.

"Marcus!" she protested.

He placed her on the bed and dropped kisses on her belly. "How are my girls?"

She giggled and pulled him down beside her. "You have to be tired. It was a long day."

But he proved he wasn't too tired! "I missed you," he said later, pulling her close. "Did you say you had some food?"

She giggled, telling him she brought him a sandwich from the deli. She slipped on her caftan and led him down the hall. They sat in the kitchen while he ate his sandwich and salad, and she munched on some salad.

"Hungry?" he teased.

"Yeah, always. I thought about calling Lilly today, but I figured I'd leave them alone. I wonder what they did last night."

He looked up from his sandwich with dancing eyes. "I know what I hope they did. I hope they had as much fun as we did."

"Lilly told me that when he proposed, he said they didn't have to consummate the marriage."

"He did? Why?"

"He was concerned. She's young, and he's eleven years older. Plus, they haven't known each other long. But she loves him. She told me so."

"Is she...prepared for marriage? Did the orphanage teach her?"

"She knew all about it. In fact, she had a thoroughly Christian understanding of covenant, along with the duties and responsibilities of the marital relationship. The day we bought her dress, I bought her a copy of the Penners' book."

"*Intended for Pleasure?* That's a good one."

"She thanked me the day of the wedding, but she didn't know if Manny wanted to."

"Manny wants to. Have you seen the way he looks at her? He eats her up! I bet they did."

"You think so?"

"I do. She's a good woman. How could he find a better one? God gives us our wives, and just as surely as He gave me you, He brought Lilly to Manny."

"I'm glad He brought me to you." Michelle circled the back of his chair and leaned to hug him. "Let's go to bed."

"Again? You insatiable woman!"

"I want to go to sleep, you insatiable man!"

He stood and slipped his arm around her as they walked down the hall. "I'll try to keep my hands off you."

Chapter Twenty-Four

THE ADOPTION

Michelle and Marcus walked into the county courthouse at ten minutes to 11:00 on Monday. They were spotted immediately by the boys, who were turned around in their seats looking for them.

Paul screamed, "Aunt Michelle! Uncle Marcus!" and flew down the aisle, despite Manny and Lilly's attempts to hang on to them. The couple picked them up and carried them to where they belonged.

Manny was walking toward them. Paul hung his head. Papa had told him to stay in his chair, but he was so excited.

"Does he have any idea what will happen here today?" Marcus asked.

"Ms. Baker, our social worker, who should be here any minute, brought us a book, and we've read it about one thousand two hundred and seventy times. Right, Paul?"

"The court says today Papa and Mama will be my father and mother," Paul informed Marcus. "But God already made it so, didn't He, Papa?"

The back door opened, and Ms. Baker walked in beside the attorney, who set his briefcase on a table and came to shake their hands. He set a stack of papers on the table, asked Manny if he had the copy of the marriage certificate, and announced that that should do it, but he needed a notarized copy for Lilly's citizenship. He turned to Marcus and Michelle, verifying their identities and clarifying how long they had known Father Manny and Lilly. He jotted a few notes, checked his papers from the Department of Human Services, and straightened the stack.

"That should do it. Any questions?" He looked at the boys, "Paul, right?"

"Yes, sir."

"I'm Mr. Manning. Can you tell me who these people are?"

"This is my papa. I came across the ocean to be his little boy. And this is my mama, because she married my papa, and she came with me from South Africa."

"You are a fine, smart boy." The attorney held out his hand to Lilly. "Manny has told me about you."

Manny put his arm around Lilly. She looked up at him, love shining in her eyes.

Marcus led Michelle to the bench in the back and leaned to whisper, "The answer to your question is yes."

She looked at him for a moment and grinned. "You think?"

"I know so. Look at them!"

Michelle's eyes softened as she regarded them. "They do glow, don't they?"

Once the bailiff called, "All rise," a few minutes later, the procedure went smoothly. The judge asked Paul if he wanted Father Manny to be his father and Lilly to be his mama, and the boy responded with enthusiasm, adding, "God already made it so."

"Then let's agree with God, young man." He pounded his gavel, announcing, "Petition granted."

With tears streaming down her cheeks, Lilly wound her arms around Manny's neck, and the two of them gathered the children into an embrace.

Michelle was surprised to see her parents in the back. Louise asked if they could take them to lunch, but Marcus needed to get back to the hospital.

Herman put his arm around Michelle. "We'll get you home." He suggested a nearby seafood place. "Our treat," he said to Manny, and the family agreed.

In the restaurant, Lilly pulled out her bag of fruit and veggies to keep the boys occupied until the food came. She placed her hand over Manny's when he reached for a second roll, and he entwined his fingers in hers. The Logans were amazed at the boys eating fish, rice, and salad.

"It's not as good as Lilly's," Manny boasted. "You'll have to come eat with us some evening."

"I'm sure it will be a treat. Marcus and Michelle tell us you're an excellent cook, Lilly."

To Michelle's amazement, Lilly didn't duck her head. She looked up at Manny and over to Herman, then replied, "Thank you."

Michelle asked if she could take a carry-out plate home for Marcus, admitting she wasn't a good cook.

Lilly placed some toys in front of the boys to occupy their attention, but she told Manny they needed to leave soon for naps. He took Paul to the bathroom, and they excused themselves. Michelle and her parents lingered over coffee, and Michelle asked her mother if she wanted to go to her checkup Wednesday.

"I don't know if they'll do a sonogram," she said, "but Marcus figures they will since the only one we've had was in Johannesburg."

Louise was thrilled, and they arranged where to meet Wednesday before returning to their car. "I can't wait to see the babies!" she said when Michelle got out of the car.

Herman had pulled up in front of the apartment house, and the valet opened the door, but her father got out to embrace her. "How much joy you bring to everyone, sweetie. You and your husband. Those boys are precious, and Manny is over the moon. Lilly's story is amazing, and once again God has awed me."

"She's special. One of God's best." She hugged him, thinking she was awed by what God had done in her family's life. She waved to George on her way to the elevator.

* * *

At 11:00 on Wednesday, she, Marcus, and Louise convened at the doctor's office.

"I hope you don't mind, Marcus. Michelle invited me."

He gave her a hug. "Of course not! You're the grandmother. Are you ready for little girls?" He pulled open the door and saw his wife checking in at the desk. "Bob told me to come down for the show," he told her.

"He's going to do a sonogram?"

"Four-D, baby!" He told Louise she wasn't going to believe this technology.

"I dread getting on the scales." But when she did, the doctor said she hadn't done badly for carrying twins, and he measured her growth. "Looks good. Are you ready?"

Marcus arranged a chair for Louise and pulled a stool up to perch on himself. He took Michelle's hand as the screen clicked on. She sucked in a breath, and he grinned, his dark eyes sparkling. "Look at them!"

"Simply amazing," Louise exclaimed. "This one looks exactly like Michelle!" She indicated the larger twin.

"They look good, Michelle," her OB said. "Real good. One's a little smaller, but they're both good size. They look healthy." The doctor took some measurements. "Definitely two girls. You told me you wanted a girl, Marcus."

"I did." Marcus scooted forward, peering intently at the screen. "I prayed for a little girl who looks like her beautiful mother. Two is twice as good."

"We'll plan more definitely later along, but the protocol is two pediatricians for twins. We hope you'll go to thirty-eight weeks, and we'll put you on bed rest, if necessary, to make that happen. Gestating twins takes patience, Dr. Logan. Give your girls every possible break you can. The longer, the better."

"I know. But they look wonderful."

"They do, but I want to see you every two weeks. You're six months along. Any twinges? No complaints?"

"My only complaint is that I'm hungry all the time. And I'm turning into a blimp."

Bob laughed. "You ain't seen nothing yet, girl! You're using those calories to grow fine, healthy girls. Right on target for twins." He looked at Marcus. "Is she behaving herself? You worried about anything?"

"She glows and looks more beautiful every day."

"You are so full of it!"

"She does get grumpy occasionally," Marcus teased, "but not so much once we got past the first trimester. Her energy picked up in the fourth month, but I figure she'll slow down a bit in a few weeks."

"She's carrying a lot of weight there, Dad. Don't let her pick up anything heavy."

"I told you!" Marcus fussed.

"I was relieved you decided not to work when I found out about the twins." Bob stood. "That's it for today. See you in two weeks." He pointed her to the appointment desk.

Louise stood up. "I'll step outside and let you get dressed."

Marcus helped her stand and took her in his arms, brushing his lips against her cheek. "It's getting exciting, Mama."

She grimaced. "Yeah, but it looks daunting."

He gave her a squeeze and then held her shirt. "We need to get you some pants. You wear the same two pair over and over."

"Can you eat lunch?"

"This was my lunch hour. I'll grab an energy bar. Take your mom to the deli."

They met Louise in the waiting room, and he repeated his suggestion. When Louise agreed, he asked if she could take Michelle home and leave him the car. Tucking her arm around her daughter, Louise said she'd be glad to do that, and Marcus waved at them as they walked off.

Michelle suggested shopping for new pants after they ate, and Louise was excited. She couldn't remember ever taking her daughter shopping. She'd taken the entire day, and she wanted to be with Michelle. They had missed so many years. All in all, it was a fun day, and the women laughed and joked. They had so many bundles that Louise insisted they'd have them delivered, reminding her daughter she wasn't supposed to carry anything. Michelle said she was as bad as Marcus, and Louise thought that was a good thing. They had a few things in her mother's trunk, which the valet hustled over and took, assuring her he'd get it to her apartment, and her mother pulled away.

She was asleep when Marcus got home and didn't hear him come in, but she stirred when he walked into their room.

He sat on the bed beside her. "I saw all those boxes and bags in the living room. Looks like you and your mom bought out the stores."

She pushed him aside and hastened to the bathroom, hearing his laughter echo behind her.

* * *

The rest of the summer passed. Michelle did spend time with Suzanne and her children and Lilly and the boys. She went over to her brother's on the weekend, always eager to see Andrew in robust health. She didn't do as much volunteer work as she had planned, but she subbed for a resident who had a death in the family for a few days. Marcus liked that.

By October, she was glad to feel the chill in the air. The summer heat bothered her more than usual. Her family was resigned to their decision to live in South Africa, and she boasted about the weather there. Marcus was surprised when she agreed not to drive, but she couldn't fit behind the wheel!

By November, she hardly wanted to go anywhere, and Bob wanted to see her every week. Marcus could get her to go see Manny and Lilly, but the drive to Washington was too far. Her family spent time at Manny's with the children until it got too cold to enjoy outside. She never complained and appreciated when Marcus would rub her back.

Chapter Twenty-Five

THE GLORIOUS ARRIVAL

As the first week in December approached, Michelle was ready for it to be over. She'd roll around in the bed, unable to get comfortable, and Marcus would lay his hand on her belly, urging the girls to be still and let their mother get some sleep. She said he could use some, as well. Bob was pleased because she hit thirty-eight weeks and told her she could go anytime now. Marcus was sleeping on the couch when she called out.

She was sitting on the edge of the tub, leaning forward, a puddle on the floor beneath her. "Can you get a towel?"

He cursed. Michelle didn't remember ever hearing him swear, but he saw her doubled over, and he didn't care about the floor; he wanted to get her to the hospital. "Bob wanted to put you in. Why didn't you stay?"

"I wanted to be home with you."

"God, don't let her have this baby on the floor. Can you stand, honey?" He called a taxi and managed to get her downstairs. The driver drove to the hospital in record time, and Marcus rushed into the ER door to get a wheel-chair. He threw the driver some large bill and called back his thanks while pushing her through the doors. She was quiet, and he asked if she was okay.

"I'm having two babies here, No, I'm not okay."

Bob met them on the floor. "I told you not to go home, Michelle."

By this time, she couldn't get her breath. Marcus coached her. "Breathe in, honey. Let it out slow."

She raised her voice and waved her hands to grab onto his arms. "Get me in the damn chair."

Marcus had never heard her utter an oath, and he caught Bob's eye. "Can we do this?" Together, they put her in the chair.

Bob raised the legs and dropped down the end, pulling up a stool. "Yep, looks like we're having a baby here."

"Funny," she growled. "You're telling me?! God, help me." She let out a huge grunt.

"Don't push! Don't push!" Bob cried.

Michelle groaned. "Please." And she cried real tears.

Bob manipulated one of the babies, getting her into place, and ordered, "Push, now!" The first baby made her way out of the birth canal, and Bob quickly handed her off with a triumphant grin. "Good job! Ready?"

Michelle whimpered. "I can't do this," she whispered. She sagged against her husband.

"Sure you can, honey," Marcus encouraged.

"God!" she cried and bore down as hard as she could.

"One more, Michelle. Give me one more."

Michelle tossed her head from side to side, and Marcus prayed.

Michelle heard her first daughter cry and tried to sit up.

"Lie down," Bob yelled. "The next one's coming."

Michelle cried out again and pushed with the last ounce of her strength, feeling her second daughter make her way into the world. She was angry, that baby was! Michelle smiled. "Let me see them," she begged.

The pediatrician laid her first daughter in her left arm. "This big girl is the small one. She's seven pounds and two ounces."

"Small? That's one good-sized full-term baby," the OB commented.

The second pediatrician was working on the other baby, who was squalling at the top of her lungs.

"Is she all right?"

The doctor chuckled. "She's mad as a wet hen, but she's perfect. Seven pounds, five ounces, Bob."

"Can you believe she didn't even tear? And they fought over which one would be first." Bob looked up at Michelle, who was drenched in sweat. "Marcus, wipe her face. Michelle, you've done a great job, but we need to get this afterbirth out of there, and you need to give me a few more pushes." The first pediatrician took Cassie, and Michelle continued to push until finally it was over.

Marcus looked at his wife, who was reaching for her babies. He shook his head before settling Michellena in his arms.

"I've never delivered finer twins!" Both pediatricians agreed with Bob. They were beautiful babies. "Let's sit her up and see if they'll take the breast."

Cassie, the littler one, was eager, latching on firmly. Michellena was still throwing a tantrum, and Marcus walked her, singing until she stopped abruptly and stared. It was so quiet that Michelle cried out, "Is she okay?"

Marcus held her so his wife could see her. "She's getting to know her papa."

Michelle's head fell against the pillow. "Bring her to me," she demanded.

He grinned. "You've got one. Can't I have this one?"

She glared at him. "Bring her here!" Babies exchanged hands, and Lena got her turn at her mama's other breast.

None of the doctors was in a hurry to leave, admiring the strong, healthy babies.

"They are long, too. The first one...you're calling her Cassie?"

"Cassandra Suzanne," Marcus said.

"She's almost twenty-one inches. What are you naming the bigger one?"

"She's Michellena Marie. That's my husband's idea of a name."

"Spell that. The way you want it on the birth certificate." After Marcus spelled it, the pediatrician showed him what he'd written, and Marcus pronounced it perfect. "She's twenty-one and a half inches. No wonder she wanted out of there."

"We're going to take these beauties to the nursery," Cassie's pediatrician said, "but I understand you want them in the room with you?"

Michelle nodded. Bob stepped up to her side. "You need to rest, Michelle."

Her eyes were fluttering. She'd never been so tired in her life. She felt the bed roll as they took her to the room.

Marcus felt for his phone, finally locating it in an outside pocket. First, he called her parents, waking them up to tell them the girls had arrived. Michelle had carried fourteen pounds, seven ounces worth of babies.

"My God," Herman exclaimed. "Is she all right?"

"She's exhausted but fine."

"I should say! We'll let her rest and come over later. I guess they came fast?"

"We had no time to call. I thought they were coming on the bathroom floor, and I think the taxi driver was praying as hard as I was that we'd make it to the hospital." Marcus paused and swallowed. "Herman, you have an incredible daughter. We serve an amazing God. This was the most miraculous thing I've ever witnessed."

Michelle smiled. She could hear her mother asking questions, but she didn't have the strength to speak, so he hung up.

Marcus bent over her and kissed her lips. "I didn't think I could love you more." His tears dripped on her cheek. "You rest now."

"I love you," she whispered.

Marcus sat on the chair, his head between his hands, praising God and rejoicing. He didn't even hear the door open.

"Amen, brother. How're you doing?"

"Bob, thanks, man."

"Don't thank me. She did an incredible job! You got a couple of winners there. Look, I know she wants them in here, but she needs to rest. We'll let her sleep until she wakes, unless one of the girls really needs her. Why don't you put that chair down and get some rest, too?"

"I called her folks, but I need to call mine."

"I called upstairs. Everyone knows." Waving, the OB ducked out the door.

Marcus called his parents to tell them the news, and his mother planned to come over Christmas break. Harry said she wasn't coming without him. He asked if his son could see any resemblances, and Marcus told him Michelle thought Michellena looked like her as a baby, and he thought Cassie looked like Alicia. He said the twins were like Jacob and Esau, fighting to come out first, but both his girls were beloved of God.

And then he slept.

Bob put a "no visitors" sign up because the entire staffs of pediatrics and oncology wanted to see Michelle and ogle the babies. Marcus asked the obstetrician if he should be concerned because of his wife's fatigue, because she let them go to the nursery despite her intentions. Bob assured him she'd had a good delivery, but it was a hard, fast one, and the girls were feeding constantly. The pediatricians told him it took more calories to lactate than gestate, and Marcus figured he'd have to bring her more food! She insisted her parents should be allowed to visit, and they crept into the room to see their granddaughters. She was amazed at her father, who crooned to Michellena and bounced Cassie, but Marcus explained later they'd enjoy these girls because the love of God was shed abroad in their hearts now.

The new father was relieved when Bob and the pediatricians kept his girls in the hospital for three days, not that it was medically indicated. All of them were thriving, but the routine was demanding. Frankly, Marcus was confounded. How could they manage?

Their first night home, Lilly and Manny were at the apartment before they got there. Lilly had cooked several meals, putting some in the freezer and placing dinner on the table as soon as they got home. He held Michellena while his wife ate, and Lilly crooned over Cassie, sitting on the couch as both boys hovered over her to see. Then he arranged the new mother with pillows, and the boys were fascinated to see both babies latch on. She fed them both at once!

Manny made the boys come to the table. Marcus and Lilly ate with them while Michelle nursed, but Lilly and Marcus jumped up to burp them. He confessed he was ready to hire help. Lilly immediately said she'd stay the night and send Manny home with the boys. Although they protested, Manny took his boys by the hand, informing them that is the way it would be, and they had to obey their mama and be good boys. They hung their heads and followed him out the door. Marcus made his wife lie down because the girls should sleep, but they kept fussing when he put them in their bassinets.

Lilly came out of the kitchen. "They miss each other," she said, putting them both in the crib in the guest room. Almost instantly, they scooted together. Michellena threw her arm around Cassie, and both babies became quiet. Marcus stared at his daughters. He'd never seen them settle. After juggling them constantly for three days, he wanted to kiss Lilly!

Michelle came to the doorway and asked what was going on. "Lilly had a word of knowledge," Marcus told her.

"They missed each other. They've been side by side all these months, and they didn't like being separated."

"What made you think of that?"

"Paul and Timothy were like that after they lost their parents. They still won't sleep unless they're in the same bed. Go rest. I'll keep an eye on them." Marcus led Michelle into their bedroom and lay down beside her while Lilly cleaned up the kitchen, singing quietly. Both exhausted parents had their first deep sleep since the girls were born, and when the babies woke up, they gurgled and scooted.

"I can't believe this," Michelle said, looking down at them. "It's a miracle."

"It makes perfect sense," Marcus replied, curving his arm around her waist. "Look at them. They're precious."

"We need to ditch those bassinets and move the crib in our room."

Once again, Michelle fed them together. She had safety pins attached to her nursing bra, a pink one for Cassie and a purple one for her sister. She moved them to alternate her daughters; one of the nurses in the hospital had taught her that.

Lilly slept in the bedroom with the girls, and they slept for two or three hours at a stretch. Marcus thought perhaps they would survive, after all! He called Manny the next morning to tell him, but he wasn't surprised, and he suggested an older woman in his congregation who had agreed to help them, and that afternoon he brought her over.

Marcus simply had to go back to work. He had a good chief resident, thank the Lord, but he was paid to be chief of oncology.

Manny drove Stella Harris, an elderly congregant who had her own grandchildren, to the apartment. He greeted his wife with a kiss. The boys wanted to see the twins again and hopped around Michelle as she held them. Stella shooed Manny's family off, promising she'd fix dinner. After they left, Marcus arrived, taking off his coat and announcing it was snowing. He shook the snow off his coat and hung it, then pulled the curtains back off the big windows. He took Lena out of her mother's arms and walked her over to the window. Michelle joined him, Cassie on her shoulder. He leaned to kiss her, and she noted his lips were cold. He nuzzled her with his nose, and she shivered. He laughed.

"Look, girls. Your very first snow!"

"I'm sure they'll remember this moment forever," Michelle teased.

Mrs. Harris called them to the table, and they put the babies in the crib, now in their bedroom, and watched their familiar pattern of nestling together; only this time Cassie threw her arm around Lena. As they walked out of the room, they heard the girls settle. The couple showed their new friend the double bed in the guest room and returned to their bedroom, explaining they grabbed sleep while the girls were down. Mrs. Harris told them to be sure and wake her because she was here to help.

Although Marcus wanted to get up and help with the girls, Michelle often snuck them out so he could sleep, and Mrs. Harris would hear her and get up. Michelle felt all she did was nurse her babies, although she tried to nurse them at the same time. She nursed and slept, nursed and slept, unless her parents came by, or her brother and his boys.

Chapter Twenty-Six

CHRISTMAS

Mrs. Harris left to go to her daughter's for Christmas, but Michelle thought she could handle it until Alicia and Harry arrived in two days. Boy, she didn't realize how much help Mrs. Harris had been, and Marcus worked late every night. When he came home, she collapsed. On the twenty-third, the Logans picked up Alicia and Harry at the airport and brought them to the apartment.

"Where is my beautiful daughter?" Harry said, calling out to Michelle. He gathered her into his arms and told her how beautiful she was. "I thought you were a new mama. Marcus said you were exhausted." He gathered her into his arms and held her close, kissing both her cheeks. Then he glanced over to Herman. "I'm sorry to steal your daughter. We have none of our own, but we claim Marie and Michelle, our sons' wives."

Alicia looked around for the babies, and Michelle led them into the master bedroom, where the girls lay, legs tangled together and heads touching.

"Marcus told us they have to sleep together. Look, Harry."

"They don't look newborn," Harry remarked. He leaned over and ran his hand over their dark curls.

"You wake them, they're yours," Michelle warned with a smile.

Lena disentangled herself and lifted her head. Harry reached in and scooped her up. "Hello, Michellena Marie. I'm Grand-Papa." Cradling her head in his hand, he stretched her out. "And this is Grand-Mama."

Cassie, feeling her sister's absence, scooted around. Michelle picked her up before she started to fuss.

Observing from the doorway, Herman wanted to know how he recognized Lena.

"Marcus said she looked like her beautiful mother. He prayed for that. But this one, little Cassie, looks like a baby picture of Alicia."

"They were both big girls, especially for twins," Herman said.

The grandparents trailed into the living room, admiring the girls. The two grandmothers sat side by side, and Louise agreed that Lena did look like Michelle.

Harry took a foot in his hand. "Look, Lena's going to be tall and stately, like her mother. Marcus must be putty in her hands."

Louise laughed. "He's putty in both their hands. I've never seen such a devoted father."

The girls began to complain before long, and Michelle arranged her pillows to feed them. Herman turned aside, but Harry, used to seeing mothers and their babies, watched, curious about the arrangement. Michelle held their heads close to her breasts and stretched their legs behind her. He was fascinated as both girls latched on, and he smiled, shaking his head.

Marcus came in with a boisterous cry. "Papa!" Father and son hugged with warm enthusiasm, slapping each other on the back and embracing again. "What do you think of our girls?" Marcus dropped a kiss on his wife's cheek and admired his nursing babies. "They eat well. They've already gained weight."

"They're magnificent, son! I thought Mama was going to pop before we got here."

"Just over three weeks, and look at them," Marcus boasted, and Harry told him Lena had lifted her head. Brilliant, his girls were brilliant. He took Cassie and brushed his lips on her tiny face before lifting her to his shoulder and burping her. Alicia scooted down on the couch to give him room, and he handed the baby to her and put his arm around Michelle. Lena let the nipple slip out of her mouth and looked up to her father's face.

"Hello, sweetheart, Papa's home." He plucked her out of Michelle's arms and burped her before settling her into his father's arms. He greeted Herman and Louise, then apologized that they didn't have Christmas decorations. They'd been a bit busy!

Louise had prepared a meal, and they traded the girls around the table. Although it was early afternoon, it was late for the fliers from South Africa, and their attempts to stifle yawns caused the Logans to excuse themselves so they could settle in.

The next day, Harry was out on the street before Marcus left, looking for Christmas tree lots. He was wearing one of his son's heavy coats, and he met him with a tree over his shoulder as Marcus was walking out of the building. Harry promised to put up Christmas by the time his son got home, but the staff took off a half day, leaving a minimal crew for Christmas Eve. Nevertheless, the lights were on the tree, and the ladies were hanging decorations. As was his custom, Marcus walked back to the crib, but he found no babies. Confused, he returned to the living room. Propped up in infant seats and staring at the lights were his girls. He squatted beside them.

"They like the lights," his mother said.

"They seem to," he agreed, and he hunkered down beside them. He described how he was sure Michelle was going to have them at home or in the taxi and how impressed the pediatricians were at the fine, healthy babies.

The next morning, Michelle and Marcus were astounded to see packages under the tree. Michelle carried stacks of wrapped packages in her arms for her in-laws, which she'd bought in the fall. Each granddaughter had diamond ear studs, and Michelle had a diamond necklace with two baby figures. After all the unwrapping, they loaded up two cars—the Logans left one for them to use—and headed to Manny and Lilly's house. Michelle rode with Marcus's papa to show him the way, and Alicia rode with her son. They found Manny in the kitchen, but he was relieved to have help cooking the turkey and sides.

"Where's Lilly?" Michelle asked.

"She's lying down with the boys. They were up at six o'clock. We did Christmas up big, so excuse the mess."

Thinking it was strange for her friend to take a nap and leave the cooking to Manny, Michelle tip-toed to the bedroom and found Lilly sound asleep.

"Is Lilly not feeling well?" she asked Manny when she came back to the kitchen. Did he look embarrassed?

"No, she's fine. Just tired. Sometimes a little nauseous." He ducked his head. "She's pregnant."

"When was this decided? You know you have to talk about these things before the wedding." With a twinkle in his eyes, Marcus quoted their pre-marital counseling.

"I never thought about it. When I was married before..." His voice trailed off.

"But your wife was sterile, not you," Marcus reminded him.

"I know, I know, but I didn't think. But she doesn't seem to mind."

"She doesn't mind, Manny," Michelle assured him. "You already have a ready-made family, and she told me she felt very loved. Before, she was cared for, but she was one of sixty children. She feels like you love only her, and the boys, of course."

Manny was overcome by emotion and sat, wiping his hand across moist eyes. "I never expected to love again. She is my world. I never dreamed I'd have a child of my own, and now I have a wonderful wife and three children."

"God restored what the locust had eaten, Manny." Harry sat beside him and took his hand. "We wanted to check you out, make sure you were good enough for our Lilly, and we find you to be even more."

Hearing sounds from the back of the house, Michelle placed Lena in Harry's arms and went to help. Soon, the boys tumbled into the living room, Timothy boasting he'd put his tee-tees in the potty, then forming a small O with his mouth when he saw unfamiliar faces.

Lilly squatted down and put her arm around him. "This is Uncle Marcus's mama and papa, Timothy, from South Africa, where you were born."

"I remember them," Paul said.

Michelle brought out a large shopping bag. "I guess you have so many new things. You might want to save this for another time."

Screeching, the boys fell upon it, but Lilly took them in her arms, and Manny asked, "What do you say, boys?" After proper thanks, the boys opened their gifts—more train cars for the train set, and dinosaurs that growled.

After Michelle nursed her babies, she left them in the grandparents' care and helped Lilly in the kitchen. The ladies chatted about how she was feeling and what to expect, and Michelle promised to be there for her, but Lilly mourned that Michelle would be gone before she gave birth.

"I'll stay until after the baby is born," Michelle promised.

Epilogue

Michelle kept her promise. Marcus had to work through July to serve the full year he had contracted, and Mrs. Harris stayed with the boys the night Manny brought Lilly to the hospital. The Logans watched the girls, and Michelle was with her friend throughout the delivery of their daughter, Michelle Alicia.

The Mansours decided to settle in Cape Town instead of Johannesburg, and they bought house. Marcus's grandfather lived in the guest house now. They found a perfect place near where Marcus taught and joined a practice. Just as Michelle had promised, their son, Edward Harold, was born in South Africa, and great-grandfather Edward was present for his christening.

Michelle's father decided to fully retire and bought a home in Hout Bay, where they lived six months out of the year. Her brother and Beatrice spent vacations in South Africa's pleasant winter, during the boys' vacations. To no one's surprise, Andrew Logan would one day attend the Anglican seminary in South Africa.

Several years after Michelle and Marcus moved to Cape Town, Manny was chosen by the Diocese to attend an Anglican conference in South Africa, and Lilly, the boys, and their daughter accompanied him. Lilly was pregnant again, and radiant. Manny handled his daughter like a professional father. They took the boys to Johannesburg, to the Orlando Home, before they returned home.

The Hope House girls came to South Africa twice, once holding an event to raise funds for a maternity home. Michelle flew to the states several times for reunions.

Michelle and Marcus had a second son, who weighed in at eleven pounds, and they decided enough was enough. Michelle was forty-one then, and she worked part-time when the children were little. By the time their younger boy was two, she became a partner in a four-person pediatric group, always devoting at least one afternoon each week to an orphanage. Eventually, she was appointed by the nation to visit every orphanage in the country twice a year and write reviews. Because of her expertise and her gentle godliness, she encouraged each one to higher standards, and their death rates dropped dramatically. Both Alicia and Harry were in their sixties when she was voted South Africa's Woman of the Year. Edward, nearing one hundred, watched the event on TV.

When South Africa lost its collective mind and seized the property of white farm owners, after much agonizing prayer, Marcus and Michelle decided to take advantage of their dual citizenship and move to the United States. Marcus cried the entire flight, and when Lena asked her mother why, she told her he was grieving for his country. They spent one winter at the Cleveland Clinic, but Marcus could not get warm the entire winter, so they moved to Houston's M.D. Anderson. Meanwhile, in South Africa, Marcus's papa bought white farms, promising to keep them in trust for when the country returned to its senses.

About the Author

Charlotte met her husband at Duke University. Married in 1962, they reared six children (four natural, one adopted, and one foster daughter). Their nine grandchildren range in age from adults to a toddler, and four are adopted. A pro-life leader for many years, Charlotte believes God creates every child.

A Phi Beta Kappa graduate of Duke, Charlotte received a Masters of Social Work from the University of North Carolina in 1966. She founded a pregnancy help ministry in 1985, and she's been a Mothers of Preschoolers (MOPS) mentor for twenty years. Her experiences as a wife, social worker, mother, pro-life leader, and MOPS mentor contribute to her inspirational fiction.

She lives with her husband, a practicing orthopedic surgeon, in rural West Virginia. She has published articles and short stories, some of them may be viewed at her website/blog: www.charlottesreaders.com. She has three novels published by Oak Tara, and many articles and short stories published in various magazines. (Her short stories are free and her books may be purchased at Amazon or at her blog.) She is on Facebook and Twitter @Charlotte Snead.

www.ingramcontent.com/pod-product-compliance
Lightning Source LLC
Chambersburg PA
CBHW071154260626
47162CB00003B/1053